When I Am Ashes

When I Am Ashes

a novel

~

Amber Rose

atmosphere press

Published by Atmosphere Press

Cover design by Nick Courtright

atmospherepress.com

Chapter 1

Paris
June 1938

Hot chocolate was Sasha's favorite addiction. Thick, melt-in-your-mouth, hot chocolate with whipped cream solved everything, but it had to be *dark* hot chocolate. Yes, definitely dark. Not instant or milk chocolate, either. Dark–created from scratch.

After her sacred ceremony of hot chocolate for breakfast, Sasha continued on to her next ritual...her daily visit to the Louvre. To escape her loneliness, Sasha fled the grey and entered the paradise of Paris' Louvre. Magic swirled in the air with the scents of old oil, dust, and the rosewater an earlier attendee left in her wake. But today would be different. Just before Sasha left the museum, she turned around and came face-to-face with a huge and startling painting she'd never seen. Its emotion ignited a dream. The devotion depicted on the canvas jumped from its gilded frame, grabbed hold of her heart and electrified her soul–metaphysical lightning. Tears she'd fought since childhood burst from a deep well inside her. Sasha's life would never be the same.

"If only I could be loved like that someday..." she whispered, and her words hung like clouds in the air...

The way those hearts pine for their beloved...a kind of sacred love. It's devotion that surpasses the heaven that is hot chocolate. A love to die for...

It was the most deeply romantic painting she'd ever seen. Sasha yearned to be *Atala,* that woman in the white dress being held with love by two men: a handsome man at her feet and a monk at her shoulders. The way that heartbroken man clutched her lower legs spoke of his undying love. Would Sasha ever be loved that way? Not if she listened to her mother. And the monk in his brown hooded robe who held *Atala's* shoulders gave Sasha a sense of spiritual peace that she missed growing up in a culturally Jewish family.

Sasha had to have that painting. A fantastical notion to pull it from the wall swept through her and tingled up her fingers. But, no. That was crazy! How could she procure a copy? As Sasha drank in the scene, memorizing every line and shadow so she could dream of this love later, it came to her–the gift shop.

Out of breath, Sasha raced down the long hall and two flights of stairs to the small gift shop in the lobby. A frantic sense of desperation slowed her down, all thumbs as she searched through the racks of postcards for that painting. Sasha rushed to the counter where a handsome young man whose employee nametag identified him as Michael gave her a pensive look when she asked about them. He said if she left him a few francs, he would mail her the postcard when it became available.

Would he really do it? She wasn't sure but the passion of the painting still burned in her heart. It was worth a try. Sasha's fingers smoothed over the buttery golden leather purse that Abie had given her for her birthday and retrieved some coins. Her hand trembled as she held them out to Michael along with her New York address which she'd scribbled on a scrap of paper. Why did she do that? She was not planning to go home.

"Please promise you'll send it," Sasha begged, as she wiped away a new fount of tears.

Michael ducked his curly, dark head and handed her a tissue from a box somewhere out of sight behind the counter. "I promise, mademoiselle."

"Thank you for your kindness," Sasha said, eyes riveted on her shoes.

She wasn't used to people being so helpful. But Sasha wasn't in New York anymore. And she never planned to go back. She ran away from home in early June and adored Paris... but she could feel the rumblings of a frightening war approaching. Hitler's Nazis were on the move. Her heart beat double-time. Where would she be safe?

Sasha was startled by a strange buzzer and a voice crackled across a hidden speaker, "The museum closes in five minutes. Please exit in an orderly fashion." The message repeated in English and two other languages she didn't recognize. Sasha scrambled to put on her burgundy raincoat and found her way out into the unusually cold, dark street.

There was a heavy downpour and everyone else in Paris seemed prepared. Sasha stood under an overhang and took in the sea of multi-colored umbrellas ebbing and flowing like jellyfish in the wind-swept air. Of course, she'd forgotten her umbrella and got drenched as she ventured out. Her solution: wait for the storm to pass with hot chocolate at a nearby café. So many cafés to choose from. Wait, this café displayed a liquid hot chocolate fountain in the window with several descending levels in a whirlpool–Café au Chocolat.

Eureka! Sasha hit the mother lode. She jotted down the name of the café. The best Parisian hot chocolate so far–simply divine. The deep magical sacred aroma in this café encouraged her mouth to water as she ordered a second cup. Yes, this hot chocolate's perfect. While she savored her delicious liquid gold, she leaned back slightly, almost sloshing the chocolate delight in her cup. Michael from the Louvre gift shop strolled into the café. Why was he here? He wasn't following her, was he? With a slight bow, Michael inquired if he could join her. She nodded yes, despite the butterflies in her stomach. She was determined to break through her long-time fear of rejection. My, what a handsome young fellow. But how handsome was his heart? Sasha loved bittersweet chocolate but not bittersweet romance.

Sasha had an immediate and deep connection to this stranger. Why this sudden attraction? Because it was Paris? Because it was 1938 and a war was coming? Because of a chance meeting? Because they both loved dark hot chocolate? Divine intervention? Because they were old souls meeting again for the first time? She would have to live the question even though she didn't have the answers.

After his third cup of cocoa, Michael confessed, "I feel drunk from this hot chocolate. Is there any alcohol in it?" he laughed.

"I don't think so, but I'm feeling it too," Sasha swooned, her eyes closed, the deep Aztec aroma melting over her.

They laughed because they were free. They laughed because they still could. They were young – no responsibilities. Paris, plus rapturous chocolate aphrodisiac, ecstasy. They'd both ordered three cups of dark hot chocolate with whipped cream on a cold, late June afternoon in the midst of a rainstorm. Neither of them had umbrellas. They were both soaked to the bone. Sasha's auburn red hair, almost black from the heavy rain, still dripped onto the table as if she'd been swimming. Michael's kind face, surrounded by his wet, black hair, became a heart.

"I really hope you don't get sick, Michael. You're still drenched. I wish we had towels."

"My turtleneck will keep me warm if we sit here for a while longer," he flirted with a wink and a smile.

"I love turtlenecks, too. I'm always cold so I wear one every day, even in the summer."

As they continued to talk, Sasha discovered that Michael had never come across the painting of *Atala* she'd just fallen in love with. He promised to find it the next day. As they continued to visit, they warmed up and dried out. When the storm passed, Michael offered to walk Sasha to her small youth hostel. He again reassured her that he'd send a postcard of the painting as soon as it became available. The grumpy concierge yelled at Sasha for coming in after her 9 p.m. curfew but she didn't care as she waved goodbye to Michael.

Would Sasha ever see him again? It was surreal. She didn't know her right from her left and she floated on cloud nine. Magical, the way it happened. An indelible ink moment in time. A forget-me-not moment–perhaps, someday to be a distant memory, or maybe not. He loves me, he loves me not. Love at first sight. Maybe they'd never see each other again. Maybe they'd be separated by time and space or by war.

***

Michael stood in front of the *Atala* painting the next morning. It took his breath away. He fell in love with it instantly. The missing passion in his soul awoke. A fierce urgency and spark led him to find Sasha again and share how much he loved the story and soul of the painting. Then it dawned on him that Sasha, with her auburn hair and pale skin, seemed very similar to *Atala*, the woman in the painting. An uncanny resemblance. Strange.

Michael couldn't wait for his workday to end. When it did, he raced over to the youth hostel.

"I'm thrilled you're here. I came to invite you to go for a walk by the river Seine. I feel a burning desire to discuss *Atala.*"

"Sure, Michael. I'll just get my shoes. Why a burning desire?"

Michael shared, his voice trembling, "It's too bad *Atala* is dead."

"Dead? No way. Are you sure?"

"Yes, I am positive, Sasha. The name of the painting is *Atala's Funeral* by Anne-Louis Girodet."

"Oh," she replied, embarrassed, "If only I could be loved like that when I am alive, not dead!" Her cheeks flushed.

"Me too, Sasha."

A man who loved dark hot chocolate and who admitted aloud that he desired to be loved like that, was probably too good to be true. She braced herself for the other shoe to drop: rejection.

Instead, they became inseparable. They were one person in two bodies. Twin souls. Her first true love. They say one never forgets their first love. What would their story be? Happily ever after, the one all women die for? Michael and Sasha spent every day together for weeks. They held hands as they strolled.

Sasha chose to share, "My deep loneliness and grief comes from the loss of my brother, my mother's favorite child, who died of cancer."

"I'm so sorry about your brother. That must've been hard."

"Yes. It's still difficult for me."

"Is your mother supportive?"

"No. That's one of the reasons I ran away from home. My mother is very mean and strict. I always have to be on a diet. Her favorite remark is, 'You're fat and ugly and no man will ever want to be with you!'"

"How cruel and untrue," said Michael, as he reached out his hand to brush a long lock of auburn hair from her face.

"Thank you, Michael," she said with silent tears.

Her gaze lingered over him. No one had ever said that to her. Maybe her mother was wrong? Sasha began to question her own self-image. Maybe she wouldn't lose everyone she loved. Looking into Michael's handsome face and his soft brown eyes that held her hostage, she'd found her one true love and never dared lose him.

"My mother is the total opposite. She's a nurse-kind and empathetic." Michael said.

"You're lucky. I'm happy for you, Michael. To be loved is such a wonderful feeling. That's why I fell in love with that painting of *Atala*-she's loved both passionately and spiritually. Thank God my father is loving. I don't know what I'd do without him. He counterbalances my mother's intense negativity with a 'one big happy family' personality. He's very warm and a big hugger. My Dad always reminds us to 'tell people we love them because you never know if you will see them again'. If I take a deep breath and concentrate, I can feel his love now... Well, it's like chocolate. Come to think of it, he loves dark chocolate, too."

There was a pregnant pause. Michael did not discuss his father and Sasha was aware it was better not to pry.

About a month after they met, Michael and Sasha spent a weekend together in a quaint hotel near the Sacré-Cœur (the Sacred Heart). Within the cocoon of that dramatic and sacred neighborhood, they declared their undying love for one another, with hopes not to duplicate Romeo and Juliet.

"Now we are one. Your breath is my breath. We have the same heart," said Sasha. She hugged him as if that hug had always been inside of her, yearning to come out.

Sasha quoted Rumi: "Lovers don't finally meet somewhere. They're in each other all along."

The light poured in through the balcony window. The crystals in the chandelier took the slanting sunlight and threw rainbows on the ceiling. The sunlight fell across the carpet, making the dust glitter. Oh, my God, Michael got down on one knee...the moment Sasha dreamt of. She held her breath.

"I love you, Sasha," Michael said. "I am devoted to you." His cheeks flushed. His voice was soft as his brown-eyed gaze caressed her.

"I'm sorry I don't have enough money saved up for a ring yet." She held her breath.

"I hope you'll accept this gift as a commitment of my eternal love for you." Michael placed a burgundy velvet box in her hand, which trembled. "Will you marry me, Sasha?"

Before she opened the box, Sasha answered with deep joy, her face aglow, "Of course, I'll marry you. Any gift you give me will be cherished."

Within the velvet box she found a heart-shaped locket on a chain, with Michael's photo on one side and a lock of his hair on the other.

She started to cry, "Oh Michael, I love it!" Sasha opened the clasp and put the locket on. She stared at herself in the mirror. "I promise I'll never take it off as long as I live."

From that moment on they spent as much time together as possible. Their love was even more powerful than their addiction to dark chocolate. Whenever Michael was free, they took to the streets. It was like they were the only people alive on the earth. They waltzed through the air without a care in the world. Cloud nine came down to meet them. The world was their kaleidoscope. Colors and smells were accentuated in the fractured moving pieces of rainbow glass. They visited all the colorful and fragrant gardens and sacred stained-glass windowed cathedrals around Paris. Michael treated her like a fairytale princess. They continued to stop at cafés along the way where they enjoyed their signature hot chocolate. They were determined to find the best hot chocolate café in Paris. This would become an immortal journey to be passed down to their children.

One day Sasha returned to her small hostel only to discover a telegram on her bed: *Emergency! Come home immediately.* A lightning bolt sliced through her heart.

Goosebumps covered her skin. She swallowed the sudden lump in her throat. She broke out in a cold sweat. With her heart racing, Sasha ran to the front desk and asked, "What's the fastest way to get back to America?" Sasha couldn't afford a plane ticket. The concierge helped her look up which shipping lines had departures in the next few days. Sasha was so conflicted. Should she leave? Should she stay? Would she ever see Michael again? If she left, how soon would she be able to return to Paris? All those questions swirled around her brain as she started to pack her suitcase, heartbroken. That telegram set off an avalanche and cascade of uncontrollable shivers that prevented her from sleeping that night.

Sasha didn't have a chance to say goodbye to Michael before she left for America. She went to the Louvre but Michael wasn't working that day. Saddened, she left him a gift with a note. She explained that she had to return to America due to a family emergency.

To leave France and step onto that boat, Sasha had to give in to bittersweet surrender. It was one of the hardest things she'd ever done in her life. And as soon as the boat left the shore, Sasha regretted her decision to leave. She spent the next three weeks on a creaky, old, damp Trans-Atlantic liner. The dark shadowy walls and grey halls exacerbated her bleak loneliness. There were several bunk beds in her room but no roommates, no one to talk to. There were very few passengers on the boat. Sasha obsessed about the emergency at home. Oh God! Fear of the unknown gripped her. It had to be something awful. Someone must have died, or was dying. A rush of fear mingled with her blood. She needed to scream but nothing came out of her mouth.

Sasha was also very seasick. She continued to suppress waves of nausea. Her consolation prize was that she had so much time to write letters.

August 6, 1938

Dearest Michael,

I'm so sorry that I wasn't able to say goodbye to you in person. I already regret leaving Paris. I'm terrified by the urgent telegram. I'm positive someone died. Please don't let it be my Dad! A million butterflies are taking wing in my stomach. I have prayed that my worst fears prove unfounded. I promise you I'll return to Paris as soon as possible. You are the love of my life! My plan is to come right back. I can't lose you. Please wait for me.

Your Beloved Soulmate, for Time and Eternity,

Sasha

P. S. I discovered there's no hot chocolate on the boat for me to drown my sorrows. What will I do? Every time I drink hot chocolate for the rest of my life, I'll feel your love melt my heart no matter what's going on. You are my knight in shining armor, my fairytale hero.

August 8, 1938

Beloved Michael,

I am so exhausted but I can't sleep. I'm hungry but I can't eat. I wish I had never left Paris. I have a bad feeling about this trip. My seasickness persists. I wish I had someone to talk to.

Love,

Your Beloved Rose of Sharon,

Your Lily of the Valley,

Sasha

August 10, 1938

Dearest Michael,

To say that I miss you is a huge understatement. You mean the world to me! In the midst of these dark, stormy days and nights at sea you are my world, my shining sunlit world after a spring rain, like the first night in Paris when we sat together sipping hot chocolate as we warmed one another's hearts. You are my first true love. Thank you for your support that I'm not fat and ugly at 110 pounds! If only I could have stayed in Paris with you. That would have allowed our love to blossom and make all our dreams come true. I still regret my decision to return to NY. Therefore, I promise that I will return to France as soon as possible.

Love,

Your Soulmate for Time and Eternity,

Sasha

When the boat finally arrived in New York, Sasha's mother, Lillian, her father's best friend Abie Gabriel, and her father's parents, Nathan and Fanny Wolf, met her at the dock. By that point she was so glad to get off the boat-that's how sick she was, both emotionally and physically. Sasha was glad to be home, despite her fears of the emergency. The boat had become her prison.

Sasha's first question was, "Where's Daddy?" And that's when her worst fears came true. No words were spoken at first... only tears and sobs.

Then Abie took her aside and whispered, "Your Dad passed away."

"What happened?" she asked.

"We'll tell you more at home."

Why did she have to wait? She couldn't take this! The drive to the apartment in Brooklyn seemed like forever. An eternity. They must've passed twelve cemeteries. The car was stifling without air conditioning on such a hot day. She was still seasick even though she was off the boat. Sasha missed her sweet Michael. If he were here, she knew he would help make everything okay. He was her chocolate, but at the moment it was intensely bittersweet. She touched her locket, hidden under her dress, and his love encircled her. She took a deep breath.

Everyone gathered around the large wooden dining room table when they arrived home. Sasha chose to sit in her father's chair to feel close to him.

"Daddy was murdered," her mother blurted out. Sasha began to cry. A thousand ants seemed to crawl over her skin.

"I don't understand... Who killed him? Where did it happen? Why? Daddy was such a good man, a kind man. I know he didn't do anything wrong. Please explain! I don't understand." A scream sliced through the confusion in her brain.

Chapter 2
Camp Siegfried

"We were surrounded by 40,000 Nazis on German Day pledging allegiance to Hitler. Just imagine! A powerful, hypnotic rally-loud, raucous, almost erotic. Chants of 'Heil Hitler', 'blood and soil', and 'Germany awake, destroy the Jews' filled the air at Camp Siegfried. Swastika flags flew with wild abandon. Portraits of Hitler encircled the camp. The Nazi salute was inescapable. Even I did it out of fear. It still gives me the shivers. I will never forget it," said Abie.

"What are you talking about, Abie? What does this have to do with Daddy?" Sasha tried to snatch hold of Abie's words and make sense of what he meant but he was talking faster than usual.

"We never should have gone. Your Dad refused to follow the crowd and he didn't give the Nazi salute. The Nazis close by became suspicious. They were sure he was a spy, an outsider. They shouted 'dirty Jew' over and over as they punched and kicked him. I froze. An avalanche of shivers ran up and down my spine. I was paralyzed. One young man in a brown-shirt uniform stabbed your father in the abdomen several times. There was blood everywhere. Someone yelled, 'Run!' A huge commotion and stampede followed. Your father was on the ground bleeding out. I shielded him with my body but we got trampled. I needed to run, scream, fight back but my body had become a frozen statue. The man who stabbed your father got away with murder. Everything slowed down and became surreal. The world didn't make sense anymore. I'm still in shock."

"Oh, God! I hope they find that man and give us justice for Daddy. But I am still confused. Help me understand, Abie. How did Daddy even find out about this camp? He never mentioned it to me."

"Murray Cohen, one of your father's students at the high school, snuck into Camp Siegfried and took pictures. He showed them to your Dad in class. Your father and I found the pictures very disturbing. We chose to check out the camp ourselves. We drove to Yaphank on Long Island to see if Murray was telling the truth. He was. And the rest is history. If I hadn't given the salute, I would be dead too."

"Oh, my God! I can't believe this! Nazis in America? I was under the impression America was safer than Europe. My world is shattered. My worst fears came true. I missed the funeral and the Shiva, didn't I?"

"Yes, you did. According to Jewish tradition, your father was buried within 24 hours of his death. The funeral and Shiva took place while you were on the boat coming home," Abie sighed, wiping his sweaty palms on his pants. "I am so sorry, sweetie."

Sasha's heartbeat throbbed in her ears. She collapsed into Abie's arms and the rest of the day was a blur.

Whenever she was alone, Sasha took her locket out and kissed it. She remembered the day Michael gave it to her in the hotel room. She should've stayed in France. She and Michael would have been together. Abie created room for Sasha on the white velvet couch and covered her up with soft, white down blankets-like Goldilocks, just right! That long, velvet couch was older than Sasha; it had been a wedding gift for her parents. Sasha cried herself to sleep that night and slept for many hours. She caught up for all the sleepless nights on the boat.

Sasha woke up in a semi-dreamlike state. Where was she? Was this all just a bad dream, a nightmare? Had her father been murdered, and would she never see him again? She could still hear his whistle as he came up the stairs after work or a long trip. Those slate stairs had an unmistakable echo. And then her mind drifted to Michael. Would she ever see him again, or would the upcoming war get in the way? Sasha couldn't hold back the tears. She cried for the two men who meant the most to her.

Sasha did not miss the irony that her mother continued to ask her if she was hungry. Her mother used to say she was too fat. Now she attempted to push food on her. "No thanks, Mom, I'm not really hungry," Sasha said, annoyed, with an exasperated sigh. This became a pattern that continued to recur day after day. Sasha stayed up late and stared into space, she slept late, and didn't feel hungry. She stewed in the salty broth of disappointment–her new obsession.

After several weeks, Sasha told her mother that she planned to go back to France.

"France? Are you crazy, Sasha?" screamed her mother as she pounded her fist on the thick oak table. "War is about to break out and Europe is not safe for you now. Hitler hates the Jews!"

Her mother didn't even let her answer. "You will enter college in the fall, just like we planned."

Promises and panic mingled with her salty tears. "I cannot begin college in the fall, Momma. What's the point? It would be a total waste of money. I just can't concentrate on anything right now."

No matter what her mother said or did, she could not change Sasha's mind. Sasha was adamant, which was out of character for her–she was usually a people pleaser. She was even stunned herself. Sasha had found her voice.

Everyone except her mother was supportive, but Sasha was the closest to Abie. He was her pal and her surrogate Dad. Together they started to read about this Camp Siegfried and the Nazi sympathizers on Long Island and NYC. The German Bund had a large organization and presence in the area and they teamed up with the KKK. Huge rallies took place at Madison Square Garden and then campers were put on trains and sent out to Yaphank, New York.

The Nazis and Klansmen marched in the streets wearing their brown shirts and Nazi regalia or white hooded sheets. Swastika flags lined the streets. The only person missing–besides her Dad–was Hitler himself. But Hitler was there in spirit. Everyone at Camp Siegfried had to swear their allegiance to Hitler. Every street nearby was named after Hitler and his henchmen. It broke Sasha's heart, as ice water trickled through her veins.

"What if Hitler wins the war and comes to America, Abie?"

"I can't let myself think about that. It takes my breath away, Sasha."

"Every day I wake up to this nightmare. What a time to be alive."

"We are living in a time when history is being written."

Sasha wrote to Michael and spilled everything out onto the page. Her kinship and closeness to Michael now consumed her. She'd never experienced this with anyone before, not even with her Dad, and that was really saying something. They were twins on a soul level. She poured her heart out to him.

"My father died because he didn't give the Nazi salute in a crowd of 40,000 Nazi sympathizers. He bled out and was trampled to death. I missed the funeral. It's too late. I can't even save him. I came back to America for nothing. I should have stayed in France. My heart is broken. I cannot survive this without you."

Later she wrote in her journal, "Daddy come back. Come back. Please come home. I do not know how to survive without you since Mom is so mean. I need you to protect me. If only Michael were here to help me. The only man I can turn to is Abie! I'll do anything. I'll be good. Please come home."

Sasha must have written those sentences hundreds or thousands of times, as her pen pushed the ink and indentation through the paper five pages deep. Sasha used up three journals in one week.

Over the next month or two, Sasha got two letters from Michael. He was very supportive. He said that he understood the loss of a father because his father died during World War I. Sasha sent him some newspaper articles about her father's death. One of the articles had a photo of her Dad.

"Can you feel his warmth, his heart, his love?" she wrote. Perhaps a rhetorical question.

It was so sweet to hear his response that Sasha cried.

August 20, 1938

Dearest Sasha,

I'm so sad for you, Sasha. I wish I could be there to hold you. It must be a terrible knife to the heart. I'm so sorry about the changes in your life right now. I'm so glad you have Abie. Please hold onto the fact I love you. And yes, I can experience your father's warmth, his heart, and his love. They came through the photo. I love his face. I have saved all your letters and the articles in a brown, wooden, ornately carved box under my bed.

Also, I may join a resistance movement and I might not be able to write very often. But no matter what, I still love and miss you and I will carry your love and your gift with me wherever I go.

Your Beloved,

Your One True Love,

Your Michael, for Time and Eternity

Through their letters they continued to pledge their love to one another over and over again. Then Michael's letters stopped, and Sasha's came back "return to sender". Abie reminded her that long-distance relationships were not easy to maintain. But nothing in her life would ever be easy again. Gone were the carefree days in Paris. Gone, but never forgotten.

In Sasha's next letter she pleaded for Michael to be careful and stay safe. Someday they would be together again, after the war. But deep down she was worried about Michael's decision to join the resistance. Would she ever see him again?

"I'm so afraid that you will die like my father, at the hands of the Nazis," she wrote.

It seemed that her first real romance was so far away. Abie secretly took Sasha down to the waterfront pier every Saturday with her suitcase. She tried to return to France, but civilians weren't allowed on cargo boats anymore. It was definitely a hot chocolate moment.

"I bought you a pretty journal because you can't write to Michael anymore, Sasha."

"Thanks, Abie. I'm not sure I can start now but I am sure I will begin soon. That way when I see Michael again, he can read how much I loved him every day."

Sasha's hopelessness was like a dark cloud that blinded her to carefree chocolate days in France with Michael. It was the end of an ecstatic, romantic love story that could've had a fairytale ending, but instead was gone forever. Sasha had lost everything: Michael and her Dad. The veil of tears that surrounded her now was the next chapter of her life. A life without Michael, and her father, her protector against her cruel mother. Unbearable. The only thing Sasha was thankful for was that her seasickness was gone.

In order to escape her mother's negativity, Sasha began to help out at the local hospital. She also spent time in the library doing research on Nazi sympathizers in the U.S. Sasha was determined, even consumed, with finding the man who murdered her father. She and Abie were on a secret mission to find that Nazi.

"I can recognize him. He is very memorable. He has a big scar on the right side of his face," Abie said.

"I will search for him forever. He will not get away with murder. I will pursue him until I take my last breath," Sasha declared.

It's one thing to have a noble quest to find her father's killer. But it's quite another thing to come face-to-face with him and survive. Would Sasha have the strength and courage to stand up to this Nazi or even be in the same room as the murderer?

Chapter 3
Peter

Brooklyn, NY
March 1939

About three months later, Sasha discovered she was pregnant with Michael's child. Her mother was furious–she slammed doors and threw dishes at the wall whenever Sasha walked into the room.

"I am so ashamed of you. I can't stand it, Sasha. What will people think? The whole neighborhood will be talking about you. You are not my daughter anymore. You're dead to me now."

She shot Sasha a venomous glare. Sasha froze. She didn't know how to respond. Her posture went limp, as if her bones had dissolved.

Sasha began to retreat inward and was racked with guilt and shame. She tried to pull the covers up over her head and hide away from the world. She daydreamed that she'd stayed in France, she and Michael eloped, and that the two of them were ecstatic about the baby. Instead she found herself in Brooklyn, without her father or Michael, hiding in her room from her controlling and cruel mother. What a shame. What could have been the happiest time in her life, instead was poisoned by the barbed wire fence her mother electrified around her heart.

Sasha's relationship with her mother was as futile as carrying water with a fork. The tension got so toxic that she moved in with her father's parents, the Wolfs. What a relief. It also allowed her to be closer to Abie, who lived in their building on the same floor. Sasha had a small room, but it was cozy. It had old-fashioned striped satin wallpaper, but the bedspread and rug were purple, her favorite color. She even got a teddy bear to cuddle with at night. It was heaven. This move allowed her to feel excited about the baby, the closest thing Sasha had to Michael.

The next time Sasha was around her mother, she said, "I wish I could marry Abie."

Sasha wasn't really serious. The truth was she dreamed she could go back to France to be with Michael. But that was impossible, so Abie was the only man to whom Sasha was close.

"Oh, my God! I'm livid, Sasha. What will people think? He's old enough to be your father. You're still looking for Daddy; pick someone your own age," she grumbled. That was the last real conversation she had with her mother before her son was born.

The whole family was very happy with the birth of Sasha's healthy baby boy, Peter, in March of 1939. Even her mother seemed more supportive and gave Sasha a baby blanket she'd crocheted. Sasha wrote to Michael that he had a son, but her letter came back "return to sender". On one level she guessed she would never see him again. But secretly, she kept her dream alive.

Sasha placed a baby picture of Peter on top of the photo of Michael in her locket. Father and son were now close to one another forever. Sasha confided in Abie about her feelings for Michael. They both agreed that Sasha might never see him again due to the war.

"I am so disappointed, but I understand, Abie."

But in her secret heart of hearts, she prayed that someday they could be together again. She desired 'one big happy family,' like her Dad used to say. Never seeing Michael again–unthinkable!

It is a Jewish tradition to name a newborn child after the most recent person in the family to die. Sasha's father's name was Philip, so she needed to choose a name for her son that began with the letter P. She chose Peter. Her great grandfather's name was Joseph. Therefore, she picked a middle name that began with J. Her son's full name was Peter Johannes Wolf.

The idea that Peter would grow up without a father, especially a father like Michael, just broke her heart. Sasha started to get ahead of herself. She was worried that she wouldn't know what to say when Peter got old enough to ask, "Where's my Daddy?" This kept her up at night. She talked it over with Abie and they agreed that unless she had definitive proof that Michael was alive, she should just say he died in the war. With kids sometimes it's best to keep it simple. To explain the French resistance to a young child might be even scarier.

Sasha did not care for Peter to grow up with an obligation to hunt down Nazis for her sake, since she lost her Dad that way. When he was older, she'd explain things in more detail if he was interested. It would be bad enough that she'd spend her whole life on a search for her father's killer and for Michael.

Sasha was determined to tell Michael about Peter but her letters didn't get through to him. There was nothing she could do. Would he have planned something different about the resistance if he'd been aware he had a son? She'd probably never know. If only she and Michael could've raised Peter together. She should have stayed in Paris. It was her deepest regret. Now it was impossible for Sasha to go back because of the war.

Sasha had a hole in her heart that Abie helped fill. They did everything together–cooked, changed diapers, shopped, played in the park, pushed Peter on the swings, bathed Peter at night, read him a story before bedtime, and sang him to sleep. Abie was a father figure for Sasha. She leaned on him when it came to her emotions. He was a godsend. Everyone in the neighborhood just assumed they were married. They were always together.

Sasha was curious why Abie had never gotten married. She'd never seen him with a girlfriend. One day she got up the courage to ask him why. Abie seemed uncomfortable at first, but then he told her the truth. "I do have a girlfriend and I love her very much...but she's married to someone else, so I don't get to see her very often."

"Oh, I'm so sorry I brought it up, Abie. It is none of my business. I feel embarrassed."

"Oh, that's okay, sweetie. But it's a secret...It would be best if you kept that information just between us..."

"Okay, mum's the word." Sasha demonstrated a quick motion to zip her lips.

Abie had many secrets he had to hide and promises he had to keep. One of those promises was given to Sasha's dad, to take good care of her. But would Abie be able to keep all his secrets and promises?

By the fall of 1940, Sasha started Brooklyn College. She had a host of babysitters to help her out: Abie, her mother, and the Wolfs. At first Sasha experienced separation-anxiety when she left Peter with someone else, but over time she got used to the idea. While Sasha went to school, Peter enjoyed the attention from all his caregivers. He was so blessed to have the kind of grandparents that loved to spoil a child. Peter was very lucky.

Once Sasha was comfortable being away from Peter, she found herself to be in a new category: a single mother and a student. She had to juggle and balance her time. As a perfectionist, Sasha found her school experience rather difficult. Her mother expected her to earn a score of 100 on every test.

"If it's in the book, you should get 100," her mother would say. Sasha hated that pressure. But things fell into place over time and she began to enjoy college.

Sasha chose to study psychology. She didn't like Freud but enjoyed Jung. She loved to learn about archetypes, myths, and the art of storytelling. She was fascinated by the good and evil in fairytales. It was hard to keep up with her studies and still take care of Peter. But she planned to complete her college education. Sasha's goal was to get her master's at the New School, which hired the best scholars who'd fled from Hitler's Germany–for example, Dr. Hannah Arendt.

Sasha was still worried about Hitler and the possibility of an upcoming war. If America entered the war, would Abie join? Sasha didn't think she could handle losing him. What if Hitler won and took over America? That seemed like the end of the world. Looking for Michael and the man who murdered her father would have to be put on the back burner. Those searches would have to wait until the war was over, and the Allies would have to win. Sasha just threw her hands up in the air. She would have to put all her secret desires on hold. She wasn't even sure if she could be in the same room with a Nazi. That would take a whole lot more courage than she had now. She often looked at herself in the mirror and wondered how she would find the courage to face a cold-blooded Nazi. But whenever she needed strength or love–just to get through a moment in time– Sasha would touch the locket Michael gave her and drink dark hot chocolate.

Chapter 4
Where is Michael?

In 1939 the war was headed to Europe. The Nazis increased in numbers and were everywhere. Hitler had become a cruel bully and a household name who began to swallow up whole countries. Michael lost his appetite. Even though Michael was Catholic he was still worried about the upcoming war and the fate of Jews, Gypsies, political prisoners, "undesirables". Michael was born in France, but his family came from Italy. His mother, Therese, came to Paris to become a nurse. Her studies were interrupted by World War I. She left school and volunteered to treat wounded soldiers. Six months after Michael was born, she finished school and began to work as a nurse at a hospital in Paris.

As World War II approached, Michael and his mother returned home to Italy to be closer to their extended family. His mother had two sisters there that Michael had never met. He enjoyed his new family. This was not a good time to feel isolated. As Michael and his mother settled into their new apartment near Assisi, Italy, he continued to write to Sasha and explained why they moved back to Italy. Michael's letters were sent back stamped "return to sender" and he didn't understand why. He was heartbroken. It had never occurred to Michael that he and Sasha would lose track of one another during the war. His dream was for them to continue to correspond and be reunited after the war, to get married and have a family.

With great sadness Michael admitted that he'd probably never see Sasha again if they couldn't stay in touch. His heart ached. He still yearned for her. He pretended to move on, but his heart longed for her, and his soul never gave up the dream. When in doubt, he drank hot chocolate. Perhaps as Shakespeare would have said, he and Sasha were "star-crossed lovers" who might never meet again, or at least not on this earthly plane. It reminded Michael of the death of *Atala* in the original painting that brought them together. Sasha was his first love. Could he put her in the past? Could he bury her like the scene in *Atala's Funeral?*

After many months of reflection and prayer, Michael was convinced that if he couldn't be with Sasha, he didn't desire to be with any other woman. Could he become a monk so he would have a sense of community and feel closer to God? He wasn't sure. He was still conflicted. He explored the monastery, St. Francis of Assisi, in his hometown. Michael had a long talk with the Abbate of the monastery. He had two important issues to discuss. The first one was his love for Sasha, his marriage proposal, her acceptance, and the fact that the war had separated them. His second concern was the use of the monastery basement as a sanctuary for Jews and others at risk.

Abbate Francesco said, "I understand your dilemma. I have never faced this issue before with anyone who planned to join the brotherhood. But you've already promised a spiritual commitment to Sasha, and she to you, that I believe takes precedence over any other spiritual agreement now especially because you are separated due to the war. We don't know if your paths will cross again. If God plans for you to return to the outside world and pursue your marriage proposal to Sasha, he will guide your heart in that direction. Since we have an understanding in advance, I have come up with a solution. All you'd have to do would be to let me know that you have taken off your robe and folded it up and I will know God's plan."

"Thank you so much. I will not make this decision lightly. I will look in the mirror deeply and search my soul."

"As for the issue about the sanctuary, tell me more."

"Would it be possible that St. Francis of Assisi monastery could save, hide, and feed the targeted victims of the Nazis and Fascists? If the monastery can't be a sanctuary, I plan to join a resistance movement."

"I love your idea, Michael, and I agree with great enthusiasm. This church will become a sanctuary. Let's set up the basement with fifteen beds, plus some extra mattresses on the floor, and create a separate kitchen with a wood-burning stove."

"Fantastic!"

"Would you still like to join the monastery, or would you like to take some time...?"

There was a long pause. Michael searched his heart.

"Yes, I am ready to join now."

"What name would you like to use?"

"I would like to use my original birth name, in Italian-Brother Michelangelo."

"I predict everyone will call you Brother Angel since your mission is to rescue Jews and other endangered people from the greedy clutches of the Nazis and the Italian Fascists."

What Brother Angel committed to do was very dangerous. He and the people he hid might end up in a concentration camp or worse. Would he ever see Sasha again? That was the most important question.

Chapter 5

What Really Happened to Sasha's Father?

Poland, 1938-1942

Sasha's father, Philip Wolf, was seriously wounded on German Day at Camp Siegfried in 1938, but he recovered in a nearby hospital. He made a plan with his best friend, Abie, to bury an empty coffin so he could fly to Poland on a desperate search for the man who tried to kill him, and who later murdered his cousin during a pogrom in a little village near Warsaw. Philip was aware of the villain's face with clarity as he rode with wild abandon on his dark, sweaty horse. The man swung a bloody club covered with nails and spikes aimed to kill, not wound. This man had a very distinctive scar on his right cheek.

Philip was sure he'd find the man easily due to that scar. But no one else in the community had witnessed this particular attack, or those who did were dead. He went to a local rabbi who said, "I think I've seen this man in Warsaw near the farmers' market. But be careful, he's dangerous." The Rabbi's warning frightened Philip but he pursued his goal as if his life depended on it. In order to keep his identity secret, he changed his name to Samuel Rosenstrauch to blend in with his relatives.

At the time, Samuel lived with his Aunt Nettie and Uncle Shea Rosenstrauch, who owned a small bakery in Zyrardow. It was their son who'd been killed in the vicious pogrom by the man with that scar on his face. Samuel vowed, "I will get justice for our family." Despite the aftermath of Krystallnacht and more pogroms, Samuel was fiercely determined to find the man who killed his cousin. He was not sure what he would do if he found him. A desire burned within Samuel to kill him for many reasons.

Samuel spent many hours near and around the farmers' market in Warsaw. He often sat on a bale of hay without any gloves, coat, or hat. Each night he came home almost frozen to death. He tried as hard as he could to find this man without any luck. He went back and forth to Warsaw every day for almost a year and then gave up. At the time he slept on top of the oven at the bakery. The winter was very cold that year and he didn't have the proper clothes to stay warm. He did everything he could to keep his spirits up, although he was beyond discouraged. Poland was not an easy place for a Jew. The pogroms continued, almost daily. The galloping sounds of wild horses forced everyone to run for cover, Samuel included. But he still peeked out to see if the man with the scar was on horseback.

Hitler entered Poland and Samuel's world turned upside down and fell apart. What would become of his family? Would they all survive? And what price would they pay?

***

Time for the survival plan. The Rosenstrauchs gathered as much food, clothing, and blankets as possible. They saved extra loaves of bread from the bakery and put them away in a protective bag. They had planned this exodus for a long time but hoped they wouldn't have to put the plan in action. There was a cave two miles away in the forest. Shadows pressed through the trees. Dangerous enemies might be lurking nearby. People who used to be neighbors could easily turn you in for being Jewish. Samuel and Uncle Shea had built a strong, heavy wooden door to the cave that could be locked with bolts from the inside. They had set up areas with beds and a root cellar to store vegetables.

They had arrangements with a local family they trusted, the Heidelbergs, to bring some bread to the cave every other day. In exchange, the Heidelberg family would inherit an established bakery, the only one in town. Samuel's family gave up a bakery that had been in their family for generations. They had to let it go to survive. And despite the fact that the Heidelbergs would earn money from the bakery, it was still a risk for them to bring food to a cave with hidden Jews. Thank God the Heidelbergs took that risk.

Samuel and his family arrived at the cave and began to set things up. There was no turning back. Out of the blue, there came a knock at the door of the cave. Scared out of their wits they were speechless. Something was wrong. They'd been careful not to be followed. Samuel cringed. He took a chance, unlocked the bolts with his right hand, and opened the door of the cave. With his hands trembling and clammy, Samuel peered out the door. The sun almost blinded him. A woman–and oh, God–the woman was pregnant! That certainly forced them into a position where it was harder to say no. On the other hand, a crying baby could bring too much unwanted attention to the cave. But how could they say no? In spite of everything, they chose to let the couple in. But that was it. They were not equipped to take in any other strangers. They also wrote out the rule: no speaking of any kind allowed inside the cave. They all shook hands.

All was quiet in the cave for weeks, months, and even years. Bread was delivered every other day in the evening. Even the smell of the bread was like Heaven. Bread meant hope. Hope meant life. Every morsel was appreciated. The birth of the child was carried out magically with a minimal amount of noise. The new baby slept most of the time. Instead of being a liability... this adorable child became another miracle of hope... Everyone loved to hold her and rock her to sleep...

But what kind of future would Poland's children and grandchildren have...?

The silence of the cave was deafening. No verbal communication. Days became weeks, months became years, and a whole year–forever. Time and space became intermingled as if eternity had turned in on itself, like a ball of yarn, unbearably tangled. Five adults and a little baby–not easy in such a small space. It was a little cave carved out by hand and shovel over thirteen months. It was basically a hole in the ground that was only supposed to be used by three adults. Now their stockpile of food and blankets had to be shared with five adults and a young child. But again, how could they have said no to a pregnant woman and her husband?

Days really did grow into weeks, weeks then turned to months, and months become years. The cave was so cold and damp. They needed more blankets. Sometimes they huddled together for hours to stay warm. Samuel came to the conclusion that this situation was like hibernation. It was so dark they didn't know if it was day or night. They had planned to read but it was too dark. And when it rained the walls of the cave became very wet. They'd never planned for that. They ached for the sun. By this point they only were aware if it was a bread day or a non-bread day. As time went on the owners of the bakery were having trouble making ends meet... so they crept through the forest and delivered bread every third day. Everyone was terrified that either the bakers or the cave dwellers or both would be discovered very soon.

Their worst nightmare came true... The bakers were betrayed by local townspeople. They were arrested by Polish officers who worked closely with the SS. The Heidelbergs ended up being badly beaten and tortured. The five adults living in the cave figured out something was wrong because they hadn't had a bread delivery in an estimated two weeks. They braced for the worst. They expected a surprise attack by the SS or the Polish police. They had no bread and no hope. It was just a matter of time.

The day arrived when the trampling sound of horses raced in their direction. They were awoken at three in the morning by Polish policemen and SS officers on horseback. Samuel's aunt and uncle were executed on the spot because they were the ones who owned the bakery. Blood splattered all over Samuel. He was in shock. The other couple visibly trembled. They did not make eye contact with the officers. They were arrested and shipped off in cattle cars to Auschwitz. When they were on the train, they asked what year it was. To their amazement it was 1942. They had been in the cave for three and a half years.

But they had bigger problems now. They weren't safe in a cave anymore. Heading to Auschwitz was a death sentence.

***

The cruel conditions in the cattle cars were criminal and just the beginning of their punishment. Fear was contagious and spread like wildfire. Where were they going? Would they be separated from family? Who would live and who would die? Packed in like sardines, they had no food or water for the entire trip. The stench of decayed bodies combined with the smell of feces and urine was enough to discourage breathing altogether. Everyone slept on their feet, leaning on one another. Samuel was beyond exhausted. The only thing that allowed him to live life was his quest and determination to find that man with the scar when the war was over. He needed to find justice for his family. Nothing else mattered. Justice was his strong moral compass.

The cattle car doors opened. People trampled over one another to get outside. The dead and half-dead bodies created a human carpet to stumble over. Samuel fell twice but he ached to make his way through the crowd. He had a strong sense of purpose. Samuel jumped out of the cattle car and bent to kiss the ground. The sunlight was so beautiful, albeit blinding because of his years in the cave. He experienced a brief moment of happiness but was jolted back to earth by a rifle butt shoving him onward. He lost track of the couple and their small child. What a shame. If only he could have stayed with them. They were the closest thing to family he had left in this world. He was forced to go to the left, get his striped pajamas, and move on to get his tattoo.

His first assignment was a lucky one. He began to work in the building that was called "Canada." He was forced to go through all the belongings that the prisoners brought with them in their suitcases. The goal was to create piles of various items–shoes, glasses, coats, candlesticks, silver, gold, watches, paper money, artwork, and even the suitcases had their own pile. An assignment in "Canada" was an easy job. You were inside, warm, and not involved in hard physical labor as most of the other inmates were forced to do outside. By this point Samuel weighed about 80 pounds so he could not have withstood the cold or heavy physical labor.

One day Samuel exited the barracks first thing in the morning, ready for a roll call. He was shocked by a Nazi guard whose face struck a nerve. He hadn't seen this man at the camp before so he must be new. Wait. Samuel was stunned by the man's familiarity. There was no mistaking him now–the man with the scar. He was the man who tried to kill him and later beat his cousin to death in that pogrom. Definitely. That scar on his right cheek was a dead giveaway. To think of all the countless hours Samuel spent looking for him...back and forth to Warsaw...only to find him here as a guard in Auschwitz. What an irony. Samuel was elated. For almost a few moments Auschwitz was like Heaven.

Without a plan Samuel rushed towards this Nazi guard and head-butted him square in his gut. Samuel knocked him clear off his feet. There he was on the ground. Once Samuel comprehended what he'd done he realized there would be trouble. He had to make a quick getaway. He bolted as fast as he could, but Nazi-scar-man got up and sic'd his huge German Shepherd on him, who bit and clawed Samuel's face, carving it into a piece of raw, red meat.

"Take him to the infirmary," said one of the other guards, "he needs stitches. I guess that will teach him not to attack a Nazi guard again," he chuckled, and Samuel was hauled off.

Waffen SS Major Schmidt, the guard Samuel attacked, was so humiliated that he pulled out his revolver and shot three random prisoners execution-style in the roll call line as a form of retaliation. He had to regain control and maintain his authority over the prisoners. Samuel spent two long months in the infirmary. He enjoyed lying in bed and all the attention from the nurses. Every day he woke up thinking up new ways to kill this guard, even if it meant he died trying.

Samuel could not believe the incredible irony that the man he had sought for almost a year ended up as a guard at Auschwitz. Samuel's life now centered on revenge. Fate had brought them together at last. It was his destiny. Samuel smiled with relish; his teeth glistened in the sun. In many ways, both men were facing death sentences, Samuel as a Jew in Auschwitz and SS Major Heinrich Schmidt who would be hunted down every day by an inmate who didn't care if he lived or died. Schmidt didn't understand the reasons Samuel was so angry with him. But at some point there would be a reckoning.

Samuel had a long hard road ahead of him if he was going to survive and accomplish his goal. Would he prevail? Would he kill this guard? Would he even survive Auschwitz? If he survived would he be able to go home and look for family and friends?

Chapter 6
Pearl Harbor

Sasha's emotions intensified on Sunday, December 7, 1941, the day that would live in infamy. The American army and navy base in Pearl Harbor was attacked by the Imperial Japanese Navy. The United States would declare war. Sasha was on a walk with Peter in the park when she ran into Abie.

"Did you hear about the attack on Pearl Harbor, Sasha?"

"No, what happened?" Her heart raced and Sasha began to shake.

"The Japanese attacked Pearl Harbor and that means we'll enter the war soon," he said with a grimace, his jaw clenched.

They both ran into the building and turned on Grandpa Wolf's radio. Yes, indeed it was true. Sasha's terror thermometer went sky-high. Her emotions rose up to the surface. What if Abie signed up? Heaven forbid. Her anxiety went through the roof! She just couldn't lose Abie; he was her lifeline. And what about Michael in a French resistance group? The world was a dangerous place. That's when the insomnia started.

For the next few days everyone was glued to Grandpa Wolf's radio. The U.S. had already declared war on the Japanese. When would the other shoe drop? Germany and Italy declared war on the U.S. on December 11th. Sasha had never lived through a war before. She was horrified by Hitler's Nazi propaganda and she worried he might win the war and take over America.

By the end of the week, Abie announced that he'd enlisted in the army. He was determined to fight against Hitler. He figured Sasha would be upset so he tried to break it to her gently. A chill went up Sasha's spine. She became hysterical–she screamed and cried in the shower hoping no one would hear. Sheer terror ran like ice water through her veins. She'd already lost her father, and the idea of losing Abie too was just out of the question, impossible.

"Please don't go, Abie," she begged, sobbed, and tugged on his shirt. "This is my worst fear. I cannot bear to lose you. You've been like a father to me. Don't leave me, please don't leave me, Abie. I cannot live without you. You are the kindest, most loving soul I know."

"I'm sorry, Sasha, I have to fight Hitler and the Nazis. They killed your father."

Abie got his uniform. He tried it on, twirled around, and tipped his hat at Sasha.

"That's not funny, Abie." Sasha hid her eyes and stuck out her tongue.

He tried to make her laugh but her smile was gone. She imagined her worst fears would come true–every man she loved would die at the hands of the Nazis. It brought back her father's gruesome death. Sasha was totally obsessed. She had nightmares and couldn't sleep for months.

On the day Abie left to join his regiment, Sasha sat outside on the stoop of the apartment building. Peter played with chalk on the sidewalk. She tried to hold back her tears but cried into a handful of tissues.

"Let's go inside, Peter. It's getting cold."

"Aww... Mom, do we have to?"

"Just for today, sweetie. I need to talk with Grandma Wolf."

"Okay. I bet you feel sad Abie left."

"I sure do, Peter."

They went into the apartment building and knocked on Grandma Wolf's door. She greeted them with a hug.

"How about some apple pie, Peter?" asked Grandma Wolf.

"Sure, Grandma. I love your homemade apple pie. He gobbled it down. "Great pie, Grandma. May I be excused? I'm gonna go play with my Lincoln Logs."

"Sure, Peter," answered Grandma. "He's so cute, Sasha," she said, looking over at her granddaughter.

"Yes, he is." Sasha smiled.

"Grandma, what am I going to do without Abie? He's been my Rock of Gibraltar. I think he's too old to go to war anyway."

"His goal is to fight Hitler."

"I know. I'm just afraid he won't come home, murdered at the hands of a Nazi like Daddy. Déjà vu."

Grandma gave her a hug. "Anytime you need a rock, I'll be here for you."

"Really?" she sighed and reached for more tissues.

"Absolutely."

"I'm scared to death when I see those swastikas and hear the anti-Semitic propaganda. Are you, Grandma?"

"I am. My parents moved here to get away from anti-Semitism and the pogroms. If we hadn't come to America, we might not be alive today."

"Hitler made me afraid to be a Jew!"

"Anytime you need a hug, come to me."

"Okay. Thanks. I will."

Would Abie ever come home? Would Michael be alive by the end of the war?

***

That first bleak winter consisted of sleet, snow, and ice. Everyone sat around the Wolfs' apartment. Peter and Sasha spent many evenings around their fireplace with hot chocolate. One night when everyone was together, Peter asked Sasha, "Is Abie my daddy?"

"No, sweetie. Your daddy died in the war." She pretended to know, because she wasn't sure. This was the conversation Sasha dreaded when Peter was born.

"Did Abie die in the war?"

"No, Peter. Abie is very much alive even though he is still in the war." She suppressed her own fluttering panic. "Your daddy died as part of the resistance movement." She wasn't going to say that. Why did she do it?

"What is the resistance movement, Mommy?" asked Peter with an inquisitive smile.

"Let's see. How do I explain it? The resistance movement is a group of people who fight against Hitler, a very mean man. So your father was very brave and died being true to himself. Your daddy's name was Michael. He died before Abie even went into the army. I know it's a little complicated, sweetie. Even though I love Abie very much, he's not your daddy. He helped me take care of you just like Grandma and Grandpa Wolf. I guess you could say Abie is your 'pretend daddy.'"

"Well done," Grandpa Wolf laughed.

As Sasha spoke about Abie, her heart began to race, and Sasha's gaze bounced from place to place. Her worst reality was that Abie would not make it home. She needed to put a positive spin on everything. Sasha became overheated and took off her sweater.

But Peter continued to ask hard questions. "When Abie comes home from the war, will he be my daddy then?"

"No, Peter. Abie's too old to be your daddy."

"Where are all these daddy questions coming from, Peter?"

"Oh...all the kids on the block make fun of me because I don't have a daddy."

"I'm sorry, Peter. Just tell them your daddy died in the war."

"But why can't I get another daddy who didn't die in the war, Mommy?" yelled Peter, wiping away tears.

"Why do you need another daddy, Peter?" Sasha asked, offering a small smile of acceptance. She chose her words with care to get the root of the problem.

"Because then all the kids on the block won't tease me anymore." Peter cried and put his head in his hands.

"What kind of things do they tease you about?"

"Oh, sometimes they just say, 'You don't have a daddy,' in a kind of sing-song way. Other times they say, 'Peter and the Wolf, Peter and the Wolf,' and then they laugh."

"Who is Peter and the Wolf anyway, someone bad?" Sasha giggled. "Peter and the Wolf is a famous musical piece that you would love. We should get a copy of it and play it for you on Grandpa's Victrola. How would you like that?"

"I would like that a lot, Mommy. I would love it!" said Peter, his face beaming. Sasha threw her arms in the air and gave Peter a big bear hug.

"I love seeing your smile, Peter."

The problem was solved when they bought Peter a record of *Peter and the Wolf.* He loved the album and played it over and over again until he had the whole thing memorized. It became an addiction, his new obsession. During the day Peter pretended he was the conductor as he waved his arms to go along with the music. At night he fell asleep to it. It was a godsend. Peter loved all the instruments and how they represented different animals in the forest. Sasha was the bird, represented by the flute, Sonia was the duck, represented by the oboe, and Ivan was the cat, represented by the clarinet. Plus, the wolf was played by the horn section.

"That's funny, Mommy...that Sasha is the bird. So *you* are the bird, Mommy, and I am Peter, and I am the wolf, too, since my name is Peter Wolf... That's too funny, Mommy. I don't have to be scared of the wolf or those bullies."

The next time the kids started to tease him on the block or on the playground Peter walked right on by, as he sang the melody of *Peter and the Wolf*. He held his head high, and never turned back.

Chapter 7
Homecoming

September 1945

As the war dragged on, Peter continued to ask "why" questions–his favorite activity. He graduated up from "Why is the sky blue?" and "Who is my daddy?" to questions about the war.

"Why does the world need to have war anyway? I don't understand. People just buy guns and kill each other? Who started this war anyway? Have there ever been any other wars? How long do wars last? Forever? What happens if we lose the war? What happens if we win the war? You must get tired of all my questions, Mommy."

"I'm not tired of your questions at all, sweetie. I am happy to answer your questions to the best of my ability. I don't have all the answers you need, Peter. It would be great to live in a world without war. World War I was supposed to be 'the war to end all wars,' yet here we are fighting World War II.

"Sometimes people can't fight their own battles against bullies. Some of those bullies get too strong for just one person to fight. At times like that they need to get together to help people who can't help themselves fight the big bullies. People like Hitler are big bullies and I'm sorry to say he's gotten millions of people to follow him. I don't understand why but now the good people of the world need to be even stronger. They need to stand up and make their voices known. They can no longer be bystanders. That way they can stop bullies from hurting their families and their children.

"So, for example, in the war that's going on right now, there's that very mean man named Hitler. Some people are going to war just to stop Hitler."

"Like what kind of bad things, Mommy?" said Peter.

"Well, I don't like the idea I might give you nightmares...that's why I am hesitant to answer your questions."

"I promise I won't have nightmares, Mommy. I'm more grown-up now and not worried about monsters or scared of the dark anymore," Peter responded, "I feel proud of myself."

"Ok, sweetie, I will try to explain more. Let's say that Hitler doesn't like people who are Jewish, or Gypsies, or maybe he just doesn't like people who disagree with him. Hitler has the power to put people like that in big jails, like big prisons, or maybe labor camps. Then Hitler and his friends make sure that the prisoners don't have enough food, clothing, toilets, soap, or water.

"Do those examples help you understand why many people have tried to stop Hitler from what he's doing?"

"Yes, Mommy. I am already having nightmares and I'm still awake. I think I'd better not ask any more questions about war–it's too scary for someone like me," said Peter, his lip trembling and his voice rising to a higher pitch than usual.

"Sweetie, when you say 'it's too scary for someone like you,' do you mean someone who's 6?"

"Yes."

"I'll tell you a secret, Peter. It is even scary for mommies, daddies, grandmas, and grandpas. The truth is that when you have bullies, like those boys who were teasing you in school–those are called bullies–when you have bullies in charge of the world, that's when you have a lot of war. That's why we need to stop bullies early in life, like in schools. If we did that, maybe we wouldn't have as many wars.

"Okay," Sasha squeezed Peter's hand affectionately. "Now let's listen to *Peter and the Wolf* on the Victrola and we can make cookies while we listen. How does that sound?"

"But Grandma and Grandpa have gone to sleep. Won't the music wake them up?" Peter asked, still fearful.

"I think it'll be okay, honey. We'll keep the music a little bit softer than usual. I'll make some hot milk and honey, too. That always helps you go to sleep."

"Okay, Mommy. I guess I shouldn't have asked about wars so close to bedtime."

"Aww so sorry, sweetie. We won't do it again."

"That's good."

"Hot milk and honey and chocolate chip cookies always make things better, right?"

"Right, Mommy."

But Peter always found interesting questions that Sasha hadn't figured out how to handle. Within her own heart she was still afraid for both Abie and Michael's wellbeing. And her nightmares came back again with a vengeance.

***

Spring 1945

The war rolled on. Panic clawed at Sasha's throat. She feared Michael and Abie were dead. Fear of the unknown. Time passed slowly but Peter got older. Sasha's new obsession–the rumors about concentration camps. Her colleagues and professors who were smuggled out of Europe just before or during the war shared the disturbing news. Sasha was petrified. She was still determined to find her father's killer but had no idea where to begin. She would have to wait until the war was over. Discouraged, in the middle of the night, she held her head in her hands. Sasha was so alone. Without Abie she was lost. She tried to talk to Grandma Wolf, but for some reason it had to be Abie. Late at night hot chocolate kept her company in the kitchen. Chocolate always solved everything, at least temporarily. She cried herself to sleep.

Insomnia became Sasha's best friend, her silent partner in crime, her obsession. She talked to her father out loud or wrote to him in her journal.

"Hey Dad, would you have gone to the war, like Abie? I bet you would have... even if you hadn't been stabbed. But how could you leave me alone? Abie doesn't have children, but *you*? How could you leave me alone with Mom? She's so mean. And you never got to meet Peter or Michael? Say, Dad, is it true what they say about those labor camps? Can you see them from Heaven? But anyway, Dad, when are you coming home?"

Sasha often woke up in the morning having slept on the kitchen table, head rested on her folded arms, her journal and a pen underneath.

When the war ended, Sasha discovered that her worst fear had *not* come true. She was her own worst enemy.

"Abie is on his way home. He's safe," Sasha screamed to Peter. She waved the letter around wildly in her upraised hand through the kitchen.

"How come he didn't write to us sooner, Mom?"

"He was in a POW camp in North Africa."

"What's a POW camp?"

"Oh, sorry, Peter. It's a prisoner of war camp."

"Abie was a prisoner of the Germans, Mom? It's amazing he's still alive."

"Oh man, I bet he's got a lot of cool stories. When will he be home?"

"I'm not sure. Maybe a few weeks?"

"I can't wait to see him."

"Me too!"

It was a Thursday when Abie strolled towards the apartment building with his duffle bag. Sasha dashed across the park. She almost tripped over her own two feet.

"I wasn't aware your homecoming was today!" She pinched herself to make sure this wasn't a dream.

"Sometimes it's nice to get good surprises, Sasha."

"Well, ain't that the truth. Always the jokester," she chuckled and gave him the biggest hug. Then Sasha burst into tears, "I didn't think you would ever come home. I was concerned you would die like Daddy!"

"Aha! That's why I had to come home to make sure your worst fears didn't come true!"

"Oh, how I've missed you, Abie. You always say just the right thing." Sasha sobbed and held on tight with both arms. "That hug is one for the books, Abie. I have to catch my breath. That was longest hug in the world. Am I a little girl who just hugged her Daddy?"

"Anything I can do to help, just ask, Sasha." Abie wiped his tears away.

"Since my worst fear didn't come true with you, do you think that Michael's still alive... if you survived?"

"Oh, wow. I'm really not sure."

"Look who's here, Peter!" Sasha switched subjects and encouraged Peter to come over.

Peter raced over, giving Abie a gigantic hug. "Abie, so glad you came home. Mom told me you survived a POW camp."

"I'm glad to be alive. It's so good to be home." Abie leaned over to pick up his duffle bag. "Boy, you're almost as tall as I am, Peter. You've really grown in four years."

"Yep, I sure have. And I'm old enough to hear all your cool stories from your POW camp."

"No problem. Maybe over a home-cooked meal?"

"Yes, of course. Let's have dinner together. How would you like some chicken soup, blintzes, and good ole *American as apple pie?*"

"You're on, Sasha. Oh, quick question, is that apple pie in a deep-dish cast-iron skillet, the way Grandma Wolf makes it?"

"Yes, it sure is. It's her recipe."

"I've dreamed of that pie for four and a half years. See you at 6 p.m."

"Peter, Abie may not tell all of those cool stories around Grandma and Grandpa Wolf at dinner."

"Yeah, right. But isn't tonight their late night at Brighton Beach?"

"Yes, you're right, Peter. They have bridge tonight. You and Abie must have planned this you could pick his brain and hear all his juicy stories."

"Aww, Ma."

***

"I couldn't wait for Peter to go to sleep so we could have our first real heart-to-heart, Abie. Thanks again for staying alive. Peter and I need you."

"That's so sweet. I missed you guys too. I had to make it home for you and that helped me stay alive." He reached out for Sasha's hand.

"It sounds like you're still hopeful about Michael based on the question you asked me earlier."

"Peter longs for a new daddy but I am not going to settle for just anybody. Several men have asked me out, but they didn't compare to Michael."

"Oh, so you told Peter his daddy already died."

"Yes, I did when he asked if you were his daddy after you left. Until I am sure that Michael is dead or married, it's impossible for me to fall in love with someone else. I need closure with Michael... Peter needs to have a father and a good role model, but I also need to be with the love of my life. I think it's very important for me to be true to myself. Nothing and no one can ever replace Michael. He was truly a one-in-a-million man. You never forget your first love."

Chapter 8

Peter Finds his Mission

September 1945

Peter started school in the fall.

"I love school and I'm happy. I have so many new friends. None of them are bullies, Mom. I love reading, math, and art. Can I invite friends to come home after school to play and show them my toys, books, and records?" asked Peter, all in one breath.

"Sure, sweetie. I'm glad you are so happy," Sasha responded.

About six months later, Peter came home and discovered Sasha's tears. "What's wrong, Mommy?"

"There was a terrible car accident."

"Was anyone hurt?"

"Yes, my mommy," Sasha sobbed while she grabbed more tissues.

"Can we go to visit her in the hospital?" Peter asked.

"I wish we could, but it's too late."

"It's not too late, Mommy it's only 4 o'clock in the afternoon."

"I mean that she already died, so she's not in the hospital," Sasha sobbed, numb all over.

"Oh Mommy, I'm so sorry this happened. It's not fair. We didn't even say goodbye."

"Right, it's totally unfair." Just like Sasha never said goodbye to her Dad or Michael, now she also wouldn't say goodbye to her mother.

"Why do bad things happen to good people?" Peter asked.

"That's a good question. I'm not sure." But a message went through her heart like a dagger. She was going to need to find a way to forgive her mother. That wouldn't be easy. Despite her negativity, Sasha did love her. But at least her mother couldn't hurt Sasha anymore.

"Let's take a walk, Mom."

"That sounds like a good idea. You're such a good boy, Peter."

"Thanks, Mom."

"Here, let's put on our jackets, scarves, hats, and mittens." A nice long walk around the playground gave Sasha a change of scenery. The cold air rushed past her cheeks. Sasha breathed deeply for the first time in a while. She hated the cold weather but today it helped her to feel that cold, windy air. Sasha was overcome by a hypersensitivity as she glanced at all the naked trees. She had a heightened sense of being alive. She was still alive, even though her mother had just died. What would she do with her freedom? What would she do with her life?

"Thanks for the suggestion of a walk, sweetie."

"Anything to help you, Mommy."

"You did. More than you could possibly understand."

"Did you tell Abie and the Wolfs?"

"Yes, I did."

"What happens next?"

"The funeral process begins. Some people wash the body, wrap her in a white sheet, put her in a pine box called a casket or coffin, and then we bury her tomorrow after a brief service. The pine wooden coffin has a carved Jewish star on top. It will be lowered into the ground. Then we'll use a shovel, and everyone gets to dig up some dirt and throw it into the grave on top of the coffin. It is an old Jewish custom."

"Can I come, Mommy?"

"Yes, of course, Peter."

"Good," he said, as he clutched his scarf. "What's it called again?"

"You mean a funeral?"

"Oh, that's it, Mommy. A funeral."

When they got home, Abie was already there. Peter ran over and hugged him. "*You're* not going to die now, are you?" He held onto Abie's shirt.

"No, buddy. I just got home from the war and I plan to stick around to take care of you and Mommy."

"Oh, that's good. I think you need to hug Mommy. She is having a hard day." Abie held Sasha and she sobbed on his shoulder.

"Does everybody die?"

"At some point, Peter," said Sasha, trying to reassure him.

"Sometimes people die in an accident, of old age, or some illness," said Abie.

"When I die it will be when I did something really courageous," said Peter, and he stuck out his chest. "I'm Superman." They all smiled.

"I am so proud of you, Peter. I'm sure you'll have a nice long life and you'll be the bravest most wonderful boy a momma could ever yearn for."

But deep down inside, Sasha had this horrible premonition that Peter would be brave and die at an early age, just like her father and Michael. Sasha trembled. If that happened, she wouldn't have a chance to say goodbye. Something new to worry about, as a chill ran up her spine. Sasha had a Ph.D. in worrying. She tried to push those ideas out of her head but sometimes death and worry went together for Sasha. She would have to stay where her feet were and not get ahead of herself.

The next morning, they bundled up for a snowy day and met the Rabbi at Pine Lawn Cemetery.

"They did everything you said they would, Mom," said Peter after he shoveled some dirt in the grave.

It was a small gathering of mostly relatives, some of whom Peter had never met like Betty, Leo, Sadie, Lucille, and Tante Gella. The Wolfs prepared a delicious meal on short notice. Peter loved the chicken soup best, which was good for a cold day.

After a few days of sitting shiva, Peter went back to school with a little note explaining his absence. He was glad the teacher did not ask him any questions. He didn't mention it to anyone and just acted as if everything was normal. Peter was glad to see his best friend, Sonny. They hung out on the playground and ate lunch together. They were in the same reading group and sometimes walked home together. Sonny lived nearby. Most of the time Peter loved school. If he was sad, he tried not to show it. He was ready to be grown up.

A few times the teacher was sick and they had a substitute. "I don't like substitutes, Mom. Most of the kids are rowdy but I am a good boy. I don't like to get in trouble."

A few weeks later he ran home to tell his Mom with excitement, "My teacher isn't sick at all–she's going to have a baby! All the kids are happy for her but we're going to have that mean substitute teacher till June. I'll be glad when the year is over."

And when the summer came, Peter told Sasha with a bright smile, "I love summer because I can go to the Brighton Beach Club with Grandma and Grandpa Wolf. You and Abie can come too. I invited Sonny to come along. I feel like I died and went to Heaven."

The summer flew by and Peter was back in school again. And that's how it went from year to year. A year of working hard, learning to read at an advanced level, and doing more complicated math, science projects, and learning about the world. Then going to Brighton Beach Club every summer.

"This is the life of Riley," said Peter. "I just love summer, Mom. I feel so relaxed and carefree. I feel like I don't have to worry about anything. It's so great to have a big family. And Brighton Beach Club is the best. Can I have some money for a hot dog, French fries, and cotton candy? And maybe a drink?"

***

One night at dinner, when Peter was in junior high school, he said, "I feel worried about something."

"What's bothering you, Peter?" asked Sasha.

"One of my homework assignments is to figure out what I'll be when I grow up. It's a hard question. I've never focused on that. What should I be when I grow up?"

"That's an interesting question, Peter," said Abie.

"What activity do you love most in the whole wide world?" Sasha asked Peter, curious how he'd respond.

"To spend time at Brighton Beach Club with your Grandma and Grandpa."

"Would you like to be a lifeguard?"

"Hmmm... not sure. I think I'd rather be with the people who are playing cards."

"You could work at a casino; they play cards there," Sasha replied with a little giggle.

"That feels kind of sleazy, Mom."

"Yeah. I think you might have to pay off the mafia, too," said Abie with a chuckle.

"Do you think you would like to be a teacher?" asked Sasha.

"Now that's more like it, but what if I had rowdy kids and bullies?" Peter scratched his head.

"I think you'd find a way to deal with them, Peter," his Mom encouraged him.

"Maybe I could teach college, then the students would be more mature."

"Yeah, right," Abie said, and they all smiled. "I guess you don't have to figure it out tonight, Peter."

"That's true but the assignment is due in two weeks. That feels like pressure, Mom."

"Oh, I see, so I guess you need to pick something and research it," Sasha said.

"Yeah I do. I am going to ask my dreams."

"That sounds like a good plan, Peter."

"By the way, Mom, dinner was delicious."

"Thanks, sweetie."

By the next day Peter had it all figured out, and he never wavered from his idea for the rest of his life. At dinner Peter asked Sasha, "Wasn't your Dad killed by a Nazi? In America, right?"

"Yes, Peter, why do you ask?"

"I think I figured out what I'd like to be when I grow up. In social studies today, we were talking about World War II and how we were so glad the Nazis lost the war. The teacher mentioned a man named Simon Wiesenthal who has a center in Linz, Austria. It is called the Jewish Historical Documentation Centre. Some Nazis escaped prosecution in Nuremberg and are probably still on the run. Since my very own Grandpa was killed by a Nazi, I owe it to him to search and hunt for those missing Nazis."

"Wow, Peter, now that's a lofty project, but if anyone can do it, you can," Sasha replied, rather stunned. She tried to hide her shock by playing with her food.

"That's a great answer to your assignment and you came up with it so fast," replied Abie. Sasha was still at a loss for words.

"Well, I have to thank my social studies teacher. He planted the seed."

Planted the seed? *Oh, my God*, Sasha screamed in silence. She was ready to kill that social studies teacher. Every hair on her head stood at attention and she tried to pull it out. Her obsessions resurrected themselves and came back with a vengeance. *Here we go again*, her heart said. Peter would place himself in danger, and he would die at the hands of the Nazis. And Sasha would never have a chance to say goodbye. Just like it happened with her father. She couldn't take it anymore.

"This premonition will be the death of me," Sasha told Abie while doing the dishes after Peter went to sleep.

"I understand, sweetie," said Abie.

Later that night while everyone was asleep, Sasha sat at the kitchen table and her head exploded in her hands. Night terrors came back and so did her best friend, insomnia.

Peter continued to research his project all through junior high and high school. He did everything else that was required of him, but he loved to research and read anything he could get his hands on related to the Nazis. They even went out to see where Camp Siegfried used to be. Sasha admitted it was rather sinister, in an eerie sort of way. She didn't have any desire to stay for a long time.

"I can't believe they had a real camp here," said Peter.

"Yep, this is where Grandpa Philip was murdered," Abie sighed. Sasha shut her eyes and held onto Abie's arm.

"But he wasn't alone, right, Abie? You were with him?"

"Yep. We were alone in a sea of 40,000 Nazis and Nazi sympathizers."

"40,000. Wow. I'm really glad he wasn't totally alone. I still can't get over all those people pledging allegiance to Hitler in 1938, right here in New York."

"The whole thing feels very uncomfortable. It still gives me the shivers, Peter. My Dad died here." She couldn't hold it in anymore. Her arms trembled. "I can't stay here any longer.

This place gives me the creeps," Sasha blurted out and ran to the car, sick to her stomach. The whole world was spinning. She could hear her heartbeat pound in her ears.

The following fall Peter entered the University of Chicago on a scholarship. He planned to major in history, but he had to take two years of core courses. This rather annoyed him since his main obsession was to study the Nazis. He did his regular coursework during the day and continued his research when his friends were off meeting girls. Peter dated from time to time, but nothing serious. He was riveted on his obsession with Nazis on the run. He burned the midnight oil every chance he got.

"I love it here, Mom," Peter said with passion in his voice when he called home. Sasha was happy for Peter but at the same time her soul was tormented. She was going to have to overcome her haunted preoccupation with Nazis killing her loved ones.

Peter was addicted to used bookstores and searched city libraries for rare books. Sometimes he got lucky. If not, he devoured the transcripts of the Nuremberg trials. He learned about Dr. Mengele and his research on twins, which was heartbreaking. He was curious how the twins were doing now. Peter also learned about the Eugenics Projects in the U.S. which disgusted and embarrassed him. On the bright side he was excited to read about Dr. Hans Munch, the only SS high ranking official and physician acquitted at the Nuremberg trials.

It was hard to keep up with all his regular assignments when his heart was wrapped up in his Nazi research. By the time he was done with his core coursework, he was able to choose his electives. He chose to study German to help him with any future translations. He also took courses on German literature including Kafka, Thomas Mann, Brecht, et al. He also delved into German and Austrian history. This allowed

Peter to focus on his passion. He learned about German culture and how to go about the hunt for Nazis.

"This is who I am, Mom," Peter told Sasha on the phone. "My adrenaline's pumping,"Peter continued. Sasha raised her hand to Heaven and begged God help keep Peter safe on his journey.

One day, Peter found out about a new movie, *The Diary of Anne Frank*. Although his mission had been clear for a long time, the movie increased his desire to be a Nazi hunter a thousand-fold. He was thrilled that Anne Frank was in love with a boy named Peter–pronounced Pay-der–whose family was also hiding in the annex. He later learned that Anne died in Bergen-Belsen shortly before the camp was liberated while her true love, Peter, escaped from another camp, joined the resistance, but was murdered. Peter's father had died as a resistance fighter too. This fueled Peter's desire even more to hunt for Nazi war criminals. He told Sasha all about his reaction to the movie the next time they talked.

"There's no stopping me now, Mom. My mission is clear and the danger is present. Nazis are still hiding or on the run. My job in this world is to find them and bring them to justice!"

Peter ended up doing his undergraduate thesis on the American Studies of Eugenics and their use in the Third Reich. He received special honors for his paper from Dr. Bettelheim. Peter discovered to his horror that Nazis directly used American Eugenic writings on controlling and eliminating groups that were considered "undesirables." There seemed to be some evidence that besides sterilization, such groups were inoculated with infectious diseases such as tuberculosis, left untreated, and observed as they died. If Peter had not been so preoccupied with being a Nazi hunter, he would have continued his obsession with American Eugenics.

Peter wrote in his journal, "I will avenge my grandfather's death at the hands of a Nazi in 1938 in America. That Nazi got away with murder. I plan to bring him and all Nazis to justice if it's the last thing I do. I'll make you proud, Mom. I'll do it for you, Mom–and Grandpa, you too!"

Chapter 9

Chocolate, Sunflowers, and Spies

After getting his B.A. with Special Honors from the University of Chicago, Peter stayed on to get his Master's in Modern German History, specializing in Nazi propaganda and the concentration camps. By now everyone was aware that Peter was a serious student who desired to be a Nazi hunter and planned to do his second year abroad to study with Professor Giovanni, who had discovered the "monastery routes" ("ratlines") in Italy that allowed many Nazis to stay there and hide in safety. They wore robes and pretended to be monks, or sailed to South America–for example, Eichmann, who'd recently been tried, found guilty, and hanged in 1962. Peter followed the whole trial on TV and read Hannah Arendt's articles about "The Banality of Evil."

As his second year began, Peter left for the University of Perugia in Italy. It had three things going for it: chocolate, Professor Giovanni, and monasteries in Rome and Bolzano, which might have Nazis hiding in them. He said goodbye to Sasha and Abie at the airport and they all had hot chocolate at a café near his gate. He promised to call them every few weeks. As Peter walked towards the gate for his plane, his Mom used a common expression, a little game they used to play together.

Sasha said, "Don't take any wooden nickels."

Peter responded, “Don’t do anything I wouldn’t do.” He brushed some tears from his eyes, turned around and waved, but then he kept on walking. He did not look back.

“I’m petrified that Peter will never come home. I feel like I’m going to faint, can we sit down?” said Sasha, out of breath.

“Of course, let’s sit down over here,” said Abie, as he pointed to a row of chairs. “You’re hyperventilating. Just breathe normally, Sasha. Take your time. Peter’s okay. It’s normal that you would be scared. Remember, I came home and your fears about me did not come true.”

Sasha sensed Abie was right but her emotions still got the best of her. Why should she be shocked? This was her weakness and something she had to overcome, a challenge.

Peter was now on a plane headed for beautiful Italy. He read most of the way and the time just flew by. Even though it was a night flight, he was too excited to sleep. He landed in Rome, rented a car, and headed straight for Perugia. He got to his dorm room and met his roommate, Billy. Peter had gotten almost no sleep on the plane, and with the time difference plus the long car ride, Peter crawled into bed with the idea he would sleep forever.

“Where is the nearest chocolate shop? I am looking for hot chocolate,” Peter asked Billy.

“But it’s summer. It’s hot out.”

“That’s okay, it’s a family tradition.”

“Alright, take a left when you go out the dorm room, go down the hall, and exit the building. Then go about three or four blocks and it’s on your left,” Billy grumbled, needing to hit the books.

Peter got dressed and followed Billy’s directions. He found it. He stared at the menu and ordered a double hot chocolate. The cashier was young but very sweet.

“Hi, I’m Peter. I came here from America to study with the famous Professor Giovanni.”

"Welcome to Perugia. My name is Maria. I study with Professor Giovanni, too. He's a monk who saved many Jews and other people during the last war. He's sitting right over there now," she said, pointing to a man with a grey beard, wearing a brown robe.

"Do you think it would be alright if I approached him now?"

"Sure, he is super nice and loves helping students."

"Thanks, Maria."

Peter went over to Professor Giovanni and introduced himself.

"Oh, I understand exactly who you are and why you're here," said the professor, as he stared right into Peter's eyes. "You are the bright young man from America who aspires to be a Nazi hunter. You have come to the right place. There are Nazis hiding in Bolzano and Rome and perhaps other places. I need a young graduate student to help me with my mission. We need to find them, hunt them down, and lock them up," he said as he ran his fingers through his beard.

"I'm your man, sir," Peter responded, and he stood up straight.

"It may involve some risk, son."

"My grandfather and other relatives were killed by Nazis."

"No wonder you are so motivated, Peter. You're famous all over the world."

"Me? Not really, Professor."

"It's true. Everyone in our field has read all your papers. And I also see you like hot chocolate."

"Yes, I do, especially *dark* hot chocolate. It's a family tradition!"

"That's interesting," the professor said as he scratched his head. The professor's heart skipped a beat–Peter's last name was Wolf. Was his mother's name Sasha? He was too embarrassed to ask. There were probably millions of Wolfs in America. So instead, he said, "If you are looking for me on my regular teaching days and you cannot find me in my office, I'll be right here in the Chocolate Shoppe. I'm addicted to *dark* hot chocolate–it reminds me of someone I love. By the way, Peter, I'm really excited to have you as my student."

"Oh, great. Thanks for your vote of confidence. When does our class begin again?"

"This coming Tuesday at 11 a.m."

"Thanks again, Professor. See you then."

After finishing his hot chocolate, Peter left the Chocolate Shoppe and meandered along the old cobblestone street.

"I'm so alive," he said to the sky.

Peter experienced the coolness on his skin as he strolled through the shady side of the street. He crossed over to the sunny side of the block. But the sun was so strong he needed sunglasses. He squinted and found his way to the college bookstore. In addition to sunglasses, Peter examined the books required for his class. He already owned most of them but there were two he didn't have. Peter purchased those. During the next few days, Peter drank hazelnut dark hot chocolate at the Chocolate Shoppe, flirted with Maria, and devoured two of the professor's new books.

Peter was so excited to finally be in Italy. He came to the right place. Giovanni was a real expert. He has done so much research. Peter couldn't wait for his class to begin. *Wow.* Giovanni listed all the monasteries throughout the war that hid Jews, Gypsies, etc. and outlined the monasteries that hid Nazis after the war. Peter had already read one of the professor's books so some of this information was a little repetitive, but that was okay. He was able to read it with a new perspective. Wait. His first book on the monastery routes was written by Professor Giovanni, but the new ones were written by Brother Angel. Why...? Peter bet Giovanni needed to protect himself. These were *real* Nazis Giovanni hunted. He had to be careful. That must be the reason he used a nom de plume. And there was something else mysterious, too. It suddenly struck him that all the professor's books were dedicated "To my BELOVED S.W." Who was S.W.?

Peter fell asleep with one of the professor's books on his lap. His lamp was still on. Billy came in a bit later and turned Peter's light off and covered him up with an extra comforter. Billy was curious what Peter was engrossed in. Billy was on a year abroad to study Italian. He planned to teach Italian and this was the year to immerse himself in it. He had studied it for a year in college. He was a bit younger than Peter.

Peter woke up bright and early on the first day of class. It was a beautiful fall day. He went to get some dark hot chocolate and a cornetto for breakfast. He did not see Maria and then he remembered it was her day off. He was sure to see her in Giovanni's first class. Peter had a backpack all set with several pens, pencils, and a large spiral notebook. He got to class early. In his family if you're on time, you're late. Peter smiled. He could hear his mother's voice echo in his head. He observed the classroom was set up like a seminar with a table and space in the middle and chairs all around it. Maria entered the room and she chose to sit next to him. He was drawn to her... or was it just her hot chocolate? Then he laughed and whispered sweet nothings in her ear.

"What do you plan to do after class?" asked Peter as he gazed into her eyes.

"I'm not sure. Is this a date?"

"Maybe," said Peter. He was like a little schoolboy, kind of shy.

Then Maria asked, "What do *you* plan to do after class?"

Peter shook with laughter. "Would you have lunch with me?" asked Peter as he touched her hand with tender grace as if to kiss it.

"Of course, I was curious if you'd ever ask."

Professor Giovanni entered the classroom and observed the lovebirds. "Incurable romantics. Oh... to be young again in Paris with my beloved, drinking hot chocolate," he said under his breath. Giovanni's shoulders dropped with a sigh as he opened his lecture notes.

The class started on time. There were twelve students in the class. Peter was right, it was a seminar. Everyone went around the room and talked a little bit about themselves and their project. One person planned to study Dr. Mengele and his experiments; another person's project was the Nuremberg Trials. Several people were focused on Hitler, but Maria and the other students planned to study WWII in general.

When it came time for Peter to speak up, he cleared his throat, and said, "My name is Peter Wolf. I came here from America. I have been focused on my topic since I was in seventh grade. I am obsessed with the hunt for Nazis on the run. I have come to believe that there are many Nazis hidden in Italian monasteries right now."

Some people seemed impressed with Peter's project and came up to him after class. Each student was given a research appointment time once a week with the professor. Peter's turned out to be on Thursday afternoons.

When class was over, Peter and Maria went out to lunch. "So what trattoria is your favorite, Maria?"

"Bella Ciao," she answered, as she skipped on the cobblestones in the old city. "It's not too far away and you can get a feel for Perugia along the way. Sometimes they have live music, too."

"Okay, that sounds great. My Italian's not very good so I appreciate the tour." Peter wasn't aware yet but Bella Ciao was not just the name of a restaurant, but also the name of a song.

Some of the streets were closed to traffic, so the pedestrians were able to enjoy the street vendors as they sold fresh vegetables and fruits. Peter's favorite booth was the one with huge sunflowers–he'd never seen any sunflowers that big in his whole life. Maria showed him a booth that had herbs: rosemary, sage, and lavender.

"Hmmm...I love these aromas. I love Italy," he said as he glanced back at those sunflowers in awe.

What a wonderful place. Peter's experience was that he died and went to Heaven! He meant it in a light-hearted way, but it was also kind of heavy. The use of the words "died" and "Heaven" in the same sentence could be a dangerous thing.

They bought some flowers, herbs, and postcards for Peter to send home. After they meandered on the cobblestone streets and glanced about the marketplace and art galleries, they arrived at the Bella Ciao trattoria. Peter told Maria that he was really enjoying her thoughtfulness. She answered, "My pleasure."

As they were eating their sandwiches, Peter asked Maria why she had chosen the University of Perugia to go to school, since she had mentioned in class she was from Rome. "The simplest answer is I had to get away from home, and Perugia had great chocolates. I got a scholarship, so that helped, too."

"What's the complicated answer?" asked Peter. He didn't let Maria off the hook.

"Well, my mother and uncle always fight and there's a lot of tension in the house."

"Oh, I see," Peter sympathized. He held her hand. "But didn't your father do anything to intervene?"

"My father died in the war," Maria answered. "I feel very embarrassed about it," she continued as she looked down at the floor.

"I'm so sorry," said Peter, as he reached for her hand again. "My father died in the war, too."

They both started to say at the same time, "We have a lot in common."

Professor Giovanni and Peter had a lot in common too. Peter met with the professor alone for the first time in his office on a rainy Thursday afternoon. Peter was drenched because he forgot his umbrella but the spiritual sunlight in the professor's office warmed his heart. Peter discovered that he would need to become a spy as part of his project. Just the word "spy" sent a shiver up his spine.

"I need your help, Peter," said the professor. "Your project is very dear to my heart. I would do it myself, but the Nazis are aware of who I am. I am choosing you due to all your powerful research and the fact that none of the Nazis hiding have seen you yet. They also are not aware that a monk from Bolzano is passionate to help us with this mission. Brother Paolo is ready to be a confidential informant and share what he has learned with you, but first Paolo must go to a monastery in Saint Hilaire, France to solidify his information. He will have to make up an excuse to the monastery in Bolzano in order to be gone for so many months. Most of all, Paolo needs to protect his sources in Saint Hilaire. There are many former Nazis hiding in Bolzano, the countryside in nearby South Tyrol, and Rome. So his safety is priority number one."

"Why is Brother Paolo taking so many risks?" asked Peter, confused, but still curious.

"I could ask you the same question," said the professor. "Brother Paolo was in a Nazi youth group during the war. He never carried a gun, but he still feels guilty about being part of that movement. So, he sees his research and giving us the names of the Nazis in hiding as way of absolution."

"Wow," said Peter, "that feels heavy."

"Yes, Peter, you have to search your soul and decide if you are ready to take on this risk because once Paolo comes back, you will be the key person to gather the information from Paolo and bring it back to me. I'm not meeting with Brother Paolo myself and I feel guilty about it. But I have done it several times already and they are very suspicious of me...

"You have never met any of them. But I have to be sure you are comfortable with these risks. You cannot mention this project to anyone in class or outside of class, even your parents by phone or mail in case they wiretap us or check our mail. Do your parents support your mission?"

"My father died in the war, but my mother and I share the same passion. But her panic attacks often paralyze and prevent her from moving forward."

"I implore you to think about this project for a week and come back to me next Thursday and tell me how you feel."

"I'm already on board!"

"I still ask you to think about it for a week and come back next Thursday and give me your well-thought-out answer. Think about what you would like to do between now and when Brother Paolo comes back. Also, we may get letters from Paolo with photographs. Those photos will allow us to do some research in advance."

"Photos would be great!" said Peter as he picked up his jacket and threw it over his shoulder.

Giovanni waved, "Ciao."

The next week Peter did some real soul searching. His mother wouldn't be happy if he took on this mission. But he was confident Brother Paolo was going forward anyway. It was quite likely Paolo would find some important names. So, if Peter didn't participate, eventually Giovanni would have to find someone else, or he might take the risk and do it again himself. Peter mulled it over as he rubbed his sweaty palms together. In spite of his fear, Peter breathed deeply. If he went forward with this project, he'd make a huge contribution to humanity. He remembered he told his Mom when he was young, that when he died, he needed to die doing something courageous and brave. In order to be true to himself, he had to say yes. Peter chose to go forward. Yet he also vacillated.

Peter had nightmares that week that gave him the shivers, but he couldn't talk it out with Maria. The two of them spent almost every day together but he found himself conflicted about whether or not to participate in the project. His inclination was to do it because he would have trouble forgiving himself if he didn't. This was what he came here to do, and Professor Giovanni trusted him with an amazing opportunity. How could he say no? But then again it was dangerous. This wasn't a movie. Shivers entered into the pit of his stomach.

Peter had breakfast at the Chocolate Shoppe every morning that week. Maria was working there every day except Tuesdays, so it was a convenient way to flirt with her. They also met for dinner each night in the University cafeteria. On Tuesday they went out for lunch after class. They took sandwiches to the park and had a picnic on a soft blanket.

Thursday afternoon arrived. Peter raced over to the professor's office and told him, "I'm ready to commit to the mission."

Giovanni replied, "I'm thrilled, but also frightened for all of us. We have to be very careful."

"Professor, as soon as we get four to five photos from Brother Paolo, I plan to go to Vienna to Simon Wiesenthal's office," Peter said with boldness.

"I agree. That's a great idea." They were on the same page and shook hands.

***

"Hi Mom, how are things going?" Peter dreaded the non-disclosure issue.

"We are all doing well here in Brooklyn. How's school?" Sasha said.

"I love my class, and the professor's fantastic. I just need you to understand in advance that I won't be able to discuss my research project with you, on the phone."

"Is it really safe?"

"Oh, yes," he lied. He hid his own shivers. "I just had to tell you right away that my professor asked me this favor. We can talk about anything else under the sun, just not that. At least not now."

"Ok, Peter. I am glad you like your professor and the university. You sound really happy."

"I am, Mom. I met a nice young woman from Rome who's shown me around Perugia."

"I'm thrilled you already met someone. That's great."

"Last week at the farmer's market they had the most amazing sunflowers in the world. They are HUGE!"

"Really? Take a picture and send it to me. Better yet, Abie and I are thinking of coming to visit you in July, and we can buy some then."

"That's the best news."

"I have to go now, Peter, but let's talk on weekends, every two to three weeks. Does that work for you?"

"Oh, yes. That's fine."

"Be careful and be safe, Peter."

"I will Mom, I understand your fears. I'll be extra careful just for you!"

When Sasha hung up, she knocked on Abie's door. "I'm scared out of my wits, Abie. I guess I am going to have to find a way to overcome my obsession. I have a feeling that whether I worry or not it won't change the outcome."

"You're probably right." Abie replied.

Chapter 10
Death and Remembrance

Fall 1963

Over the next few months, Peter and Maria got very close. The weather was getting colder so they couldn't have picnics outside. They both had roommates, which meant no privacy. They focused on their own individual research. Maria had other classes and extra homework. That left Peter free to do more of his own private research.

But on November 23rd, Peter's world was rocked. As usual he went to the Chocolate Shoppe to have breakfast with Maria. But it turned out that nothing was going to be usual anymore.

The New York Times headline read: KENNEDY IS KILLED BY SNIPER AS HE RIDES IN CAR IN DALLAS; JOHNSON SWORN IN ON PLANE. Under Kennedy's photo was a story titled "Why America Weeps." Peter cried, devastated.

"I need to call my mom tonight. Probably at about 10 p.m. our time; that should be about 1 p.m. their time."

"I am so sorry, Peter." Maria reached out to grab his hand.

"Thanks, Maria."

"You're so welcome, Peter. Just tell me what you need."

"Wait. Come to think of it, Peter, I believe there's a TV in the common room in the dorm. Maybe it has international news. I have a break coming up. How about I walk you over there and we can check out the TV?"

"Thanks, Maria. I think I'll go back to the dorm now and see if that TV is available. If not, I don't think I can wait till 10 p.m. to call my mom."

"But isn't it like 1 a.m. her time now?"

"I get it...but she won't mind the call, under the circumstances," said Peter, on the edge of tears.

"Oh yes, you're right. I'll find you later."

"Okay," said Peter, very distracted. He wiped his tears away with his sleeve.

Peter chose to call his mom right away. When he got back to his dorm the payphone in the hall was available. Peter reached her.

"I'm so glad you called, Peter," she said. "I just found out." They had a good cry together.

"I am heartbroken for those poor little Kennedy kids. They will grow up without a father. I understand what that's like. Thank God for Abie. But it's important to me that you understand on a deep level how much I appreciate your love, support, and encouragement," Peter said.

"Thanks," Sasha tried not to cry but reached for some tissues.

"Send my love to Abie and the Wolfs. I'm sorry I called so late."

"It's okay, I'm happy you called, Peter; I'll send your love to everyone."

After he hung up the phone Peter was more relaxed. He went to check out the TV Maria had mentioned. He wasn't the only one who was driven to take in the news. Maybe thirty to forty students were gathered around the television and they had it turned up fairly loud. It was in English with Italian subtitles. Peter stayed glued to that TV for the next few days until the funeral was over. Peter hadn't used that television since he'd arrived.

It was quite a shock to see both famous people and regular folks cry in the streets. The TV showed people in all different cities mourning in their own way. For example, in the Bronx, people were kneeling on the sidewalks, praying with their rosaries. People all over the world prayed and cried.

Peter told Maria, holding back tears, "It's so hard to watch Mrs. Kennedy all dressed in black as she walks alongside Robert Kennedy and the two little Kennedys, John Jr. and Caroline. The coffin was draped in black and it was on a wagon driven by two horses. There was a horse led alongside the coffin. It was a cold, dreary day. And a day people would never forget."

Time seemed to drag on after the funeral. For Peter, things never came back to normal. He continued with his research, but he said to Maria, "I'm in a melancholy mood and numb all over."

But time marched on with or without Peter. Christmas was just around the corner. Maria invited Peter home to Rome for the holidays, but he'd recently gotten five photographs from Brother Paolo. Peter created an arrangement to visit Simon Wiesenthal. He needed to take a train–or several trains–to Vienna.

"I'm sorry, Maria, it's the project. We'll have to spend the holidays apart, but we'll be together in spirit." Maria nodded.

Peter boarded the train in Perugia with a backpack filled with sandwiches, a book and a large plaid thermos of dark hot chocolate. He would have to switch at Venice, Innsbruck, and then he would catch a train to Vienna. Outside the windows were all fogged up. He breathed on one and used his finger to draw a heart for Maria on the foggy window. When the fog lifted, the landscape seemed like one big tree with lights. All the little towns sparkled with their Christmas decorations. All the trees glistened like icicle fireworks due to an ice storm the day before. Peter was glad he did not drive to Vienna. The train would cost him a couple of extra days. But it was worth it not to worry about icy roads over the mountainous countryside.

Peter had to be especially careful now with his secret photos from Brother Paolo. He was on edge and jumped at any little unexpected noise. He fidgeted; he was a bundle of nerves. Peter had sewn a makeshift pocket onto the inside of his shirt to keep them safe. He was wearing a woolen Merino sweater and a pea coat. Maria had–in secret–knitted him a warm scarf and hat to match. Peter might have appeared like an American tourist or had he graduated to be an Italian? Would anyone suspect he was a spy? Was he safe? Had anyone followed him? He hadn't been aware of any suspicious strangers.

Peter slept on and off in between sandwiches and hot chocolate. He arrived in Vienna on time. Wow. Vienna at Christmas time. It was like a fairytale storybook: outdoor skating rinks, decorations lighting up all the streets. Peter found his hotel and got his first good night's sleep in two days. He was much safer in the hotel room than on the train. Here he could lock the door. He double-checked to be sure his photos were well hidden.

The next morning, Peter took a cab to Wiesenthal's office. They became fast friends.

"Here are the five photos that Brother Paolo sent us."

"Wundebar! I'm thrilled." said Wiesenthal, as he held his magnifying glass over the secret photos. "I have good news."

"Yes?" Peter waited with bated breath. He leaned over the photos with Simon.

"I recognize them all!" He took out a pencil and labeled each photo on the back with the name, rank, and what camp they were at. Peter was shocked by how much Wiesenthal held in his brain and how quickly he identified each photo.

Simon explained, "I am the deputy for the dead." He gave Peter back the five photos, and Peter put them in his secret pocket right away.

Simon Wiesenthal was truly an expert. His brain was worth millions. Peter smiled like the Cheshire cat.

"Would you like to spend some time looking at my whole photograph collection, Peter?"

"Yes, would I ever," Peter said, as he suppressed a desire to jump through the roof. Simon asked if Peter was in the mood for any coffee or tea? "By any chance do you happen to have hot chocolate?"

"Oh yes, we do. And I will join you."

Simon's assistant brought them two cups of hot chocolate as they perused a series of photo albums. "I am very proud of my collection, Peter."

"I can see why. Your photos are so well organized. I'm so impressed. A whole thick album on the Mengele twins. Another album on the Nazis who have not been caught yet, including Mengele himself. Do you mind if I copy down a list of names of the Nazis on the run and put it in my secret pocket?"

"Oh, no, I don't mind at all. I trust you, Peter, and Professor Giovanni. Before I forget, I'm sorry about your grandfather and any other relatives you lost in the Holocaust."

"Thank you. Coming from you that means the world to me." They hugged one another.

Peter copied down the names of Nazis still in hiding and tried his best to memorize their faces. That was hard to do because there were so many of them, but he could at least familiarize himself with them. "I look forward to coming back with more pictures soon so we can continue our work together. At some point down the road I think we'll be able to give you these photos for your collection."

"Marvelous," said Simon, touching his heart. The two men shook hands and Peter returned to his hotel. He still had one of his sandwiches left and a bit of hot chocolate in his thermos. He went to bed at 7 p.m. because he had an early train to catch.

Peter took the early bird train to Innsbruck and retraced his itinerary backwards. He slept almost the whole way home but managed not to miss his connections. He was happy to get home so he could sleep in his own bed. He called Giovanni the next morning and they met in his office.

"I cannot wait to see the names and places of the Nazis that Wiesenthal identified," the professor said.

"Simon is a very impressive man. He's a gem, one in a million. He has an amazing collection of photo books of both witnesses and perpetrators. I feel honored that Simon showed them all to me, over hot chocolate, naturally. So, here are Brother Paolo's photos, with the names, places, etc. written on the back in pencil. Plus, I created a list of all the Nazis Simon believes are on the run at this very moment."

"Wow, thanks. Good work, Peter."

The five secret photos that Paolo had sent them became the focal point of Peter's next step for his research project. "It is your assignment to find out everything you can about these five men–and I mean everything," said the professor, his voice passionate and strident.

"I will. That's a promise, and I keep my promises."

"Thank you, my son. Oh, and one more thing, do you think you were followed, Peter? Just checking."

"No, I do not believe so. I was very careful."

"Okay, that's great." They shook hands as two spies and collaborators. Peter was off to the races–his heart throbbed as he ran to the library. *Knowledge is power*. This was the art of the game–a human chessboard.

After dinner Peter called Maria to see how she was doing. "I'm fine. I just miss you. When are you coming back?"

"I'm back already, Maria."

"Now that I found out you're in Perugia, I'll come back tomorrow."

"Terrific. I can't wait to see you!"

"Me too!"

Peter remembered he had to find some wrapping paper for the scarf he'd bought for Maria on his trip. He was so glad there was a gift shop near the University that was open the next day. That way he could wrap Maria's present before she arrived.

"Welcome home, Maria," said Peter, holding his arms open wide.

"Thanks so much, Peter. It feels so good to be home."

"Here's a little present I got for you."

"It's beautiful!" Maria tried it on and walked over to the mirror. "It even goes with the outfit I am wearing right now. I'm going to leave it on."

"Great. So glad you like it. How was your Christmas with your mother?"

"It was okay until my uncle showed up. Those two fight like crazy. That's why I left to begin with. It's a horrible environment to relax in, do my homework, or bring friends over."

"Oh. I'm so sorry. It makes me realize how lucky I am to have my mom, my grandparents, and Abie."

"Who's Abie?"

"He was my grandfather's best friend, so he helped raise me."

"I see. I guess sometimes you just get lucky, Peter."

"Yes, and when you don't feel lucky, you make your own family by surrounding yourself with people who love you."

Maria could not wait for those three magic words and asked Peter, "Is that your way of saying you love me?"

"Come here," said Peter. He took Maria in his arms and hugged her for a long time. "I do love you, Maria," Peter whispered in her ear.

"I love you too, Peter," Maria said with her eyes closed. Billy had taken his girlfriend on vacation, so they had the room to themselves for the night before his return. Peter and Maria spent the night in each other's arms and woke up the next morning to the sound of birds chirping outside Peter's window.

Would they have a lifetime in each other's arms listening to birds in the morning? Peter wasn't sure. His mission was a dangerous one.

Chapter 11

Haunted

A few days later the spring semester started. Peter and Maria would have loved to have a few more days to relax and lounge around. Maria had to go back to work at the Chocolate Shoppe. They ended up with breakfast together most mornings. That always started the day off right. The history class didn't meet that semester, but students could sign up for an individual research project with Professor Giovanni. Peter signed up. Maria did not. Peter met with his professor on Thursday afternoons again.

"I have continued my research and I am haunted by two brothers. Their photos spooked me at Wiesenthal's office. Their last name is Schmidt. Heinrich and Friedrich. They gave me the willies," Peter confessed as he took a deep breath. "I am hoping one of them shows up in the next batch of pictures we get from Brother Paolo. If I could wave a magic wand I'd like to see *both* of their pictures show up," Peter said, his eyes sparkling. "Heinrich has a big facial scar and was a guard at Auschwitz. Friedrich was at Theresienstadt." Peter sounded wistful, his voice thickening with emotion.

"Maybe we'll get lucky. I feel hopeful," Giovanni replied as he stroked his beard. "Why do you think you feel haunted by them, Peter?" asked the professor, leaning forward, waiting for Peter's answer.

"I'm not totally sure. My grandfather was killed by a Nazi with a scar. Also, I just have a funny feeling about them being brothers, I guess," said Peter, swallowing excessively. "Have you gotten any notes from Brother Paolo recently?"

"No, I haven't, which scares me a little," said Giovanni as he shifted in his chair, unable to get comfortable. "I think I will send a birthday card to him, even though it's not his birthday. I won't sign my name, but it will have a Perugia postmark. I'll send him a smoke signal without words. What do you think of that idea, Peter?" Giovanni asked, clutching his hands.

"I think it's a great idea," Peter said with confidence. Peter was so pleased his professor respected his opinion and trusted him with this mission. He was curious why the two of them were such a good team. They brainstormed together and supported each other as if they'd known each other all their lives. He was pleased yet baffled. And when in doubt they always had dark hot chocolate.

A month later Giovanni received an envelope with no return address. He assumed it was from Brother Paolo. He called Peter, pacing in his office. "Come right away, Peter. I got something from Brother Paolo and I need you to be here when I open it."

Peter dropped everything, euphoric. This was the very moment he'd yearned for. Peter got goosebumps on his arms. He raced all the way from the dorm to the professor's office as if he were flying a kite on a windy day. Peter was like a kid in a candy store, almost out of breath. The two men opened the envelope with care. They prayed they would have four or five new photos.

Lo and behold, they got their wish. "Take a look at them Peter, be methodical and take your time," said the professor.

"Oh my God," Peter did a double-take. "I can't believe this. I'm flabbergasted. I got my wish. Now we're on a roll," Peter exclaimed and bounced on his toes. "This is Heinrich Schmidt, the one with the scar. This photo was taken at Auschwitz and the second picture is his brother Friedrich Schmidt-taken at Theresienstadt!"

"Wow," they both said simultaneously, hugging one another. They laughed and cried.

"Boy, Peter, I have to hand it to you. You have an amazing intuition. All the work you did this last month was not done in vain. Heinrich Schmidt even has that same scar you remembered. Great work. Great memory, my boy," said Giovanni, as he danced in place. "Let's have hot chocolate to celebrate."

Peter continued to trust his intuition. No one and nothing could stop him now. He almost jumped out of his skin with excitement. This project was seductive. He kept his research going. Who cared if he only slept a few hours each night? He was on fire, thrusting his fist skyward.

Chapter 12
Bolzano

The next few months raced by. Brother Paolo sent more photos and Peter continued to research each and every one. Maria was almost done with her classes and they started to plan a vacation together in August when she could get some time off work. Sasha and Abie talked about a visit in July. Peter was excited.

On Sunday morning, June 7th, Maria sat Peter down and, biting her lip, said, "I need to talk with you, Peter."

"You're not breaking up with me, are you?" Peter panicked and backed away with raised hands.

"No, sweetie, not at all!"

"That's good," said Peter, relieved, with a sigh.

"Well," Maria said shyly, wiping her hands on her skirt, "I'm not sure how to bring this up."

"Take your time," Peter said anxiously as he rocked in place.

"I am very sorry, but I think there is a possibility that I might be pregnant."

"That's fantastic," Peter exclaimed, his heart racing with joy.

"Are you sure it's okay?"

"Absolutely," said Peter as he crushed Maria with a bear hug.

"First of all, I love you," Peter shouted with euphoria, his face and neck flushed with color. "My plan was to ask you to marry me on our vacation in August. I've been saving up for the ring. If you are pregnant, we'll just tell everyone and have a big wedding... Would you like a big wedding?" asked Peter hesitantly, his hands starting to tremble.

Maria boldly blurted out, "Yes."

"So it's all good," Peter reassured her, holding her hands in his.

"We'll wait and see if you're pregnant and if so, we can make plans right away. But wait. We can actually make plans either way."

"Thank you so much for being so nice about this, Peter. I was afraid you might be mad at me," she said, glancing down at the floor.

"Are you kidding? I could never be mad at you, Maria, especially not about something like this."

"Well, some guys might be upset ...."

"Well, I'm not just some guy. And you're one in a million," he said as he got down on one knee, holding up a piece of Perugian chocolate, "Will you marry me, Maria?"

"Yes, I will, yes," Maria laughed, blushing. "Now I have another question for you," said Maria. "This one is an easy question compared to the last topic. My mother would love to meet you and she has invited us down for an early Sunday dinner around 3 p.m."

"Sure, that sounds great," Peter said, blissfully throwing the piece of chocolate into the air. Maria caught it on the first try and burst out with a deep laugh. There were both punch-drunk.

"What kind of flowers does your mother like?" Peter asked.

"HUGE sunflowers because she feels they're so cheerful."

"Okay, let's go to the market before we leave," said Peter, grinning from ear to ear.

An hour later Peter was almost ready to leave when there was a knock at the door. He assumed it was Maria and Peter nonchalantly opened the door. Instead of Maria there was a monk he did not recognize standing in his doorway. He passed Peter a note and then he left without a word. Peter glanced down at the slip of paper with apprehension. *Call this number at 4:30 p.m. today.* He wasn't sure what this was all about, but assumed it was related to Brother Paolo. He would have to figure out a way to call while he was at Maria's mother's house. He would have to find a graceful way to do it, he thought as he ran his hands through his wavy black hair.

A few minutes later Maria came by. They stopped to get the sunflowers and then left for Rome. They smiled and discussed the wedding and the baby the whole way to Rome. They decided not to say anything to her mother at this time. "So if I look over at you across the table tonight and you're smiling, Maria, I'm going to think of the Mona Lisa with her sly smile," Peter joked.

Peter enjoyed and was very comfortable with Maria's mother, who insisted he call her Anna. She loved the sunflowers and put them in a vase on the table right away. She'd baked a delicious lasagna which was the best Peter had ever devoured. Maria vaguely mentioned Peter's research, noting that he was in search of Nazis in hiding.

"That's an interesting topic, but I don't like to talk about Nazis," Anna said. Peter changed the subject.

Before dessert Peter glanced down at his watch. It was almost 4:30. "Do you mind if I make a quick phone call?" Peter asked Anna, tapping his foot under the table.

"No, not at all," she said.

Peter went to use the bathroom first. There was a phone in the kitchen. After Peter used the bathroom, he pulled out the scrap of paper and dialed the number.

A man answered and whispered, "Hello."

"Hi this is Peter and I was told..." but before he could finish his sentence, the man said, "I am aware of who you are. I will meet you this Wednesday at 3 p.m. in the rose garden of the Bolzano Monastery. I am the Brother who sent you photos. I am back now."

"Ok, Brother Paolo, I'll meet you there," said Peter, conflicted, tightening his grip on the phone.

"Make sure you aren't followed, Peter."

"Ok, I'll be careful," Peter replied, frightened, his back up against the wall. "Ciao."

This was an unusual turn of events. Peter was not sure whether to be terrified or happy, or maybe both. Brother Paolo was home now and couldn't wait to see him. This was the beginning of a new era. Peter got more excited, his insides vibrating, as he took his seat back at the table. And more would be revealed. Peter smiled with curiosity. This was great. Peter would see Paolo on Wednesday and he could follow up with Giovanni on Thursday. Perfect. That would work out well. Peter needed to inform Giovanni about his plans. Peter was very confident.

It was starting to get late, so Peter and Maria were getting ready to leave when someone opened the front door. It was Maria's uncle. When Peter went to shake his hand, he glanced up at her uncle's face and was sure the man had a distinct scar on his right cheek. Peter tried to catch his breath. He had just come face-to-face with Heinrich Schmidt, the senior guard at Auschwitz, one of the Nazis in hiding he had been searching for. Peter shook his hand and tried to act normal. But he was desperate to make a mad dash out of there. He was in total shock and disbelief–blindsided. The room started to spin. Almost in spite of himself, without meaning to, Peter had found one of the Nazis on his list–a Nazi he'd been haunted by, nonetheless. Could it be his grandfather's killer?

Oh, my God! Peter tried not to fall apart but he was in a panic as every muscle in his body went rigid. He couldn't even tell Maria what was bothering him. Maria fell asleep in the car shortly after they left. The good news was Peter didn't have to make small talk anymore, the bad news–he was shaking inside. Peter jumped out of his own skin, all alone in the world. Cold sweat glued his shirt to his back. Peter couldn't wait to call his professor right away. But, for now, Peter had to concentrate on the road.

Peter's panic escalated, ripping his heart in two, but he had to act like everything was normal in case Maria woke up. He clenched the steering wheel as if his life depended upon it. He had to calm down. He forced himself to take deep breaths. At the moment he was just driving back to Perugia and they were going to get home late. He would have to call the professor tomorrow. Giovanni would be able to help Peter calm down–or at least he counted on it. Wow. What a bombshell. Adrenaline shot through Peter's veins like ice water. Panic swelled up inside him, threatening to swallow him whole.

Peter wasn't prepared for having to meet Brother Paolo so soon, and he had no way to guess that Maria's uncle was Heinrich Schmidt. Two asteroids had just collided in his brain and exploded. It was too much for him to handle. Peter scratched his head and was glad when his brain didn't fall out. When he was anxious he sang the alphabet song silently.

Peter needed to focus on the road, focus on the road. Take one minute at a time. This had been his whole life's mission. Peter had prepared for this since seventh grade. He had to be ready for the wildest ride of his life. *It's okay to be scared. Just hold onto the prize, hold on.* Peter tried to talk himself down from the biggest panic attack of his life. It was like talking someone down who was standing on the edge of a rooftop getting ready to jump. Peter now understood why his Mom was so scared of him hunting Nazis. This wasn't a movie. This was very real. Peter had to be the hero so his mother would be proud of him. But he also had to survive and make it home to tell the tale. Peter couldn't let his mother's fears come true. Peter fought off a sense of paralysis as his right lower lip went into a spasm.

Peter pulled into the parking lot of their dorm and the car stopped. Maria woke up, startled. Peter helped her up to her room, kissed her on the forehead, and then raced up the stairs. Thank God Billy was asleep because Peter's mind was traveling faster than the speed of light. He could still hear the sound of the tires grinding on the road. Would sleep come easy? He needed to escape from his fear. As he washed his face and stared in the mirror, a wave of panic swept across his face. He had to be brave. He threw on his pajamas. As soon as his head hit the pillow he collapsed from exhaustion.

Peter overslept the next morning and did not wake up till noon. He had to call Giovanni immediately. "Can we to meet this afternoon?"

"Yes, of course. Is everything alright?"

"I better not say anything on the phone," said Peter as he clenched and unclenched his fists. "I'm just a bit scared."

"Okay, whatever it is, we'll talk it out, Peter."

"I pray we can. You're the only one who can help me."

"Okay, no problem."

"See you soon. Ciao."

Peter took a quick shower, got dressed, stopped to pick up hot chocolate, and headed to the professor's office. "I need a hug," said Peter, out of breath after he'd raced over and climbed the stairs to the office.

"One hug, coming right up," Giovanni said with a sweet smile. "What's going on, my son?" asked the professor, touching Peter's shoulder.

"First, I was handed a note to call someone yesterday at 4:30 p.m., so I did, and it was Brother Paolo."

"Great, son. That's fantastic news."

"He plans to meet me in the rose garden in Bolzano this Wednesday."

"*Wow*. That's fantastic. Brother Paolo did ask me how he could get in touch with you, so it seems this was his plan. But it seems that there's something else that's heavy on your heart, my friend, am I right?" asked Giovanni, worried. The professor leaned towards Peter as his monk's hood fell forward, covering his face.

"Yes, what I'm going to tell you next was even more unexpected and intense. I'm terrified, can you tell? I went to Maria's house in Rome yesterday and her mother was very nice. But just as we were leaving, Maria's uncle opened the door and sauntered in and..." Peter began. He had to take a deep breath. He got ready to reveal his secret.

"And...?" asked Giovanni, trying to encourage Peter to continue.

"And... her uncle is a Nazi in hiding. I mean in plain sight. Heinrich Schmidt, scar and all!"

"You've got to be kidding..."

"Nope, it's Heinrich, I am positive."

"Oh, now I see why you didn't tell me on the phone. That was a smart move because they might tap the line. I can see why you're still in shock. What an incredible stroke of good luck. But downright nerve-wracking," said Professor Giovanni, "I'm just flabbergasted."

"Indeed," said Peter, still on an adrenaline rush. "I was so shocked I started to tremble, but I think I hid it well. I didn't say anything about it to Maria on the way home. But I will never go back there again. I can tell you that much," said Peter, still traumatized by his experience. "For a man who killed so many thousands of prisoners at Auschwitz, killing one more Jew would be like swatting a fly for him. I was looking at the scarred face of evil."

"We'll set it up so you never have to go back."

"Thanks. That's a relief."

"Be at ease, my son. We'll take good care of you. Just make sure at all times that you're not followed. That's rule number one."

"I will, sir, I promise. Is there a rule number two?" asked Peter, laughing nervously to cover his anxiety.

"Yes. Rule number two–do not talk to anyone else about this."

"No problem. You're the only person I could've told. I just had to get this off my chest."

"I understand, Peter. Oh, and rule number three–when in doubt, drink hot chocolate. I'll see you Thursday at our regular research time, after you see Brother Paolo. But don't hesitate to contact me at any time, day or night. This is the number for night calls."

Peter's anxiety eased after his heart-to-heart with his professor. He went back to the Chocolate Shoppe to give Maria a hug and see if she had any cornetti left. "Yes, we do, sweetheart. How many?"

"Maybe three," said Peter. All of a sudden he was famished.

"Well, promise me you will have a healthy dinner. Let's eat together at the cafeteria tonight. We will both have protein, vegetables, and not too many sweets."

"Okay, it's a date," Peter said as he winked at her. He spent the rest of the afternoon in his room. A cardinal built a nest outside the window while Peter munched away on his cornetti. Peter and Maria met at five for an early dinner. They had broiled chicken, a large salad, green beans, and braised carrots. Peter had to admit, for cafeteria food it was excellent. And he was so full he had no room for dessert.

The next day he spent a few hours at the school library and tied up loose ends before leaving the next day bright and early for Bolzano. He went back to his room to pack but when he put something away in his desk, his finger experienced something sharp. What was it? He bent over to check it out.

He couldn't see anything. Now he was curious. He would have to take everything out of this drawer. Peter discovered that there was a secret compartment. It wasn't visible to the naked eye. You could only find it by feeling it with your fingers.

On a whim, Peter wrote a letter to the people in his life who had great meaning to him–his mother, Abie, the Wolfs, Maria, Professor Giovanni, and Simon Wiesenthal. This was a good idea on the chance that something happened to him, due to the nature of his research. At least the people Peter loved would each have a note. So he spent a few hours writing the letters and then slipped them into the secret compartment. He was conflicted about writing these letters. Was he being melodramatic? Probably nothing bad would happen to him, but he must have inherited some of his mother's obsessions. Peter's heart was guided to write the letters, to let each person understand how grateful he was for them.

He waved to Maria in the school cafeteria. He put some extra food on his plate and returned to the line to get some more bread and an apple. "I need to put together some sandwiches for my trip tomorrow and put them in the little refrigerator in the hall next to my room." Peter spent some quality time with Maria but reminded her that he had to get up very early and would be gone all day. It was for his research, so she did not pry.

Peter left in the middle of the night to be sure not to be late to meet Paolo in the rose garden. So many questions swirled in his brain, but Paolo would have a specific agenda for their meeting that involved the Nazis, whose photos he sent him. Peter just had to tell him about Heinrich Schmidt. The men in all those photos were hiding in Bolzano or possibly Rome. Peter vacillated between excitement and apprehension.

He left at 2 a.m., long before the sun came up, to be sure no one was following him. He tried to focus on the scenery after the sun rose. He had all his directions written out and his backpack was filled with sandwiches and an apple. Peter stopped at a little café that was open and he paid to fill up his plaid thermos with hot chocolate and also put gas in his rental car.

Peter daydreamed about his Master's thesis on all the Nazis he would have found by then. It was so real now. He leaned his head back as he drank his hot chocolate. Peter was curious if this meeting with Brother Paolo was going to lead to the capture of any Nazis right away. If Brother Paolo's information was not related to Heinrich Schmidt, then Peter was willing to expose Heinrich Schmidt with Professor Giovanni. Peter understood where Heinrich could be found. All the research he'd ever done since seventh grade led up to this very pivotal moment in his life. He couldn't wait to discover how everything would come together like a puzzle. He was more curious now than shaking in his boots. Thank God.

Peter stopped at the side of the road by a scenic spot to eat one of his sandwiches and drink some hot chocolate. He was determined to make sure nobody followed him, so he kept an eye on the cars as they went by. He started to drive again and munched on his apple. The mountainsides had peaks and valleys. He prayed they weren't the Valley of the Shadow of Death. Then he started to sing the Partisan version of *Bella Ciao*, first under his breath then at the top of his lungs. It helped him feel strong and pass the time.

Several hours later, he arrived in Bolzano. Peter had to follow the directions to get to the monastery. At one point he got lost, but he dared not ask for help. This area of Italy was often considered more German than Italian. He did not speak Italian or German that well. He would stand out like a sore thumb–as an outsider. Peter turned around and found his way back to the signs for the monastery and a small parking lot. It was 2:45 p.m. He got there in time. He sighed with relief. Peter couldn't be late. He sat and had another sandwich and the rest of his hot chocolate. Peter would be so much smarter when he drove home.

Ten minutes later, Peter walked up the north path to the monastery and started to look around for the rose garden. He found it and sat down on a bench. The aroma of the roses preceded them. So many different varieties of roses and colors. They were divine. Perfect for a rose garden at a monastery–almost Heaven. At 3 p.m. Brother Paolo sat down beside him and whispered, "Do not say a word. And don't move!" Peter held his breath.

Paolo yelled out at the top of his lungs, "S-T-O-P!"

A monk started to hit Peter on top of the head with a huge rock. Peter fell to the ground, unconscious. Then Brother Paolo was stabbed with a knife in the abdomen and also fell to the ground. He bled out. The perpetrator went back and stabbed Peter in the heart just to be sure he would die. The killer fled.

A local gardener in overalls ran over. He had seen the whole thing from a distance, but he didn't recognize anyone. He had just arrived the day before to help out with the rose garden. He ran back to the garden shed and called the police and said there had been an attack on the monastery grounds. "I think we need two ambulances because two men have been stabbed. Hurry."

The ambulances arrived and the police were right behind them. Peter was loaded into the ambulance first. He had a weak pulse and was covered in blood, fading in and out of consciousness, moaning, "Mom-mee." Brother Paolo was placed in the second ambulance, with no pulse. He was unconscious.

The ambulances took Peter and Brother Paolo to the nearest hospital. They rushed through the streets, sirens blaring, at top speed. The police followed the ambulances after they set up crime scene tape and interviewed the local gardener. Once the two wounded men were moved onto hospital gurneys in the ER, some detectives were given Peter's wallet, which was found by on the ground by the ambulance crew. It was not clear if this was a robbery gone bad or a deliberate attack on the two men. Peter's wallet contained his mother's emergency contact numbers in New York.

The Italian police called Peter's mother in America. "I am looking for Peter Wolf's mother. Have I reached the right number?"

"His mother Sasha is outside in the garden," said Grandma Wolf. "May I ask who's calling?"

"Yes, of course. This is Sergeant Brucelli from the Bolzano police department in Italy. Her son Peter was involved in an accident. She needs to fly to his bedside."

"Oh, my goodness. Thanks for the information, officer. How bad is it?"

"Sorry, Ma'am. We cannot elaborate." Grandma tried to ask more questions, but the officer refused to answer.

Grandma knocked on Abie's apartment door. "I am so glad you're home. Something terrible has happened."

"What's wrong?"

"I just got a call for Sasha from the Italian police. It seems Peter's been involved in an accident. They need her to come to Italy right away to be at his bedside."

"Oh no, that doesn't sound good. Where's Sasha now?"

"She's outside in the garden tending the roses. I think we should go down together."

"Okay, Grandma. Let me just put on my shoes."

The pair approached Sasha. There was no right way to break the news. "Sweetie, Peter has been in an accident and you need to fly to Italy right away."

"I'll go with you, Sasha," said Abie.

"How serious is it? What did the officer say exactly?" asked Sasha, in between tears.

"They just said to hurry to be at his bedside."

Sasha was inconsolable. “Oh, God! No, not my Peter. I was sure this would happen. I never should have let him go to Italy.”

“Let’s pray that it’s not too bad,” said Grandma.

“I’ll buy the tickets,” said Abie, “while you go and pack, Sasha.”

Chapter 13
The Investigation

Peter's girlfriend Maria also got a call from the police, so she rushed up to the hospital in Bolzano. But despite the long drive, Maria had to sit in the waiting room for many hours. The doctors refused to answer any questions because she was not a relative. Maria found a little alcove near the information center. She collapsed, hysterical, into a soft, empty chair. Her makeup smeared as tears flowed down her cheeks like rain, the tissues in her hand now covered with black mascara.

Maria called her mother but there was no answer. Next, she called her professor at the University, but he was not at his desk. She had to face it. She was alone. She needed her Peter. But Peter was too injured to speak to her. Shivers went up and down her spine and took over her body. Maria became frozen and crawled up in a ball on the chair and covered herself with her jacket.

A policeman came by to question Maria at the hospital. But she explained she had been at the University in Perugia at the time the attack took place, so she didn't witness anything. Maria did remember that Peter had mentioned he'd planned to go up to Bolzano, but she wasn't sure which day. "Why was Peter so determined to go to Bolzano?" they asked.

"He's been doing some research on Nazi war criminals. There was a rumor that some Nazis might be hiding in the monasteries in Bolzano and Rome," Maria responded.

"Oh, I see. Thank you very much, Maria."

"Excuse me, sir, can you tell me anything about Peter's condition at this time?" asked Maria.

"No, I'm sorry, Maria, the doctors cannot reveal anything until the arrival of Peter's family from America."

"Okay, thanks." Maria folded up her purse for a makeshift pillow and attempted to go back to sleep. Peter's mother must be devastated. Maria was aware that his mother feared the Nazis because her father was murdered by one in America.

Maria wasn't able to fall back asleep and she figured it would be a long time before Peter's mother arrived. She came to the conclusion that she might as well drive from Bolzano back to her dorm in Perugia. She sobbed the whole way. Peter was such a sweet young man. Her mother even liked him, and her mother never liked any of her university friends. As she drove back to her dorm so many memories of Peter flooded her mind, in no particular order. The first day she met him at the Chocolate Shoppe and the last day flashed past her eyes.... She and Peter loved the sounds of the birds outside his window and in the park. She still could picture the way the light came through the trees.

Maria reminisced about Peter's sweet smile and his blue eyes that sparkled. They had so many plans to travel together during the summer, perhaps to Switzerland and France. If only she'd been aware that he'd planned a trip to Bolzano this week, maybe she could have stopped this event. On the other hand, she might have been hurt, too. When they had eaten dinner at her mom's on Sunday night, he mentioned that he was pretty sure he was going up to Bolzano very soon. Peter had called Brother Paolo from her mother's house perhaps to make arrangements to go to Bolzano...? How could she have forgotten? She should have told the detective that. Oh well...

Peter was hurt and there was nothing she could do about it except cry.

When she got back to her dorm room, Maria had a plan to call the hospital. She pretended to be Peter's sister to check on the status of her brother. They passed the call on to the hospital counselor who told her that Peter had passed away. Then she hung up the phone and screamed, "*No...*" and cried into her pillow.

Several hours later Maria went to get something to eat and she happened to see Peter's roommate, Billy, in the hall. He could tell she'd been crying. "What's the matter, kiddo?" Billy asked, since he was king of the rumor club.

"I guess you haven't gotten the news yet. Your roommate was just murdered." she said.

"What? You're kidding, right?" Billy joked, in disbelief.

"I'm not kidding, Billy," said Maria. Grief stricken, she wiped her tears away.

"What happened? Who killed him?"

Maria said, "Someone up in Bolzano."

"Ah, man. That's terrible."

When Billy gave her a hug, she asked, "Can I sleep in Peter's bed for a few nights to feel close to him?"

"Yes, of course."

Maria forgot about getting something to eat and instead crawled under the covers in Peter's bed. She could still catch a whiff of him on his sheets and pillowcase. This must be a mistake. He can't be dead. She must be in the middle of a horrible dream. Maria prayed as hard as she could on her rosary. She crawled into a fetal position and fell into a deep sleep.

If only it could be just a bad dream, but it was real. Maria did not eat or drink for several days. She just needed to hide out to escape the nightmare she'd inherited–the one that had taken away her hopes and dreams.

***

Some detectives had gotten a warrant to search the premises of the Bolzano monastery and the grounds. They searched for anything out of the ordinary or suspicious. Their focus was a search for the knife that created the wounds Peter and Brother Paolo sustained. But all the monks closed ranks and covered for one another. They all had solid alibis. All monks were present at the monastery. No one was missing. Police were unable to collect fingerprints because of the way the warrant was written. The local gardener gave his fingerprints.

The next day Sasha and Abie arrived in Rome. Abie got some sleep on the plane, but Sasha didn't. Instead, she cried or stared into space the whole trip. In spite of her big black sunglasses, it was obvious to everyone around her that she was very distraught. For someone who was always impeccably dressed, her clothes were disheveled, dirty, and wrinkled. Sasha tried to reconstruct in her mind the last time she spoke to Peter. Was it Monday or Tuesday? What did they talk about? Did he mention Bolzano? In the back of her mind she was aware of the answers to these questions? But now her mind was a total blank. Sometimes she was numb from the shock of it all. Other times, she needed to scream, but nothing came out of her mouth. Her fear that Peter died at the hands of a Nazi overwhelmed her. But they said it was an accident, so maybe he was still alive... Just maybe. She needed Peter to be alive and survive.

Abie rented a car at the airport in Rome and they drove straight to Bolzano, a full day's drive. The scenery was a picture postcard but neither of them appreciated it. They went straight to the hospital. They introduced themselves as Peter Wolf's family. "The police told us to come to the hospital."

The receptionist nodded and said in halting English, "Let me check for you." About ten minutes later, they were escorted into a small office to meet with a doctor.

"How is Peter doing?" Sasha asked, in a high-pitched, nervous voice.

"How serious is it?" asked Abie.

The doctor cleared his throat and said, "I am so sorry to tell you... Peter didn't make it."

"What do you mean he didn't make it?" Sasha exclaimed, blindsided. "What really happened to Peter?"

At that point the doctor explained, "Peter was hit on the head and stabbed in the heart several times. He was rushed to the hospital, but his injuries were so severe that he didn't survive the attack. The doctors tried but couldn't save him."

Sasha fell to her knees–inconsolable. Abie tried to choke back tears.

"The police need to talk with you," the doctor said, but Sasha shook her head no.

"Of course, take your time," said the doctor, leaning forward. "Just tell me when you feel ready and I will make the arrangements."

"I don't think I'll ever be ready," Sasha whispered to Abie. "My worst fears came true. He died at the hands of a Nazi and will never come home...Just like Daddy. And no one but you took me seriously."

"I understand, sweetheart. I guess at some point it might help us to understand what happened."

"Yes, but just not right now!" Sasha fell apart. "My life is over. Doesn't anybody see how desperate I am?" she muttered so low, Abie didn't even hear her.

She was clinging to life by a slender thread. Sasha was glad she wasn't alone but she really needed Michael. Where was Peter? What happened? Why did he take this risk? He understood her fears. How could he put himself at risk?

"Abie, where's the bathroom? I'm going to be sick."

"Right across the hall, honey."

Sasha started to stand up, but the shock was too much for her to bear. She collapsed to her knees again and leaned over the edge of a chair.

"Why Peter? He was such a good boy? This doesn't make any sense... and it's NOT FAIR! ... First my father was stabbed by a knife and now Peter," Sasha sobbed.

Her tears burned as they poured down her cheeks. She couldn't breathe. "I'm helpless... It's too much for a mother to bear. The old shouldn't bury the young."

Abie sat down on the floor and put his arms around Sasha. He held her for a long time. Sasha was sure Abie was also hurting on a very deep level. Abie had helped raise Peter and considered him to be his grandson. Sasha tried to be there for Abie, but she didn't have the strength.

Two hours later Sasha asked Abie, "What if it's not Peter...? We need to identify the body...maybe there's some mistake."

Abie went up to the receptionist again. "We would like to identify the body to make sure it's really Peter."

The doctor was paged and arrived a few minutes later. He escorted them down to the morgue. Peter's wallet had been found next to the body, so the police were almost certain that the victim was Peter Wolf. But Sasha still held out hope that someone else was in the morgue. Maybe the murderer had just placed Peter's wallet on the ground to throw the police off track for the real motive.

They both shivered as they went down to the morgue. Sasha was unable to go in. Her knees buckled and she ended up on the floor. Abie took a deep breath and followed the doctor into the room. Abie pulled the white sheet back to uncover the face of the deceased. There was no doubt. It really was their Peter. His face seemed calm and peaceful, but bloody. "Were there any defensive wounds?" Abie asked as his voice cracked.

"No. It seems that Peter was struck from behind first by a blunt object, perhaps a heavy rock or a metal pipe. The medical examiner thinks he was stabbed several times afterwards in his heart while he was lying on the ground. So that's why we think Peter had no defensive wounds. He didn't see it coming."

"I see," said Abie, his head bent down, his hands caressing Peter's face. "Thank you, Doctor. You have been most kind." Now he had to break the news to Sasha.

Abie found his way into the waiting room but collapsed in a chair. Sasha had prepared herself for the worst, but maybe there'd been a terrible mistake. Abie took her hands in his and stroked them. Sasha lifted her head up and said, "It's Peter, isn't it?" He just nodded yes... They did the only thing they could do. They just held onto each other as tight as they could and sobbed. It was a parent's worst nightmare.

Several hours later the police showed up. They were working two homicides now... Neither Peter nor Brother Paolo had survived the attack. Sergeant Brucelli now understood Peter Wolf was doing research on Nazi war criminals. Everyone who followed the Eichmann trial was aware that Eichmann had hidden in the Bolzano monastery before making his way to South America. Peter must have been onto something if he went to Bolzano and was murdered. Someone was determined to prevent Peter from getting the answers he needed. Sergeant Brucelli was convinced that Peter's murder was part of a cover-up within the monastery itself. How could they do a background check of all the monks at that monastery? Brucelli tried to piece the puzzle together. He figured it was time to talk with Peter's parents to see if they could shed some light on this mystery.

"Hello, Mr. and Mrs. Wolf," said Brucelli, crouching down to make eye contact. "I am sorry to bother you at a time like this, but I have to catch Peter's killer. Are you aware of the reason Peter went to that specific monastery?"

Abie took shaky breaths and replied, "All we can say is that Peter was in search of Nazi war criminals. He was convinced they hid in the Bolzano monastery. Peter planned to visit the monastery this summer."

Brucelli replied as he tilted his head to the side, "By any chance do you have the names of any suspected criminals?"

"No, sir. By the way, I'm an old friend of the family and I'm just kind of a surrogate father for Sasha here, since her father was killed in 1938. You can call her Sasha, and just call me Abie."

"Sure. So, Abie, may I ask you where Peter was told this rumor?"

"Yes, Peter studied the monastery routes with Professor Giovanni but had been given instructions not to give out any details in writing or over the phone about his project," Abie replied, annoyed with all the questions. "We can't help you, Sergeant and we'd appreciate it if you'd be kind enough to give us some privacy at this time of grief."

"Of course, Abie...I'm so sorry to have bothered you and Sasha. Please accept my apology. I am so sorry for your loss." Sergeant Brucelli left the waiting room. He now had the name of Peter's professor, which he wrote down on a scrap of paper. He planned to check in with the professor as soon as possible.

Abie and Sasha stayed over for a few days in a suite at a local inn near the hospital. When they arrived, Sasha went straight to bed. She'd been up for at least forty-eight hours. Abie tried to sleep...but any sleep he got was choppy. When he woke up in the morning he didn't feel rested. He called the Wolfs and gave them the bad news. He figured it would be a very painful conversation. They had already lost their son to a stabbing and now their great-grandson had suffered the same fate at the hands of a Nazi.

How would Abie and Sasha find a way to come to grips with this nightmare? This was a real watershed moment in their lives–a turning point, a door of no return. They could not turn the clock's hands backwards. How would they go on? Would the murderer be caught?

Sasha's guilt settled deep in her bones. Peter had sacrificed himself to complete her personal noble quest. He inherited and chose to pursue Sasha's quest and promises to herself. She should have died instead of Peter. How would she ever forgive herself? Sasha's heart leapt like a stallion into her throat. She could barely swallow or breathe. Blood drained from her face. Sasha's attempt to cross the divide via tightrope failed. She should be dead instead of Peter. She should be walking over her own grave.

Sasha had to carry on – the grieving mother, all the while she flinched–the mother in the mirror who had the word "guilty" written in blood on her forehead. Sasha's scarlet letter would be *G* for guilty.

Chapter 14
When I Am Ashes

It was time for Abie and Sasha to discuss funeral arrangements–in this case, cremation. They could always plan a memorial when they got back to America. Many years ago, when Peter first went to college, the three of them had an important discussion about cremation. They all said they desired to be cremated rather than buried in the ground. All of their closest relatives had been buried in cemeteries, so it was quite unusual that they all had a strong commitment to break with tradition.

They needed to find a local funeral home in Bolzano that did cremation. The manager at the inn recommended one nearby. Abie and Sasha rushed over before they lost their nerve. They spoke with the director about their situation. They picked out a plain pine coffin with a Jewish star carved on top. Sasha wanted to jump into the coffin and die with Peter. But Peter needed her to stay alive to finish the quest. It was a very emotional experience. The director helped with all the arrangements for Peter's body to be brought from the morgue, since the police said it could be released. He said the ashes would be ready the next day. They chose a dark, ornately carved, wooden box to store Peter's ashes.

In spite of the fact that so many of Sasha's relatives in Europe had died in crematoriums in the Holocaust... she and Abie understood it was important to honor Peter's wishes. They went back to the inn and Sasha went straight to bed. She wrapped herself in the grey sheets and thick grey comforter as Abie stood by the curtains, staring out the window at the bleak, grey sky.

The next morning, Sasha woke up with a fantastic idea that helped her smile. "Let's go to Paris. It's time to spread Peter's ashes in the Seine. There's no reason to be in Italy right now...The police have no suspects; they are at a stalemate. Let's just escape."

"I am so happy that you are excited about something," said Abie. "I'll do anything to make you happy."

They picked up the ashes and drove to Milan to catch the next flight to Paris.

It has often been said that when people experience the death of a loved one, they may have momentary glimpses of what it would feel like to live each moment with more fullness than usual. They are no longer on "automatic pilot" mode. They feel more alive. Each magical moment is experienced like a child: each tree, every blossom, each heartbeat, mountains, pastureland, wildflowers, churches, houses that appeared like ancient castles, a purple and rose-colored sunset. Sasha was very attentive to every detail as they drove to Milan. In the midst of death and sorrow, Sasha figured out an unusual way to feel more alive, even though this sounded impossible.

Upon arrival in Paris, they found a hotel on the Left Bank near the Luxembourg Gardens. The next day Abie woke up before Sasha and was careful not to wake her. Sleep had always been so important to her. Once she was awake Abie slowly opened up the drapes to let the light in.

They had breakfast at an outdoor café. They both ordered croissants. Abie ordered a café au lait and Sasha had her signature dark hot chocolate. This café placed a little leaf of dark chocolate on each croissant plate. While drinking her hot chocolate, she reminisced that Peter was conceived in Paris... so it was a perfect idea to spread his ashes in the Seine near where she and Michael took so many of their long walks.

Sasha excused herself and went into the ladies' room. When she looked at herself in the mirror, all of a sudden Sasha experienced a tremendous wave of guilt. How could she spread Peter's ashes without Michael there to participate in the ceremony? She really loved Michael and she still missed him terribly. Of course, Abie was with her and loved Peter like a grandson, but Michael was her first love, her soulmate, and Peter's father. She fell deeply in love with him and then they were separated by an emer-gency and a war. Why did she think of this now? Was it just the grief talking, or because Michael was Peter's bio-logical father and he was totally unaware of it? She had to find Michael. She took a deep breath and tried not to cry.

Sasha returned to her table and was distracted by a street juggler who rode around on his unicycle. Sasha took a deep breath and finished her croissant. After breakfast she chose to go to the Louvre. She needed to show Abie the amazing painting she fell in love with so many years ago, the canvas of *Atala's Funeral* that started Sasha's journey. They searched all over the museum and much to her chagrin they couldn't find it anywhere.

"I cannot believe we have spent the whole day in search of *Atala*," Sasha said, discouraged.

"Perhaps it's being restored right now, Sasha." And the very moment Abie said that, she turned around and the painting jumped out of its gilded frame again, the way it did the very first time she experienced it.... Sasha burst into tears.

Sasha had forgotten just how huge it was. Abie fell in love with it too. "I can't imagine anyone not loving this painting, Abie," as she wiped her tears away.

"It is quite striking," he said as he took a step backwards to get a better view.

"The first time I experienced it, I said, 'If only I could be loved like that someday...'"

"Yes, and someday you will," said Abie.

A strange buzzer and a voice crackled across a hidden speaker, "The museum closes in five minutes. Please exit in an orderly fashion."

Déjà vu all over again. She and Abie rushed down to the gift shop. It was still open and a miracle happened. They had the postcard in stock, the very postcard she'd asked Michael to mail her that she never received. Sasha allowed herself a brief moment to pretend her sweet Michael stood behind that counter and then she came back to reality. While she paid for the postcard the saleswoman remarked, "This is a very popular painting."

"Yes, I'm sure it is. I fell in love with it twenty-five years ago and I've never forgotten it."

"Oh, is that so? Are you aware that this painting is based on a novel by the famous French writer, Chateaubriand?"

"Really?" exclaimed Sasha, and her eyes opened wide.

"Yes, and I'm sure you can find it in any local bookstore in Paris..."

Sasha was beside herself. "Did you hear that, Abie?" and before he could even reply she said, "We *must* find that book *now.*"

Abie humored her and they found the nearest book-store that was still open. She was thrilled that they had a paperback version of the book in French.

"In case I can't sleep tonight I'll have something special to read," she smiled and held the book close to her heart. Sasha found ways to distract herself from the reason she came to Paris in the first place. She crawled into bed and started to read her new book.

"Do you need to order room service, Sasha?"

"Thanks, Abie, but I'm not hungry right now. The novel is my dinner."

Abie was aware that Sasha wasn't hungry these days. Death would do that to you. The death diet. Abie had a heavy heart. He ordered French onion soup and crawled into bed himself. It had been a long day. Sasha was asleep and the new book had dropped out of her hands and onto the carpet.

The following day Sasha woke up with the most important next step in her healing journey.

"I must find Michael," she told Abie, feeling a shiver run up her spine. "He's Peter's biological father. Even though he's not aware he had a son and he wasn't there to raise him, I feel it's crucial that Michael be here to help spread Peter's ashes."

"Okay. But how will we find him?"

"We need to go back to the gift shop at the Louvre and see if anyone remembers him. It's a long shot, for twenty-five years have gone by and World War II intervened... but it's worth a try. I cannot believe I didn't think of it yesterday."

So they headed back to the museum. This time there was a different salesclerk at the gift shop, a young man named Pierre who had just started to work there.

"I just checked with my supervisor who's worked here for ages, but even she doesn't remember anyone named Michael from 1938."

Sasha was beyond disappointed. But she also noticed that the salesclerk's name was Pierre–Peter in French. She figured this was a lucky sign.

"Any other ideas, my dear?" asked Abie.

Sasha paused for a minute and then came up with a brilliant idea! "I think we should place an ad in *Le Monde* and see if Michael responds."

So over breakfast at their favorite café they started to draft the advertisement. *In search of a man I met in the summer of 1938 in the Louvre. We both fell in love with the same painting.*

If you are this person, please contact Sasha at the Hotel du Luxembourg. REWARD.

They placed the ad then went back to the hotel. Sasha told the front desk, "Please take phone messages, do not put the calls through to the room, unless they are from America or Italy." Sasha worried about too many calls all day and night.

On the first day that the ad appeared in the paper, Sasha started to receive phone messages. But each time she returned the call she was disappointed because none of them were named Michael. After the second day yielded no success, they changed the ad to reflect the fact that the man's name was Michael and left the rest of the ad the same. She received a flurry of messages where the man's name was Michael. She called each man back but none of them could name the painting they'd fallen in love with. She gave them a chance to describe the painting... but no one came even close nor could they name the location in the Louvre where they'd first met.

"What a disappointment. It's hopeless," said Sasha as she sagged back in her chair. "I'm never going to find Michael."

"Let's take out the word *REWARD*. At least that way anyone who's answering isn't doing it for the money, Sasha."

"Great idea, Abie." Sasha called the paper and changed the ad once again.

They tried to stay busy. They took long walks by the Seine and visited many cathedrals with beautiful stained-glass windows–Notre Dame, Chartres, and Rheims. They even took a three-day trip to Mt. Saint Michel. They also went to colorful and fragrant gardens: Versailles, Fontainebleau, Monet's Giverny. They tried out different cafés to find the best hot chocolate in Paris. They explored some outdoor markets. Sasha bought a silk scarf and Abie bought himself a black beret that had the name Paris embroidered on the back.

"We've been in France for almost ten days and no one has answered the new ad. I give up!" Sasha exclaimed in the car, as she pounded on the steering wheel. "I'm never going to find

Michael," she admitted, heartbroken, feeling as if a knife stabbed her heart.

Abie expressed his fears, taking a deep breath, "Perhaps Michael died in the resistance in World War II or maybe...just maybe...he's not reading French newspapers, because he's not even in France right now."

"Well, I won't wait around Paris for a ghost to show up on my doorstep," she sighed, on the verge of tears.

At that very moment in time, Abie was right. Michael was not able to read any French newspapers. He wasn't in the mood to read any newspapers at all. Michael was sitting by the bedside of his dying mother in Italy. He was aware her long battle with cancer was nearing an end. As he reached out to hold her hand, a sigh escaped his lips. Michael's heart cried silent tears. Her passing might be any day now. He reached for some tissues by the bed. He'd been by her side for the last two weeks, but he'd lost track of time. He wasn't sure what day of the week it was, as he dreamed of heaven, his eyes skyward.

"Come close, my son. I need to tell you an important secret," said Michael's mother, Therese. Michael leaned forward and strained to hear his mother's weak voice.

"Okay, Mother... this must be a very important secret."

"Yes, it is, my son. On the one hand I've wanted to tell you about this for so long but on the other hand, I was determined to take this secret to my grave," his mother said, her frail voice trembling.

"Okay, Mother."

"I am troubled because I lied to you."

"Why, Momma?" There was a pregnant pause.

"I told you that we were Catholic. But we are actually Jews hiding as Catholics due to extreme anti-Semitism."

"Oh, that's interesting, considering I am a monk. I will have to talk with the Abbate about that. It's okay, Momma. Don't worry. I am not upset to learn the news."

"That's good. Since I have a sense that the Lord will call me home any day now...I guess this is my deathbed confession. I hope that I haven't upset you, my son, and that you will forgive me."

"Of course, Mother. You don't have to apologize."

"Thank you, my son...I have wanted to tell you this for a very long time."

"It's okay, Mother. That must have been a heavy burden to carry that secret for such a long time."

"Yes," she said as her weak voice trailed off.

"Why don't you rest for a while. It's almost your bedtime. I will stay here until you fall asleep."

"I love you, son."

"I love you too, Mother," Michael whispered in a dreamy sort of way, as he looked skyward, almost asleep.

No wonder Michael had such a strong need to save Jews, Gypsies, and other 'undesirables' during World War II. And he did succeed in his mission. But he would definitely have to explain this to the Abbate.

Michael left after his mother fell asleep. He knew in his heart this was going to be the last time he'd see her alive. He was so glad she shared the secret. Now everything made sense. Michael received a call from the hospital that his mother passed away at 3:45 a.m. A wave of sadness crept over him. He followed his mother's wishes and she was cremated the next day. Michael needed to buy a ticket to Paris. He promised he'd spread his mother's ashes in the Seine because that's where she used to walk with him as a baby.

Therese's ashes were placed in an ornately carved, brown wooden box. Ironically, while Michael flew from Italy to Paris to spread his mother's ashes, he had no way to guess that Sasha and Abie flew back on the same day and at the same time from Paris to Italy. They had not spread Peter's ashes. How strange. The "star-crossed" lovers crisscrossed in the air.

Michael took a taxi from the airport to a small hotel by the Seine. He'd planned to spread his mother's ashes the next day. Before he went to sleep Michael took a walk by the Seine, for old time's sake. Life would have been so different if Sasha had stayed in France. They would've had a family. Michael wouldn't be alone right now. Maybe they could've eloped. But they might've been separated during the war. They both might've been sent to different concentration camps and their children might have been taken away as well. He would've been frantic to find out if they were still alive. It would've been a nightmare.

If Sasha had stayed, Michael would not have become a monk. Sasha used to say she could have been a nun, in spite of the fact that she was Jewish. Michael recalled that Sasha said she desired to live in a church because she loved stained-glass windows. But in reality, Michael was the one who lived in a monastery now and had become a monk. And he just found out he was Jewish.

Michael was comforted by the role he played as he saved Jews and Gypsies in his monastery in Assisi during the war. Michael wept as Sasha's face flashed in front of him. The loss of his mother brought up emotions of his first loss, the loss of his soulmate and beloved Sasha. As Michael walked along the Seine, he lost Sasha all over again... It was unbearable. He sobbed, curled up on a bench, and shivered with a lump in his throat. Somewhere around midnight Michael walked back to his hotel and fell asleep.

The next day Michael wrote Sasha a long letter. He professed his love for her. He explained why he was in Paris, why he became a monk, what he did in the war, and his work on the monastery routes now. He confessed that not a day went by when he didn't think of her and described how much he missed her. Michael explained he was still in love with her and never stopped loving her.

After he sealed the letter, he walked over to the gift shop at the Louvre.

Michael told Pierre, the sweet young man behind the counter, "I worked here as a salesclerk in the gift shop in the summer of 1938..."

Pierre's eyes grew wide. "Wow!"

Michael got up the courage and asked, as his hands trembled, "Can I ask you a favor? The chances are slim..." Michael said with hesitation as he leaned in towards the counter, "but on the off-chance that an American woman named Sasha Wolf comes into this gift shop, who asks for a man named Michael, would you give her this letter?"

"Sure," Pierre agreed. "Everyone loves a good romantic story," the salesclerk smiled.

After Michael left the gift shop Pierre vaguely remembered that a couple came in the other day who asked for a man who'd worked in the gift shop many years ago, but he couldn't recall the man's name and he didn't think that the woman was an American because she spoke French fluently and her accent was impeccable. Then Pierre got distracted by a pretty female customer. He forgot all about the romantic fairytale and the letter.

Michael was desperate for Sasha to get that letter...Now he was determined to find her. But where would he start? Would he have to fly back to New York again for their paths to cross? He stopped and had some hot chocolate.

Chapter 15
The Evidence

An exasperated Sasha returned to Italy. Out of frustration she called Sergeant Brucelli.

"Are there any new developments in the murder investigation, Sergeant?"

"I was just about to call you, Sasha," Brucelli replied.

"Oh, really? What's going on?" she asked.

"Late this afternoon two hikers on a trail near Bolzano called to say a monk's body was in a nearby stream. After they got closer, they used a stick to try to pull the man to safety...But they soon discovered that they hadn't found a monk at all-only his brown robe in the stream. It was caught on some branches. Their long stick pulled the robe ashore. The hikers were still concerned that maybe a monk had fallen into the water and perhaps if they dislodged the robe from the branches they might find the monk's body in the water underneath.

"But they only found the robe. It's possible that they may have disturbed some hidden clues by removing the robe the way they did. Our guess is this, either the monk took off the robe and threw it in the stream to get rid of some evidence or that perhaps the monk did attempt suicide. It remains to be seen whether the monk did indeed commit suicide by drowning or merely disrobed and fled the scene, escaping on foot into the woods. We now have a robe which may or may not be the robe of the monk who killed Peter and Brother Paolo. But we still do not have the key piece of evidence we need to solve this mystery–the knife."

"I'm glad we chose to come back to Italy, Sergeant. Sounds like things have shifted. I just figured I'd tell you that we're back in Bolzano. We were not really ready to spread Peter's ashes just yet."

"Okay. Thanks for your call, Sasha."

"Oh, just one more thing..." Sasha added as she tightened her grip on the phone. "I've been focused on the idea that Peter was killed first and Brother Paolo was killed second because he witnessed the crime and had to be killed. But what if Brother Paolo was the intended victim and Peter was killed because he witnessed the crime? That would put a whole new spin on the case, right?" Sasha asked, pacing back and forth in her hotel room.

"Yes, indeed, Sasha, we've tried to think of all possibilities. For example, was the gardener's testimony accurate? Or did the gardener kill both men...and make up the rest of the story? But even if we assume that the gardener is innocent, we have to keep in mind that witnesses can sometimes mix up the order of things or be unreliable. We may never find out who was killed first.

"Or what if both Peter and Brother Paolo were in touch in advance? What if Brother Paolo was aware of a Nazi war criminal hiding in the Bolzano monastery or a monastery in Rome and perhaps he and Peter arranged in advance to meet in the garden? That's a possibility, too. Then perhaps, the monk who was the Nazi war criminal somehow was aware that Brother Paolo and Peter had planned to meet at the rose garden on that day. Then maybe the Nazi war criminal, dressed as a monk, waited in the rose garden for Peter and Brother Paolo to meet up and killed them both."

"Wow," said Sasha... "there are so many possibilities. How in the world do you figure it out?"

"That's my job, Sasha. I will not rest until this case is solved...as long as I live and breathe. Let me tell you the most important reason why. I am part Jewish myself and I lost family to the Nazis and Fascists! So I have a personal stake in this case. Unless we can wave a magic wand and pull a confession out of thin air... our best chance is to find that knife. That is the key to unraveling this whole mystery.

"My entire team continues to search the stream and forest near the discovery of the monk's robe. Please understand that we'll work day and night to find that knife. Trust me. Soon we'll have fingerprints of all the monks in Bolzano, plus the gardener, and everyone who came in contact with Peter. We've brainstormed about alternate theories that may fit the crime. Please don't give up, Sasha."

"I am trying not to," said Sasha with a heavy heart. "It's so hard," she continued as her eyes filled with tears.

Brucelli replied, "I understand."

Upon her return to Bolzano, Sasha had a resurgence of nightmares. Her own screams awoke her in the middle of the night. Sometimes she tried to save Peter from being stabbed in Italy, even though she was in America when it happened. Other times she tried to protect her father who was stabbed in America while she was in Paris. But in the worst nightmares often Sasha had to choose between finding Michael or saving Peter. Peter was the only thing Sasha had left of her relationship with Michael, except the locket and hot chocolate. With Peter's death she lost an extra connection to Michael. The earth was being pulled out from under her and she lost her balance. She couldn't save Peter, so all she could do was try to find Michael and save him.

Her traumas had now gotten interwoven in her dreams, which doubled the intensity in her life. Sasha became afraid to go to sleep.

“My grief is overwhelming,” she kept repeating to Abie, dripping with cold sweat. “It’s too much. I can’t take it anymore. I’ll never see Peter get married or have children. Oh...no!” she panicked. “I just realized that I’ll never be a grandmother...” she said. “My heart is breaking. I’ve always waited patiently to be a grandmother!”

How would Sasha survive this much grief? Would punishing the murderer be enough for her? Would she ever find Michael or be able to save him in some way? What would she do with the rest of her life?

***

Ten days after Sasha and Abie returned to Bolzano, Brucelli called.

“Sasha, we’ve had a break in the case. A search party of a dozen men who’d combed the woods by the stream stumbled upon an abandoned hunting cabin. They took it apart board by board and by some miracle, underneath a trap door, they found a large serrated bread knife buried under some leaves. There was still blood on the knife.”

Sasha almost fainted from the news.

“They sealed the knife in a plastic bag and brought it to the coroner’s office to see if it was the murder weapon they’d desperately searched for. After several hours, the medical examiner came forward with his determination and...” Brucelli took a breath, “we now understand conclusively that this knife matches the wounds created by the murder weapon in the double homicide. The actual murder weapon has been found.”

“That’s fantastic,” Sasha said with enthusiasm. She allowed herself to enjoy the good news. “Are there any fingerprints?”

“Yes. There are several. Now comes the painstaking process to determine whose fingerprints they are. Again, it is imperative to collect the fingerprints of everyone who was connected to either Peter Wolf or Brother Paolo. Several detectives were dispatched once again to collect fingerprints from the monks at the Bolzano monastery and this time they have a search warrant that requires each monk be fingerprinted."

"That's fabulous," she said, elated, a big smile on her face.

"We also double-checked with the gardener to see if he recalled anything else. Two detectives were sent out to collect fingerprints of everyone Peter had come in contact with at the university, in particular his roommate and his girlfriend. I also attempted to reach Peter's professor at the university, but he was unavailable. I left a detailed message for him to contact me as soon as possible," explained Brucelli, sounding out of breath.

"I hope I haven't given you too much information for you to handle. We'll keep you posted on any big developments, Sasha."

"Okay. Thanks for all the information. I am glad you didn't hold back anything, Sergeant."

Brucelli went to collect Peter's roommate's fingerprints.

"I was in Perugia at the time of the attack. Do I have to give you my fingerprints?" asked Billy as he broke into a sweat.

"It would look pretty suspicious if you refused to give us your prints," Brucelli told him, his hands on his hips. Billy gave the detective his fingerprints.

The next order of business was to get the fingerprints of Peter's girlfriend. She wasn't in her dormitory in Perugia. The university gave Brucelli a phone number in Rome where she sometimes lived with her mother. Maria answered the phone and said she would be happy to give her fingerprints if it helped the investigation. Two detectives were dispatched to Rome to collect them. That was a big relief to Brucelli–one less thing to complicate matters. He was aware that this case might make his career.

Maria's mother, Anna, crossed her arms and, apparently eavesdropping, asked, "Who was that on the phone?"

"Just some detectives who will come down to collect my fingerprints related to Peter's murder investigation."

"Why in the world would they need your fingerprints? You loved that young man and you were in Perugia when he was killed anyway," her mother complained. "I hate the police. They are just plain nasty most of the time. They better not ask me for my fingerprints, because I'll just refuse. And besides, I only met Peter once when you brought him to dinner that Sunday night. Plus, I was in Rome when he was killed in Bolzano so why would they need my fingerprints?" asked Anna, with a blank stare.

"First of all, Mother, they did not even mention your fingerprints and second of all it makes you look guilty if you refuse," said Maria.

"Okay," said Anna, annoyed, "they just better be nice!"

Maria greeted the detectives at the door and they sat down at the dining room table to take her prints. Maria's mother was in the kitchen when the detectives arrived and offered the gentlemen some coffee and pastries.

"Thanks very much, Mrs. Romano," said the younger detective.

"It's the least I can do for you fine gentlemen. What a shame about that poor boy Peter, he seemed like such a perfect young gentleman. Who on earth would desire to kill him? I only met him once, but I could tell he was an honest young man–just the kind of boy I would pick for my Maria. How is the investigation going anyway?" asked Anna.

"Oh, we just need fingerprints to rule out the innocent people who had contact with Peter."

"Oh, Mrs. Romano, since you said you met Peter, we need your fingerprints as well," said Detective Amaro.

"Is that really necessary? I only met him once," said Anna, backing away.

"Yes, I'm sorry to bother you, but we have been asked to collect fingerprints of anyone who was in contact with Peter. I am sorry to trouble you, Mrs. Romano."

"Okay," Anna complained, "That's rather annoying. I give up," said Anna, frustrated. The detectives took her prints.

When the detectives finished their coffee and pastries they had to rush back to the police station. Maria walked them to the door and said, "Have a safe journey."

When the two detectives got in the car they were relieved. "Boy, Mrs. Romano seems to dislike policemen, although she went out of her way to be very nice. She seems conflicted."

"Yeah, passive-aggressive."

"Exactly. Or maybe she was just in a crabby mood."

It took a while to get back the results of the fingerprints because they were latent and only partial prints... So that rendered the elimination of suspects more difficult. Sergeant Brucelli called in an expert in fingerprint analysis. After three weeks' examination of the collected fingerprints and the fingerprints of those in the blood on the knife, the analyst came to an unusual conclusion.

***

The entire police force in the Bolzano area–all 15 of them–and a few detectives from Perugia gathered together to hear the news. Brucelli was proud to make the announcement.

"I believe that we have three distinct fingerprints. Two of them match fingerprints we've already collected, and one set of prints does not match, so those are the 'mystery prints,'" said Brucelli as he puffed out his chest.

He continued, in a louder voice, "After careful consideration, I believe that the knife in question came from the kitchen of Peter Wolf's girlfriend. Let me clarify, from Maria Romano's childhood home near Rome, not her dorm."

The detectives were stunned. "So far I can't think of a motive that would provoke a reaction such as murder from Peter's girlfriend or for that matter, her mother," said Brucelli, puzzled, as he scratched his head.

Detective Amaro, who was an assistant to Brucelli, bragged with a grin, "Maria's mother, Anna, has a history of run-ins with the law in the past–petty theft, shoplifting, prostitution, etc."

"But murder is a huge leap from misdemeanors," Brucelli said, his heart racing.

Detective Bacci, who had taken Anna's prints, stated, his face and neck flushed, "She seemed to have a love-hate relationship with the police, kind of passive-aggressive. What's her story?"

The police were stumped as to what would Maria's and or Anna's motives be. The key to unlock the door of this mysterious double homicide was probably the third set of fingerprints, the person whose prints hadn't been collected yet. They needed to reach Peter's professor in order to set up an appointment to check his fingerprints. But he wasn't in.

"Keep calling," Brucelli shouted, "I wonder if he ran away. Stay on top of it, guys."

Detective Bacci reached Professor Giovanni, "I am sorry to inform you that one of your students passed away. We have tried to reach you many times."

"Oh, no," wept the professor as he fell to his knees. "This is terrible news. I pray it's not Peter," the professor whispered.

"Are you still there, Professor Giovanni?" said Bacci.

"Yes, I'm still here," Giovanni said, clearing his throat.

"It was Peter Wolf, the student from America."

"Oh, my goodness...Oh, how awful...I'm just heartbroken," he cried out in shock, grief-stricken.

"I am sorry for your loss, sir...um...Would you be able to come into one of our offices and give us your fingerprints, sir?

We just need to eliminate everyone who came into contact with Peter."

"Oh, of course I will come. I am near Perugia right now. Do you have any offices nearby?"

"Oh, yes, sir," said the detective, and he gave the professor directions to the nearest office.

Professor Giovanni hung up. "I feel like I've been struck by lightning. A real jolt to the heart. Oh, my God. Oh, Peter. I'm sorry, my son. It should have been me. Why did I give you this assignment? I never should have given it to you. What a brave boy. The courage of a lion."

The professor grabbed a pillow and blanket and curled into a fetal position and tried to sleep on the floor. "I should have died instead of you, Peter. Please forgive me." The overwhelming guilt ripped through his heart.

The next day Brucelli asked, "Has anyone been able to track down Peter's professor yet?"

"Yes," replied Bacci, "I spoke to him yesterday. He has an appointment this afternoon to give us his prints."

Then Brucelli called his men to action, "If the professor's fingerprints are not the third set of prints, we have to connect the dots... We must find the third person whose prints are on that knife. Okay, men... go out and get some more leads."

Professor Giovanni arrived promptly at 1 p.m. He was devastated by Peter's death. He seemed like he hadn't slept a wink. He'd been out of town and had just returned the day before, when he discovered the gut-wrenching news from Detective Bacci on the phone. The professor was heartbroken. He sobbed and blew his nose while Brucelli took his fingerprints. He really seemed distraught, unless he was a good actor.

"Professor, do you understand why Peter went to Bolzano?"

His body crumpling forward, Professor Giovanni answered, "Peter was doing a research paper on the possibility of Nazi war criminals hiding out in certain monasteries in Rome and Bolzano. If Peter's research turned out to be supportable, this would be a stunning revelation that would shake up the Catholic Church."

Brucelli then followed up, in a quieter voice than normal, "Do you think Peter was onto something, Professor?"

"Yes, I do sir," said Giovanni, his voice cracking. "From my own research I am aware there's an underground network called the 'monastery routes.' There were at least two monasteries in Italy that had a pattern of hiding Nazi war criminals, most of whom were on their way to South America, like Eichmann and Mengele. One of the monasteries was in Bolzano and the other was in Rome.

"With the help of the Catholic Church and Bishop Alois Hudal, the criminals got false ID papers from the International Red Cross Committee. Once their papers arrived, most of them went to Genoa and left Europe on a boat bound for South America. But I believe some of them didn't leave Italy, so they remained in hiding as monks in those monasteries."

Brucelli thanked Professor Giovanni and told him that their conversation had been helpful and profound.

And then the professor asked Brucelli a question, "Did anyone else die in the attack?"

"It was a double homicide. Peter and a monk were both stabbed with the same knife. The gardener was aware of the whole event and he said another monk in a brown robe did it," Brucelli, answered, curious why the professor asked.

"Was it Brother Paolo?"

"Yes, actually it was."

Professor Giovanni collapsed.

Chapter 16

"Shake the Tree"

Two days later, Sergeant Brucelli gathered his team to inform them of the newest update.

"It has been determined that the professor's fingerprints are not the unidentified prints on the knife. So, the third set of prints are still a mystery."

The Sergeant was glad Giovanni's prints were not on the knife. He was fascinated that the professor seemed almost as devastated as Sasha. Brucelli took a deep breath and tried to conceive of what it would be like to lose a child.

Then the Sergeant came back to reality. As he walked over to Amaro he said, "Any guest in the home of Anna and Maria Romano could have left fingerprints on that knife to slice a loaf of bread but that wouldn't convince a jury they were guilty. The real killer could have worn gloves."

"You're right, Sarge," Amaro agreed.

Bacci approached Brucelli, confused. "Sir, can you speculate about the motive that either Anna or Maria would have to kill Peter and Brother Paolo?"

"No, I can't, Bacci," Brucelli replied, annoyed, with a fixed stare. "But we've got to come up with a plan to 'shake the tree' and see if any fruit falls off."

"I am concerned that may be a challenge," said Bacci. Brucelli steeled himself, stood up straight, determined to move forward with the investigation.

Brucelli, Bacci, and Amaro drove to Rome and dropped by unannounced to update Anna and Maria on the progress of the investigation.

"I am curious to see how they react when we tell them their prints are on the murder weapon. Maybe they'll give something away," said Brucelli, as he clutched the steering wheel tighter.

Anna served pastries and coffee again as they all sat around the dining room table. Brucelli explained, with a clenched jaw, "Well, ladies, we have good news and bad news: the good news is that we have found the knife that killed Peter and Brother Paolo."

Both women gasped and simultaneously exclaimed, "Really?"

The detectives noticed that both women stared at each other when they spoke.

"Yes," replied Brucelli, as he studied their facial expressions. "The bad news is we've analyzed the fingerprints and both of your fingerprints are on the murder weapon."

The two women gasped. "How can that be?" asked Maria, her eyes bulging wide.

"That's impossible," Anna said as she stared at Maria.

"But Sergeant, how is that even possible? I didn't go with Peter to Bolzano." Maria asked as she covered her mouth with her palm. "I was in Perugia the day Peter and that monk were killed," Maria explained in disbelief. "And I was home in Rome that day. I wasn't anywhere near Bolzano," Anna shouted as she pounded the dining room table.

Brucelli and his detectives tried to analyze Anna and Maria's facial expressions and body language. Were they both involved in the murders? Or perhaps one was directly involved and the other one was part of a coverup? Brucelli was unsure as he rubbed his chin.

"It was obvious that both of their fingerprints could surely be on the knife if it came from their kitchen," Brucelli said under his breath.

They used that knife to slice loaves of bread every day for years. It's possible these two women had nothing to do with the murders and someone else took the knife from their house. So maybe they helped who it was and they're part of a coverup? Or maybe they don't have any knowledge about it. Brucelli was frustrated. If he couldn't link them to the murders without a shadow of a doubt, an accusation would not stick in court.

"Well," Brucelli asked, raising his voice, "do either of you have witnesses that can swear that you were not in Bolzano that day?"

Maria answered, her arms shaking, "I had a bad flu so I spent the whole day in bed."

"Did anyone see you that day?" asked Brucelli with impatience as he folded his arms across his chest.

"No, I don't think so," replied Maria, her chin trembling.

"And how about you Anna? Was anyone with you?" Brucelli continued his relentless probe.

"I was at home all day. I baked all day, but I was alone. I don't remember anybody in the house with me that day," said Anna, her head tilted to the side. Neither woman had a solid alibi. They continued to watch the women's facial expressions and body language.

"Were there any other prints on the knife?" asked Maria.

"Yes, as a matter of fact there was a third set of fingerprints, but so far we have been unable to identify that person yet," answered Brucelli as he tried to hide his frustration.

"Well, the murderer must be the other person," said Anna, "unless the other prints belonged to Peter... But that would mean that Peter killed himself." She laughed at her own joke, which was inappropriate and in rather poor taste.

Maria cringed at her mother's ridiculous remark, so she quickly interrupted, "We would have no reason to kill our Peter or that monk." Maria made a mental note that she needed to tell Brucelli that her mother had a history of passive-aggressive tendencies and psychotic breaks.

The detectives glanced at each other. "We have no direct evidence that links the mother or daughter to the crime," Brucelli whispered to his team, his back towards the women. "But let's bring them down to the station as part of our 'shake the tree' experiment. There's a strong possibility that either or both of these women participated in the double murders in some way," he continued, determined, his hands in his pockets.

"Or perhaps they are aware of the person who committed this crime. Our goal must be to figure out who the mystery fingerprints belong to. Then we'll have a better chance to solve this case."

"We better keep the two women separated so they don't have time for collusion, to discuss or change their stories," Amaro noted to the team. Brucelli and Bacci nodded their heads.

Sergeant Brucelli stood up and turned around. He stated to Anna, his hands on his hips, "Anna Romano, I hereby place you under arrest on suspicion of murder in the double homicide of Peter Wolf and Brother Paolo. You have the right to remain silent. Anything you say can and will be used against you in a court of law. You have the right to an attorney. If you cannot afford an attorney one will be provided for you. Please place your hands behind your back."

Upon hearing those words Anna became visibly shaken. Then all of a sudden, she switched to extreme violence.

"Leave my daughter out of this," she screamed in a high-pitched shrill voice. Brucelli was shocked at Anna's comment. Was Anna protecting her daughter?

Anna's inappropriate behavior escalated. She refused to be handcuffed and threw china plates on the table and then at the wall. The sound of shattered porcelain echoed in the silent room. She was out of control. Maria touched her mother's shoulder and tried to calm her down. Anna's face got very red and flushed and then she collapsed.

Maria bent down and said, "Give her some air."

As Anna came to, she screamed and flailed her arms around, "Dear God, help me. My heart, my chest, and my arms are killing me. I need help, I can't breathe... I need my medicine."

Brucelli and his colleagues were sure that Anna faked her pain so she wouldn't be handcuffed and taken down to the station. They handcuffed her anyway and carried her out to the police car.

Maria ran after them and shouted, "Are you okay, Mom?"

"Please detectives... My mother has a heart condition. Let me give you her medicine," she yelled, but nobody seemed to listen.

After the first squad car left for the station with Anna, Brucelli gave the same order to Maria: "Maria Romano, I hereby place you under arrest on suspicion of murder in the double homicide of Peter Wolf and Brother Paolo. You have the right to remain silent. Anything you say can and will be used against you in a court of law. You have the right to an attorney. If you cannot afford an attorney one will be provided for you. Please place your hands behind your back."

Maria cooperated and placed her hands behind her back. Her hands were ice cold. "Sergeant, I feel a cold sweat coming over me, and I feel nauseated." Brucelli placed Maria in another squad car anyway.

Maria started to sob, tremble, and then shake in the back of the police car. "I just lost my sweet boyfriend and now you have accused me of murder," she yelled. "I don't believe this. I did not kill anyone. I loved Peter so much. And I never met Brother Paolo. I am innocent, officer. But please, sir, please help my mother," she begged. Maria started to hyperventilate as she stared out the window. Her pleas were ignored–her words fell on deaf ears.

Maria was taken down to the police station. When she arrived, there was a big commotion. She was horrified that her mother was being dragged across the room. She was unable to stand up.

Anna yelled, "I need help. I need a doctor. Someone please help me."

But nobody seemed to care. Maria begged a policeman near her, "Please help me. My mother needs medical attention. She had a heart condition and needs her medicine," Maria pleaded, as she gasped for air herself.

But it seemed like everyone was under the impression her mother was just faking to get attention. Maria's eyes filled with tears. Some of the officers laughed. Discouraged, Maria closed her eyes and prayed.

About ten minutes later a supervisor took one look at Anna and called an ambulance to make sure she got proper medical attention. When the ambulance arrived the EMTs demanded that the police release Anna to them to go to the hospital. After a heated discussion the police allowed Anna to go, handcuffed to a policeman. The police still were convinced Anna had displayed one hell of a performance, but they allowed the hospital to check her out.

"Thank God," Maria said, grateful her prayers were answered.

Brucelli started to hammer Maria about her relationship with Peter. His questions came at her like a barrage of bullets. He did that on purpose to try to rattle her. As those questions got more and more personal, and as Maria was also concerned about her mother, Maria broke down, fell to her knees, and became hysterical.

"Can't you see I'm falling apart?" she said to Brucelli. "I can't believe this."

"I need you to be able to trust me and help me solve this case, Maria," said Brucelli.

"I do not trust anyone at this station right now. I feel defeated," she said with vacant eyes.

"Sergeant, I feel startled by my mother's bizarre reaction. I am starting to question the possibility that my mother might be aware of something related to Peter's death." Maria cringed, eyes closed, whispered, "Do I dare even consider that maybe my own mother killed those two men and if so... why?"

"What a myriad of crazy things! I've never seen my mother behave this way. My family has some deep, dark secrets ...but I don't understand what they are. One day my uncle yelled at my mother in the kitchen. As soon as I came into the room, he stopped ... and after a brief pause they yelled at each other but in a foreign language, one I did not understand. I am not sure if I should mention this to you, but I've chosen to be honest. I feel dizzy and am seeing black spots in front of my eyes. I better lean back against the wall."

"Let me get you a glass of juice," said Brucelli.

"Thanks."

Brucelli asked Maria, "Are you less dizzy after having the juice?"

"Yes, I am. Thanks. But I really miss Peter and I feel so lonely. Sometimes I can't remember what's real and what's part of the dream-like state. It's probably a combination of dehydration and real panic. I have heart palpitations and my chest is tingling. I just think it's a panic attack."

"Do you need to see a doctor?" asked Brucelli.

"No, I don't think so." She rotated her shoulders to loosen up. Maria did not feel like she wanted to tell Brucelli she might be pregnant.

"What's the worst possibility you can think of related to your mother, Maria?"

"Maybe some of our secrets from my mother's past, have something to do with Peter's death... or Brother Paolo's demise? It's strange but I feel a fierce urgency to protect my mother.... I feel like my head is going to explode." Maria was silent for a few minutes.

"Okay, I did it! I did it!" Maria confessed.

Maria's confession came out of the blue. But it seemed obvious that she was choosing to take the blame to cover up her own mother's crimes.

Brucelli stated with boldness, puffing out his chest, "I refuse to believe you, Maria. I do not accept your confession. You are just trying to protect your mother. She's an actress."

After Maria protested for another thirty minutes, she gave up. She needed to speak to her lawyer.

Anna arrived at the local hospital. The police had called ahead to warn the doctors to be careful with their diagnosis because the patient's illness might not be real. The police were convinced Anna was faking. Dr. Lombardo was assigned to Anna's case. At this point Anna was weak. The doctor checked her pulse, listened to her heart, and then her lungs.

"Is she still alive, Doc?" asked the policeman who was handcuffed to her. He'd started to get concerned.

Dr. Lombardo said, "Yes, she's alive but just barely. Her pulse is very sparse and weak. I believe she may have just had a heart attack."

"Oh, wow," said the officer, "we just guessed she was pretending."

"No, Anna's condition is very real. She is extremely dehydrated. She needs fluids and several heart medications. I think you got her here just in time. But she's going to have to stay at the hospital until we can stabilize her," the doctor replied sternly, putting the stethoscope around his neck.

"Oh, no," said the officer. "Well, I need to call the sergeant in charge of the case to bring him up to speed. Can I borrow a phone?"

A nurse gave the policeman directions to the closest telephone down the hall. The officer uncuffed himself from Anna's wrist. He took care not to wake her.

The policeman reached Sergeant Brucelli and said, weak in the knees, "Anna is hanging on by a thread. Looks like a heart attack, sir. The doctor recommended we suspend our questions at this time."

"Okay. Thanks, officer. Maria has started to cave in and crumble due to my barrage of questions," Brucelli said, determined, as he pressed his lips together.

But it wasn't true. Brucelli was pretty stuck and didn't see a way forward. Maria had refused to talk anymore. She'd chosen to wait for her lawyer to arrive. And now Anna was not available for questions for a while based on her doctor's request. Brucelli, frustrated at this stalemate, pounded his fist on the wooden desk. They had to regroup. The Sergeant rubbed his hands on his face. They had to find the person with the "mystery fingerprints."

How in the world would they find this person? It could be anyone. And it could just be a guest at the Romano home who had cut a slice of bread. The real murderer probably wore gloves. Brucelli couldn't figure out how he was going to overcome this obstacle.

***

After Anna received some fluids and heart medicine, she started to revive a bit. Her fingers and toes started to tingle. Anna discovered that she was in a very bright room. She twirled her hair, a nervous habit. Anna closed her eyes so they wouldn't be burned by the sun. This bright light was just too strong for her.

"Where am I?" she muttered. "I don't remember how I got to this sunny place. Have I just been born? Maybe that's why the light seems so bright after I came out of the dark womb...I have no idea who I am or where I am. I have no memory. I'm like a blank slate," she mumbled, enjoying a sense of peace. There was no one in the room to answer her questions.

Anna became childlike. She just had a good dream. "I am on a dream vacation where nothing goes wrong," she whispered. "It's glorious and divine. The flowers are so fragrant. The colors are like eye candy. Perhaps I'm at the beach. I can hear the waves along the shore. I love the fresh, salty sea air as it flows through me."

Anna no longer had any pain or shortness of breath. She was carefree, youthful, and innocent. "This is the way life ought to be," she continued to whisper in an empty room, smiling. "What in the world gets in the way?"

At that moment in time if someone had asked Anna what her name was, she would have been speechless; she would not have remembered. For the moment her life was simple and uncomplicated. She liked it that way. She had no memory of anything that had transpired during the last few days or months.

When the nurses came around to check her vital signs, she pushed them away because they invaded her place of innocence and sweetness. After a while she swam along the shoreline... long, deep strokes. It was almost like a baby who learned to crawl. She could feel herself glide. So peaceful, so calm. She'd died and gone to Heaven. Hallelujah.

And then...darkness fell on the landscape. Anna did not have a clue where she was. She had no landmarks to go by and it was completely dark. Pitch black. Not even a sliver of light. Time for her inner child to get used to the dark. This must be like going back into the womb. Anna took slow, deep breaths.

But it was still peaceful and calm... She could hear her mother's heartbeat. And all was well with the world. She stayed like this for days. And then....

BOOM! The light went on again and it was way too bright.

"Why are you here, Anna?" the nurse asked, shocked.

"Me?" asked Anna.

"Yes, you, Anna. We have been on a search for you over the last two days. How did you get in here?"

"What do you mean?" Anna asked.

"We've been frantic. You disappeared for two whole days. How did you end up in a fetal position locked in an old supply room closet?"

"I have no idea."

"Let's get you back in bed. You need some more fluids. You are very dehydrated and you need your heart medicine," the nurse said, relieved. "How could I lose a patient on my watch," the nurse muttered under her breath, "and a criminal under investigation, my Lord!"

So that is how Anna emerged from the closet. But was she guilty? And, if not, who killed Peter and Brother Paolo? How would Brucelli figure it out?

***

Anna now had no memory of who she was and what was going on in her life. Brucelli was concerned that Anna was feigning amnesia. The doctor said he thought that Anna might've had a mental breakdown or a psychotic break.

"Could that cause amnesia?" asked Brucelli.

"Perhaps," said Doctor Lombardo, in a rush.

"It might cause short-term memory loss but maybe not the loss of long-term memory. Does Anna have any children, Sergeant?"

"Yes, she has a daughter, Maria."

The doctor recommended that they bring Maria in to see Anna. "Let's see if Anna recognizes her own daughter."

By this point Maria was no longer considered a suspect, so Brucelli called her. "Your mother has experienced some short-term memory loss. I'd like to bring you in to see if she recognizes you at all."

"Okay. I have been frantic to get any news about my mother since I had been forbidden to see her or even call. When can I come?" Maria asked.

"How about tomorrow?" Brucelli answered, feeling guilty.

"Great."

Brucelli and several officers would be meeting Maria at the hospital the next day.

"We need to make sure there is no collusion between Anna and Maria. We have to watch those two women like hawks. Even if they are not the murderers, they might have been part of a coverup. Let's watch and be on the lookout for any signs that either woman slips and gives us a clue. We need to find out who the other fingerprints belong to. But this visit is just meant to determine whether Anna recognizes Maria. You get it, officers?" Brucelli barked, frustrated, as he stuffed his hands in his pockets.

"Yes, sir," his men replied. The officers waited by Anna's door until Maria entered and followed her in.

Maria walked into her mother's room carrying a bouquet of flowers. Anna's immediate response was, "Oh, thank you, nurse, for those pretty...ummmm..."

"Flowers," Maria answered with love. The policemen just observed from the back of the room.

"How are you feeling, Mom?"

"Oh, that's right, those pretty things are called mums," Anna replied with a smile.

Maria asked, "Don't you recognize me, Mother?"

"Oh, my mother died a long time ago in another country," said Anna, at which point Maria started to cry.

"Why do you cry, little girl? I'm sorry I don't have any candy for you," said Anna in a childlike voice. Maria threw the flowers on the floor and dashed out of the room as she sobbed.

The detectives followed Maria out but Brucelli stayed to see what would happen next.

The officers tried to comfort Maria, but she said through tears, "I've lost my boyfriend and now my mother. It's too much."

It seemed clear to the officers that Maria and Anna had not colluded with one another unless they had some kind of bizarre pre-arranged code.

Anna's nurse entered the room with a vase to put the flowers in, but Anna yelled, "They're dirty because they were on the floor. We need to throw them away."

The nurse picked them up and threw them into the garbage can in the room. "Did you enjoy seeing your daughter?" the nurse asked Anna.

Anna shouted, "Daughter? Daughter? I never had a daughter."

"But Anna," said the nurse, "your daughter just brought you these flowers."

"Well, she must have been mixed up and came to the wrong room." Anna said, her face flushed. "Get rid of those flowers," Anna yelled, as she threw her arm up in the air. "Do you hear me? Those flowers are ugly and dirty. Throw them away... far, far away. I can't see them again. And that crazy lady who brought them in...I don't need to see her again," Anna ranted.

Brucelli left the room convinced that Anna did not recognize her daughter.

He became aware of a pattern where Anna was very nice and then she would have a mood swing and become very violent and would have to be restrained. They couldn't risk her to pull out her IVs or hide in a closet again. Anna's pattern of being saccharine sweet one minute and then flip into violence the next concerned Brucelli.

"Is this a normal occurrence?" the Sergeant asked Dr. Lombardo.

"It's hard to say. Everyone is so very different. But I believe Anna has gone through an extreme shock. That might be the cause of her erratic behavior."

Brucelli was curious what that shock might have been. Was it just being accused of murder? Or was it something else?

Brucelli grasped at straws. He asked Maria if she was aware of any people who would recognize Anna from years ago, since Anna's long-term memory might be better than her short-term memory.

Maria replied with great hesitation, "My uncle might be a possibility."

"Okay," said Brucelli, anxious for a break in the case. "Can you get ahold of him and see if he will come in?"

"I'll try, but my mom and uncle don't always get along."

Would bringing in Maria's uncle be the break in the case Brucelli needed–or would it just muddy the waters? He definitely had to be present during their interaction. This should be interesting.

Chapter 17

Family Secrets and Cracking the Code

A few days later, Maria's uncle stopped by the hospital. He went straight to Anna's room but was stopped by Brucelli first. The two men shook hands and Brucelli explained, with firm instructions, "Anna is in a fragile place so please do not bring up anything traumatic or negative."

Uncle agreed and then sauntered into Anna's room. "Hello dear," he said to Anna, looking like a Don Juan. Anna immediately sat up in bed and started to fuss with her hair.

"Hi, Uncle," said Anna, embarrassed that she might look disheveled. They seemed genuinely glad to see each other.

"At least she recognizes him," Maria said to Brucelli in the back of the room. But then Anna and Uncle launched into another language. Brucelli was thrown by this and asked the hospital for an interpreter. Uncle and Anna embraced and reminisced about old times... and then Anna talked about a family secret.

They spoke in Polish, but there was no translator available at the hospital at that time. Uncle and Anna got into a heated conversation and they screamed at one another.

Uncle yelled, washing his hands of her, "You whore," and stomped out of the room.

He slammed the door and escaped the hospital before Brucelli and his men had a chance to catch up with him. Anna started to sob uncontrollably. Maria stood in the back of the room as the whole event unfolded. Maria didn't speak or understand the language her mother and uncle used. She had no clue what happened. But she assumed it was the same language they used at home.

Brucelli grilled Maria. "What language were they speaking?"

"I have no idea what just happened or what language they just spoke, sir."

"Is that man your mother's uncle or your uncle?" Brucelli asked curtly, bristling with frustration.

"He's my uncle, I think."

"Well, is he your mother's brother or your father's brother?" Brucelli pressured her.

"I'm not sure," said Maria, ashamed, "I should be able to guess the answer, but I can't. All I am aware of is that my father died right after the war, so I never had any real knowledge of him...and Uncle was always just Uncle to me. I don't even know his name," Maria said.

Brucelli did not understand. How could she not even be able to guess the answer to that question? Something was amiss.

Anna and Uncle had known each other forever based on their body language, but at the end of the conversation they had a dramatic disconnect. Brucelli was curious why Uncle left in such an abrupt manner and whether it might have anything to do with the shock Dr. Lombardo mentioned. So Brucelli went over to Anna. Her eyes were still red and tears streamed like rivers down her cheeks.

"It seems like that man hurt your feelings," said Brucelli as he leaned closer to Anna.

"Yes, he did," replied Anna, wiping her tears away.

"What were you two talking about?" Brucelli asked as he tilted his head to the side.

"He called me a bad name," Anna said, raising her voice.

"What kind of bad name?" asked Brucelli with excitement. He chomped at the bit to get a morsel to chew on.

"I can't talk about it!" yelled Anna, "I am too embarrassed." She hid her head in her hands.

"I'm sorry, Anna."

"Leave me alone. I can't see anyone right now," Anna started to yell again as she waved her arms towards the ceiling.

Two days passed and Brucelli was still stunned by Anna's response to Uncle. She recognized him, so that was good news about her memory loss. At least she still had some long-term memories... Maybe it was just her short-term memory that seemed to have disappeared. But Brucelli tried to piece together what Dr. Lombardo said about a shock that could cause a mental breakdown, amnesia, a heart attack, and a short-term memory loss, juxtaposed to the incident with Uncle. What if Uncle had something to do with this sudden shock or the murder? Brucelli also tried to figure out what language the two were speaking.

He sat down with Detective Amaro to discuss the pieces of the puzzle. They played devil's advocate with one another. "What if Anna killed Peter and Brother Paolo?"

"What would her motive be?"

"I'm not sure."

"Did Uncle have anything to do with this tragedy or the shock Anna had experienced?"

"That's a good question."

"Okay. Here's another consideration. Let's assume, and it's a *big* assumption, that Anna committed the double homicide and did not flee the area. She went back to Rome and carried on with her regular life, baking as usual."

"Right. A killer would have left the country."

Brucelli gave Dr. Lombardo a call and asked, "Is it possible that Anna experienced a shock of some kind before the murders took place in Bolzano? And if so–and it is a really big if–is it possible that Anna was in shock and slid into some kind of fugue state, committed the murders, and then came home and spent the afternoon and evening baking pastries with no memory of what she had just done?"

"Anything's possible," said Dr. Lombardo, "but you might need to consult a psychiatrist since that's not my specialty."

"Oh, that's a great idea," Brucelli said with excitement. He could not give up. "Can you recommend a good one?"

"Well, Dr. Rabino is excellent but he's out of town on vacation for several more days," said Lombardo as he stroked his beard.

"Anna has good rapport with you, Dr. Lombardo. Would you be able to ask her some questions for us?" Brucelli bumbled like a bull in a china shop.

He needed to find techniques to speed up the process. Brucelli was very uncomfortable asking the doctor to do this... He wasn't sure if it bordered on unethical behavior, but he was determined and even desperate to crack this case wide open.

"Well, what kind of questions?" asked Dr. Lombardo.

"Perhaps you could ask her if she drove to Bolzano and baked pastries on the same day?"

"Well, that sounds easy. I'll give it a try."

The next day, Dr. Lombardo asked, "Anna, would like to go for a stroll around the hospital grounds?"

"I don't think I can walk that far."

"I'll push you in a wheelchair."

"Okay," Anna agreed.

The nurse helped Anna put on a new gown and a robe and off they went out into the fresh Italian air. "This is fun," said Anna in a childlike voice. "Can we do this again?"

"Sure," Lombardo replied; he would ask a nurse to do it next time. "So, Anna, did you get any bad news before you drove up to Bolzano?"

"Bolzano?" replied Anna, "is that some kind of new sandwich?"

At this point the doctor felt that a meaningful conversation with Anna seemed out of the question. But he tried to reach her from a different angle. "What was it like to see Uncle again?"

"Oh...I hate that man and he called me a bad name," said Anna. "Let's talk about the weather. The wind is perfect to fly a kite. Can we fly a kite next time?" Dr. Lombardo said he would check on that as he wheeled her back into the hospital.

Lombardo told Brucelli that Anna was not a reliable source of information. "Even if she did kill those men in Bolzano, I doubt, at this point, she would remember very much. I do not think that she is competent to stand trial if accused."

Brucelli was disappointed but he was aware it was a long shot. "How am I ever going to unravel this case?" he said under his breath.

After Anna was brought back to her room, she had a strange conversation with her new nurse, Giulietta.

She started, "I should feel guilty about Bolzano but I don't remember anything. The only thing I'm aware of is that I have to protect some family secrets and I am afraid to tell anyone... But I remember them for a few seconds and then I forget them. It makes me feel crazy and like a bad person."

Giulietta encouraged Anna to go on.

"I forgot everything except that Uncle forced me to do it. No... wait... that's not right... I did it to protect Uncle."

Then Giulietta asked her what she did.

"I don't remember... but I have to protect Uncle at any cost or he'll kill me."

"That sounds like a nightmare," said Giulietta with compassion.

"I'll need to hide. The police will find out and put me in jail for a long time or even kill me," said Anna. "I can't freak out; I'll never come back from it."

She put her head in her hands and then she switched into her childlike mode. She asked for milk and cookies and her coloring book and crayons.

***

Giulietta called Brucelli and asked him to come in to meet with her, despite her misgivings.

"I have some information that Anna gave me about Bolzano and Uncle," she told Brucelli on the phone.

He was thrilled, changed into civilian clothes so he could be a plain-clothes policeman, and raced over to the hospital. Giulietta gave Brucelli most of the details Anna shared but he needed to hear them himself–otherwise it might be considered hearsay in a court of law.

Since it seemed like Anna only trusted her new nurse, Giulietta, Brucelli arranged for Giulietta to wear a wire and see if she could elicit some of those same details from the day before.

"Hi, Anna, how are you feeling today? Are you still scared of Uncle?" Giulietta probed.

"I am not sure why but I have to protect Uncle, otherwise I will die," said Anna. She shivered. "Sometimes I feel guilty about Bolzano but I don't understand why. I do not ever understand Bolzano and so when I hear that name I just ask to play with my coloring books. The only thing I am sure of is that I have to protect our family secrets and I will die if I tell them to anyone...

"But every time they come into my mind, I forget them right away. The problem is that I cannot forget them altogether so they drive me crazy and I feel very guilty," said Anna, fidgeting with her gown.

"Did Uncle push you to do something?" Giulietta asked.

"Uncle forced me to do a lot of things which I try to forget... He even pressured me to do Bolzano.... No... wait... that's not right... I did Bolanzo to protect Uncle. I have to protect Uncle or he'll kill me. If the police find out they will put me in jail for a long time or even kill me," said Anna. "You won't tell the police, will you?"

Giulietta had already told the police. What should she say next? "Well, I think the police would understand if you explained it the way you did now. They would like to protect you from Uncle," said Giulietta.

"Oh, great, that's good to be aware of."

"Can I ask you one last question?"

"Well, maybe," Anna answered, unsure. Giulietta asked the most difficult questions.

"Do you have any idea who killed Brother Paolo and Peter?"

"Noooooo, that's too... too.... I can't talk about that. I'll get in trouble," Anna said, her voice starting to quiver. She switched into her childlike self and changed the subject. "Can I have my milk and cookies and my coloring books and crayons?"

Brucelli was still unsure of himself but the puzzle forced him to be patient. When he was back at the station he told Amaro what happened with Anna.

"It seems a good possibility that Anna was involved in the Bolzano double homicide in some way...but I am not positive. Did Anna and Uncle go to Bolzano together? Was this some kind of strange coverup or did Anna truly have a breakdown?"

"Why don't you ask Maria what she thinks?" Amaro suggested.

"Great idea. Thanks," said Brucelli.

Brucelli called Maria and asked if she could drop by the office to answer some questions.

"Sure."

When she arrived, Brucelli brought her back to his new office. "Do you think your mother had any previous tendencies towards instability?"

"Looking back on it, my mother seemed quite strong and together except when Uncle came around. That's when she became more childlike and submissive. I always found it strange. When Uncle was there we had to be on our best behavior. He was an ominous figure who loomed large. He always gave me the chills. I tried to avoid him. He and my mother fought all the time. That's one of the reasons I went to a college out of town.

"Uncle used to tell all these scary war stories that gave me night terrors. I tended to stay in my room when he came over."

"Did he ever sleep over, Maria?"

"Yes, he slept over many times. I think he and my mom have a love-hate relationship. For the most part they did not get along."

"Did they ever sleep in the same room?" Brucelli continued to probe.

"I don't think so...I think he slept on the couch.... He was asleep on the couch when I woke up each morning."

"Do you ever think they had an affair?"

"I don't think so," Maria answered, surprised.

"When was the last time he was at your house?"

"That's a good question," said Maria. "I think it was the Sunday night before Peter was killed."

"Do you think either your uncle or your mother would be the kind of people who could stab two men with a knife and get away with it? Perhaps one could have done it and the other covered it up. Or one was the driver and the other one was the murderer?"

"Well, anything is possible, I guess," said Maria. "I am shocked by the question. I just can't picture my mother being able to do it. Uncle, yes... but not Mother. She liked Peter. The only thing that seemed to bother her was Peter's project."

"And what project might that be?" asked Brucelli, although he was pretty sure of the answer.

"Peter was fascinated by the idea that some Nazi war criminals might be still be hiding within Italian monasteries. Our professor told us that after the war many former Nazis followed the monastery routes on their way to South America. Some of the Nazis stayed in those same Italian monasteries and did not sail to another continent."

"Why do you think that Peter was so fascinated by this?"

"Well, I guess it's okay to share this since Peter has gone to Heaven... He kept this secret from his classmates. Peter's grandfather and some other relatives were killed by Nazis."

"Why would Peter keep this a secret?" Brucelli continued to press her for answers.

"He couldn't handle people's pity. I think our professor was aware and took Peter under his wing... and I found out because he was my boyfriend," Maria answered.

"Our professor was very knowledgeable about the Nazis on the run. I think he did his Ph.D. on these 'monastery routes.' And everyone is now aware Eichmann came through the monastery in Bolzano."

"I see," said Brucelli. He had momentarily forgotten Eichmann's secret hiding place. He continued to ask Maria questions in order to uncover any vital clues. "So which monasteries were part of these 'monastery routes' you mentioned?"

"Well, Bolzano, and I think a monastery in Rome itself," Maria said with hesitation as she tried to recall.

"Did you ever find out the name of the monastery in Rome that was part of the monastery routes?" Brucelli asked.

"I would have to double-check my notes, sir...I don't recall the name offhand," Maria said, "I'm embarrassed."

"Oh, that's okay... maybe just call me with the name of the monastery, Maria."

Brucelli tried to seem casual about the monastery in Rome but he now had to get fingerprints of all the monks in that Roman monastery. He needed to find those unidentified prints on the knife. He was irritated with himself that he had not considered this sooner... but now he couldn't remember if it had come up earlier. Maybe the professor had mentioned it but now he wasn't sure. And perhaps since Maria and Anna had lived in Rome for awhile there might be a connection to that Roman monastery. On the other hand, the answer to the double homicide might be found in the Bolzano monastery since that's where the crime occurred.

"Why do you think it seemed to bother your mother when Peter brought up his project?"

"I'm not really sure. If I had to guess I would say it was because I think my father was killed in the war. Maybe it was hard for my mother to listen to anything about the Germans," Maria answered, although she hesitated.

"I am sorry to ask you this question, Maria, but it might be important. Do you think your father was a Nazi?" Brucelli asked because it was the first thing that came to mind.

"I don't think my mother would associate with Nazis. She always shied away from discussion about the war and seemed to be very frightened of the Germans. I don't think Mother would have had anything to do with them. She lived in Warsaw during the war and just sold vegetables. I think she was terrified of the Nazis so she just kept her head down. She was the kind of person who did not like to make waves. She was scared to get in trouble.

"Is it okay if we finish these questions on another day?" asked Maria. "I'm not feeling very well. I must have some kind of stomach flu and I don't plan to give it to you." She smiled.

"Oh, sure, my dear. You must take care of yourself. All of this must be an awful strain on you. The loss of your Peter and now your mother's strange behavior."

"It's quite stressful and bizarre," Maria said as she grabbed her sweater and purse on the way out the door. Brucelli stood up and waved goodbye.

Maria really needed to lie down, but she had a bit of a drive ahead of her in the midst of rush hour. She just needed them to catch Peter's killer, but all of this was so intense. It's too much. Maria had no one to talk to–no one to confide in. How would she ever manage to get through this? She couldn't talk to her mother. If only she could talk with Peter. He was her rock. Maybe she should look for a therapist, or a loving mother figure right now. She didn't see any of those on the horizon. And this annoying flu kept coming and going. She just couldn't shake it... Several of her classmates had experienced similar flu-like symptoms recently but Maria's was stress-related or psychosomatic. Too many deaths and then her mother's bizarre behavior led her to feel embarrassed and unsettled. Maria needed a best friend–but for tonight her teddy bear would have to suffice.

As Maria drove up to her house she was so relieved to be home. She just headed straight to bed. She pulled the covers over her head to get away from everything and everyone. But would Brucelli be able to catch the murderer? She dreaded the idea that her mother was involved. She needed to tell Peter all about it and then she recalled that he wasn't there. So instead she pretended she was headed to a faraway land where everything was okay. *Why aren't there telephones in Heaven?* she thought to herself.

***

A couple of hours later Brucelli was still at his desk. He tried to sort out the puzzle pieces of this unusual double homicide. He didn't have enough information. He ordered some ravioli from a restaurant down the street and figured he'd work for another hour or two. After a while he discovered he'd read the same paragraph over and over again. He was unable to absorb anything, so he figured it was time to head out to his local motel room. On nights like this he didn't have the energy to drive all the way back to Bolzano where he lived, so he had taken a room down the block near the station in Rome, close to the hospital where Anna was being held. Brucelli grabbed his jacket and briefcase and said goodnight to the officers who were still on duty.

"See you tomorrow, Sarge," said the desk clerk, as Brucelli waved good night.

"Ciao."

Brucelli skipped down the grey wooden staircase on the way to his old beat-up car. He was so pre-occupied by the case that he didn't even notice a group of men as they approached him. He was caught off guard when they surrounded him. They pushed and shoved him from all directions. One punched him in his left eye while another knocked him to the ground and held him down with a shiny black boot.

Brucelli glanced up to see if he recognized any of the attackers. One man had a scar. His vision was blurry. He did not trust his eyes. But his ears were working just fine.

"Stay away from the monasteries–they are off-limits, you get it?" the men repeated, while they punched and kicked him again.

"This is your warning," they screamed, "next time we aim to kill. Do you get it?"

"I get it," Brucelli whispered, doubled over in pain.

Soon they were gone and so was his briefcase. He was a trained policeman. How did he miss their approach? It was dark, yes... but he should have been on his guard in a dark alley. This was a murder investigation and he'd better wake up.

Bruised and embarrassed, Brucelli climbed back up those grey wooden stairs and hobbled through the back entrance to the police station, minus his briefcase with all his notes. Damn it. Brucelli was so mad at himself. That was pretty stupid to take his notes home with him.

"Sarge, are you okay? What happened?" asked the desk clerk.

"I just got jumped by some Nazis–or, at least some Nazi sympathizers."

One of the officers called for an ambulance. As sirens blared Brucelli was taken to the emergency room a few floors down from Anna's room. He gave strict instructions for there to be a 24-hour guard stationed in front of Anna's room. Anna was the closest thing to a witness or a suspect that they had. Her safety must be guarded at all costs.

Brucelli wouldn't remember anything after giving that order because he was rushed up to surgery with a few broken ribs and a ruptured spleen. It was one hell of a beating. But Brucelli went from cracking the code to cracking his ribs. Would it be worth it? He must be close to solving that jigsaw puzzle.

Chapter 18
Unsafe / Safe

Brucelli's surgery went well but all he obsessed about as he came out of the anesthesia was that he needed to crack the code. There was a thread that tied everything together but at the moment it was a thread that was part of a ball of yarn that was twisted and twirled and all mixed up. As he floated in and out of consciousness, he was aware that the tangled ball of yarn was the key to the whole story. It had to be unraveled.

As soon as he was onto the answer for the puzzle, a nurse came in to take his temperature and check his blood pressure. He worried he would lose clarity.

"If I could only have an hour or two of total silence, peace, and quiet, I could solve this mystery," he complained.

But his fellow officers came in like a stream with flowers, cards, and sweets. "You'll be up in no time," they all said with encouragement.

"Well, it only hurts when I laugh," said Brucelli, which created a lighthearted dynamic and they all laughed even more.

"When can I go back to work, Dr. Florentini?"

"Oh, perhaps in a few more days... but you will be on desk duty for awhile," said his doctor, then asked, "What's the rush?"

"An unsolved double homicide," said Brucelli. "One of our witnesses, or perhaps suspects, is hospitalized on the third floor of this building."

"Oh, Sarge, someone attempted to injure Anna yesterday," said a local officer.

"But that's impossible," Brucelli said, "I asked for 24-hour coverage of her room before I went into surgery. How in the world did this happen?"

"It took place during an officer shift change. Someone dressed like an orderly went into her room and pulled out a knife...but just before he attempted to stab Anna, an off-duty policeman intervened."

"Did they apprehend the 'orderly'?"

"Yes indeed, sir, he is a local man, named Daniello Moreno, who has a string of misdemeanors."

"He claimed someone gave him one thousand dollars to stab Miss Anna. But he claimed he could not describe the man because he met the man in a confessional booth where the drapes were closed."

"Oh, I see," said Brucelli. "There seems to be a theme here. The men who roughed me up said to stay away from monasteries and the man who got the money to stab Anna received it from someone in a church confessional."

"It's too much of a coincidence to ignore. I think it's imperative to get the name of the monastery in Rome that Maria was told might be hiding Nazi war criminals and then we have to fingerprint everyone in that monastery," Brucelli insisted.

"Okay, sir, I will call Maria on your behalf today and get the name of that monastery. Then I will get a warrant for the fingerprints. Once the warrant is ready we can send several men out to collect those fingerprints."

"Great. What I now believe," began Brucelli, "is that there may be more than one Nazi war criminal hiding in those two monasteries. The fingerprints on the knife will be the key, otherwise we have nothing else to tie any monk to this double homicide."

"What if the unidentified fingerprints on the knife belonged to a casual acquaintance of the Romano family who just used the knife to cut some bread and the real killer was wearing gloves during the murder?" asked Bacci.

"I already considered that. Then we have a big problem," said Brucelli, furious, pulling his hair out. "We have to pray that scenario does not come to pass!" Brucelli threw up his hands.

Frustrated that he was stuck in a hospital bed, Brucelli was worried the murderer was tipped off and had already left the country. The clock was ticking. Delay could create a disastrous outcome.

Maria received a phone call from Bacci, who asked her for the name of the monastery that might have harbored Nazi war criminals.

"I checked my notes from class and I found that name of the Franciscan monastery, Via Sicilia, which was considered a transit station for Nazis on the way to Genoa where they would find their way onto a ship to South America. I hope this helps the investigation."

"I'm sure it'll help," said Bacci. "I'll give this information to Sergeant Brucelli and he'll begin acting on it as soon as he recovers."

"Recovers?" asked Maria.

"Oh, yes, he was attacked by some Nazis or Nazi sympathizers several days ago."

"Oh, my goodness. Please send him my best wishes for a speedy recovery."

"I promise I will."

Maria had lounged around in bed for a couple of days. She tried to catch up on sleep and needed to hide from the outside world. But finding out that Brucelli had been attacked got her out of bed speedily. She stumbled into the bathroom to take a nice, warm shower. She had moments when she forgot about her new "normal" life... but then everything would hit her like a ton of bricks. That's when she tried to crawl out of her skin. Everything seemed like a heavy burden. Too heavy for her shoulders to carry. She dropped to her knees on the shower floor–the water falling was like rain on her skin or was the water more like hot beads of tears from Peter in Heaven?

Several hours later Maria had just finished her breakfast and headed down the street to the flower shop. She bought two bouquets of flowers, one for Brucelli and one for her mother. The hospital wasn't very far away so it was only a short drive. She visited Brucelli first. She appeared at his door as she held both bouquets and he burst out in laughter and then clasped his ribs, "You didn't have to buy me two bouquets."

"I didn't. The other one is for my mother."

"Oh, Maria, have a seat. Everything's okay, but when I was in surgery for my ruptured spleen, someone attempted to attack your mother with a knife."

Maria gasped. "Is she okay?"

"Yes. An off-duty policeman caught the guy in time, but we feel like this is a serious threat and we need to take major precautions. I had requested round-the-clock police guards in front of her room before I went into surgery, but this happened just as the officers did a shift change. So it's obvious the 'enemies' figured out how to infiltrate our system. Maybe there's a mole.

"I think we need to come up with a more secure plan. This hospital has a locked unit for emotionally traumatized patients. I have consulted with your mother's psychiatrist, Dr. Rabino, and we think we should move her to that locked ward. She seems to be in the middle of a mental breakdown of some kind. She is frightened of Uncle, and said he forced her do Bolzano, and then she changed the story, that she did Bolzano to protect Uncle. I'm not sure what to believe at this point, but it's clear that your mother has been traumatized and that she's terrified of Uncle, and yet still feels a need to protect him.

"Can you think of any reason why Uncle would need to harm your mother?" Brucelli asked.

"Mother was always afraid of Uncle, I never understood why. She seemed to be always under his thumb and threatened by him. They used to have screaming matches which was my cue to leave the room," Maria answered.

"I am happy you plan to move my mother to a locked ward. That makes sense. What confuses me is whether or not she had anything to do with Peter's death. I cannot even begin to understand why. And if she did it, did she act alone?" Maria wondered aloud. "Did Uncle have anything to do with it? Did it have anything to do with our family secrets? This is all going to have to come out into the open, I guess.

"I am about to go upstairs to give her some flowers, I guess we shall see if she recognizes me."

"I hope she does," said Brucelli. "But please, keep in mind that we are all very aware your mother was under a great deal of emotional stress at the time of Peter and Brother Paolo's murders. And if by some chance your mother was an accomplice in the double homicide, we will make sure she is well taken care of. Dr. Rabino already told me she is not fit or competent to stand trial at all ...so the best thing we can do is to make sure she is in a location where she cannot harm herself and where she is safe from outside injuries."

"Thank you," said Maria. "I really appreciate your help. Get well soon." Maria waved goodbye and headed up the stairs to her mother's room.

"Hello, Mother," said Maria in a cheerful voice. "I brought you your favorite flowers."

"Thank you, nurse, can you please put them in a vase for me?" said Anna.

"Of course, Anna," said Maria, as she stepped into the role as a nurse.

"I wonder who sent you these lovely flowers?" said Maria.

"Oh, I am sure Uncle sent them. He is very thoughtful that way," said Anna, as if nothing had happened.

"Are you scared of Uncle?" Maria asked as she tried to gather some new information.

"Well sometimes I am and other times I need to protect him. I don't really understand why," said Anna.

"What reason would you have to protect him?" asked Maria. She wanted to understand.

"Well, like everyone, we have some family secrets that just cannot come out. Too many people would get hurt," said Anna, shivering.

"That must be hard," said Maria, trying to connect.

"That's for sure. Got to keep them buried," Anna replied as she pulled the covers up.

"Do you need me to ask Dr. Rabino for any medicines that will help you with scary feelings?" asked Maria. She tried to find the right words.

"It would be nice if they actually worked," Anna complained with sarcasm, sticking out her tongue.

"Okay, I'll see if I can get your medication changed," Maria said, praying that might make a difference.

Maria ran into Dr. Rabino in the hall. She asked about the possibility to make a change in her mother's medication.

"I'm willing to think about it," he said, conflicted, "but please understand that your mother seems to have had a mental breakdown and it may take her a while to recover, if she can. For now, we can try to take the edge off her anxiety and depression, but I feel I cannot make any promises."

"Thank you for your honesty, Doctor. I understand," Maria replied with a lump in her throat. "Just one more thing before you go. Sergeant Brucelli spoke to me about a possible move of my mother to a safer floor, the locked mental health unit. Would that be possible?"

“Yes, dear. We have space and staff to accommodate your mother. All we need is your written request. My secretary can help you fill out the paperwork. Once that is done, your mother can be moved to Unit B.”

“Thank you so much, Dr. Rabino.”

“You are very welcome, my dear.”

“I will go to your office now and fill out the paperwork.”

Maria needed her mother to be safe. Would the locked ward solve the problem? Maria wondered what the family secrets were. Did the family secrets have anything to do with Peter’s murder? She shivered at the idea of it.

Chapter 19

The Bedroom

June 8, 1964

If only Maria had known that a casual early Sunday dinner at her mother's would provoke the following episode the next morning, she might have been able to prevent the double homicide.

Anna and Uncle were in the middle of their morning coffee when Anna brought up a difficult topic. "Uncle," Anna started with shortness of breath. "I'm concerned about Maria's boyfriend, Peter."

"Yes," answered Uncle, as he continued to read his morning paper.

"Well," Anna began, "he is doing some research at the University on Nazis hiding in Italian monasteries."

"And..." replied Uncle nonchalantly. There was a pregnant pause. "What do you need me to do about it?"

"Oh, I'm not sure," she said, "I just figured you might need to have the information."

"Hmmm," mumbled Uncle as he glanced back at his paper.

"Well, didn't you mention Brother Paolo being one of your friends in the war?"

"And what if I did?" said Uncle, annoyed with Anna.

"Well Peter mentioned that he was going to meet Brother Paolo in Bolzano on Wednesday, I think."

"I see," said Uncle, looking up from the paper, now a bit concerned. "Hmmm... that could be a problem, I suppose. Unless you take care of *all* my problems," Uncle said, looking at Anna with a sly grin that always meant one thing.

"No, Uncle! Not again, please, please just this once," begged Anna.

"Now, Anna, you must be a good girl and take care of your uncle or something terrible will happen to you," he said.

Suddenly, Uncle slammed down his newspaper, which jarred the table and spilled his coffee. He stood up and raised his voice and yelled, "Get in that bedroom before I..."

Chapter 20

Unraveling the Secret Yarn

The time for Anna to be safe was long overdue. Many, many years overdue. Anna was moved to Unit B, the locked ward in the hospital. All staff had been instructed to be aware of any strangers or substitute personnel coming and going into the Unit.

"Please note," said Dr. Rabino at the morning conference meeting, "Anna Romano may be a witness, suspect, or accomplice in a double homicide. She is in a very fragile and volatile state. We must not alarm her in any way. I will work with the police on a series of hypnosis sessions to see if we can gather more information on the Bolzano homicides as well as any earlier traumatic events in Anna's life. If you notice the door to her room or any other room has a sign that says 'session in progress,' please honor that request and do not knock on the door or enter. Be sensitive in relation to any comments you make to Anna and be sure to listen for any important clues that relate to the following topics: Bolzano, Peter, Brother Paolo, Uncle, Maria, or Nazi war criminals. Those subjects may shed important light on a current police investigation. If you hear anything important, please bring it to my attention STAT. It may literally be a matter of life or death. Thank you, everyone. Our staff meeting is over and you can return to your normal morning duties."

Anna had agreed in writing to undergo hypnosis with the goal of uncovering any traumatic experiences that might be related to the man known as "Uncle." Anna was informed that in exchange for any testimonies or disclosures revealed by her during the hypnosis sessions, she would not be punished by jail time or the death penalty. Basically, Anna had immunity.

Anna was not only cooperating with authorities, but had suffered a nervous breakdown and been ruled not competent to stand trial. Anna also signed a written statement agreeing that Sergeant Brucelli as well as other detectives could be in the room as long as they did not disrupt the process. In addition, Maria signed the document as a family member and witness to her mother's signature.

Dr. Rabino arranged for Anna to be seated in a lounge chair with soft pillows and a comforter during her sessions. Once Anna was in a trance-like relaxation state, Dr. Rabino presented a series of questions he and Brucelli had composed.

"Anna, are you now comfortable and ready to begin our session?" asked Dr. Rabino.

"Yes, I am."

"Please state your name for the record."

"Anna Romano."

"How are you related to the man referred to as 'Uncle'?"

"Not sure. I have known him for a long time."

"Has he ever hurt you, emotionally or physically?"

"Well, after the war he forced me to do things I did not care to do."

"Can you give us some examples?"

"No, I feel too shivery."

"Okay, we can come back to that later. When Uncle first came to see you in the hospital, the two of you spoke in another language–what language were you speaking?"

"Polish."

"Why did you speak in Polish?"

"Because we have family secrets and we can't let the police or Maria become aware of them."

"At the very end, Uncle said a few words to you and then walked out the door. He slammed it behind him. Do you recall what he said and why?"

"Hmmm... I am sorry, I do not recollect that conversation."

"That's okay. Maybe you could tell me some of those family secrets."

"Oh, dear... that seems very scary."

"Okay... do any of those secrets seem less scary? "

"Yes, well, Uncle did some mean things during the war."

"What country was he in during the war?

"Poland, I think, but not Warsaw."

"What about Germany?"

"Yes, I think maybe Germany, too."

"What did he do during the war?"

"I think he hurt people because later he bragged a lot."

"What did he brag about?"

"Oh, he killed people, shot them, and other things..."

"What kind of other things?"

"Hurt them, tied them up, tried to get information but hurt them at the same time...There's a word for it but I forgot it."

"Was the word maybe 'torture'?"

"Yes, that's it. But he used to drink a lot after the war and then he would brag so I am not sure what was really true."

"Did he ever mention being a Nazi, or did he pledge allegiance to Hitler?"

"Oh, yes, sir. I'm sure he was a Nazi because he had a Nazi uniform, some medals, and a tie tack with a swastika on it."

"That's very helpful, Anna. So, would that be one of the family secrets, that Uncle was a Nazi?'

"I think so. BUT I am not 100% positive. I just know he hurt a lot of people."

"Okay... Well, were you a Nazi too, Anna?"

"Me? Oh, no. I lived in Warsaw and sold vegetables. I froze around the Germans. I just kept to myself and sold vegetables from a cart and sometimes a roadside stand."

"Okay, can we skip to Bolzano?"

"Oh, no...Bolzano is too scary...can I have my milk and cookies and coloring books now?"

"Sure, Anna. Let's stop for today."

Anna seemed very happy with her snacks and crayons.

It was a good beginning, Dr. Rabino and Brucelli agreed. But Brucelli was in a rush to get more answers about Bolzano and the murders. Would Anna's hypnosis help him get the answers he needed? How long would he have to wait? He worried the murderer would leave the country. Or maybe he was already gone.

Chapter 21
"Never Again"

It had been a while since Brucelli had any meaningful contact with Sasha and Abie, so he put it on his to-do list for the day. They had moved to a hotel in Rome because that's where all the action seemed to be. Brucelli asked to meet with them to bring them up to speed. They arrived at the police station at about 9:30 a.m. Sasha was nervous and afraid there might be some negative news. Brucelli attempted to explain some of the strange updates related to Anna, as well as his own attack. Abie and Sasha were heartbroken to hear all this terrible news. Sasha was overwhelmed. She could not believe that Peter's girlfriend's mother was probably a co-conspirator in Peter's murder. It was unbelievable. Oh, God, no. It couldn't be.

Up until then Sasha had only been aware of good things about Maria and her mother. Peter seemed to like them very much. What a betrayal. What has happened to this world? Sasha cried silent tears, devastated, with a heavy heart.

"You cannot trust anyone. You think you are safe whether you're in the lion's den or the wolf's lair," Sasha blurted out, cold and numb.

"These Nazis... they are everywhere. I need to scream," yelled Sasha. "If they ganged up on you, Sergeant, broke your ribs and ruptured your spleen, are Abie and I in any danger? Are we targets? Do you think that the Nazis believe that Peter may have told us something about their network or specific names of war criminals hiding in Bolzano or Rome? Oh, my God, this is terrible." A shiver spiraled down Sasha's spine.

"I am not sure," Brucelli replied, unable to reassure them. "Would you like me to arrange for 24-hour protection?" he asked.

Abie and Sasha stared at one another. "What do you think, Sergeant?"

"Well, it couldn't hurt," he answered, "let's be cautiously optimistic."

"Okay, I guess you should go ahead and set it up," said Abie.

"All right," said Brucelli as he jotted down some notes.

"We also have some preliminary information that a man who Anna and Maria call 'Uncle' is likely to be a Nazi war criminal. But this information comes from a hypnosis session so we cannot deny or confirm this yet," Brucelli stated, maintaining eye contact with Sasha and Abie.

"This is too much of a coincidence. First my father was killed by a Nazi in America and now my son is killed, probably by a Nazi war criminal, in Italy... This is just too much for a daughter and mother to bear. Why me? I am not strong enough to handle this. I didn't even know there were so many Nazis left in Italy. But I guess Peter and his professor were aware of all that. I understand now why his professor asked Peter not to tell us anything on the phone or in a letter. The professor tried to protect us, I suppose, but I never should have let this happen."

"When will it ever end? 'Where have all the flowers gone?' We said never again... What part of 'never again' don't people understand? I can't handle this. I need to go back to the hotel now. Can you please take me home, Abie?"

"Yes, my dear. Of course," Abie replied. And with that they left the station. Sergeant Brucelli arranged for a 24-hour protection team to start in the morning.

On the way back to the hotel Sasha looked at herself in the car mirror. She was determined to overcome her inner obstacles, wounds, scars, and fatal flaws. She deeply questioned herself. Was she the brave Sasha who said she'd hunt down her father's murderer until her last breath? And what about Peter's murderer? Or was she just going to give up? No! No matter what the cost or what she had to sacrifice, she had to be strong and carry on. Peter needed her not to give up. She must not lose hope. And despite the skeletons in her closet, Sasha must find Michael. She did not have any idea where she would find the strength to do this... but somehow she had to find out what happened to him. Even if he were dead, she wanted to at least put flowers on his grave. She needed closure.

***

After Sasha and Abie left, Sergeant Brucelli got a phone call from Professor Giovanni.

"How are you doing, Professor?"

"Well, I'm rather upset at the moment because someone seems to have broken into my office and stolen all my files and research papers."

"Oh, no," Brucelli exclaimed, stunned by the news. "Did you lose all of your research on the monastery routes where the Nazi war criminals are hiding, like in Bolzano and Rome?"

"Yes, so I guess they got what they came for. And if that wasn't enough, they gave me a strong warning. They painted in blood 'You're NEXT!' across my wall," said the professor, "my skin is bristling. If they desired to scare me, they succeeded."

"Oh, my God," said Brucelli as he pushed his chair back, stood up, and then began to pace back and forth by his desk. "I am so sorry, professor."

Giovanni then asked the next logical question, "Is there something going on within the investigation that I should know about, Sergeant?"

"Yes," admitted Brucelli. "I apologize. I am so sorry I have been out of touch. Forgive me. I was attacked by a group of Nazis so I needed some surgery."

"Oh, I'm sorry to hear that, Sergeant Brucelli."

"Thanks. We are starting to crack the code and chisel away at the secrets within secrets. We have not identified the third set of fingerprints on the knife yet, but it's clear that Maria's mother seems to have been involved in the double homicide in some way, and perhaps with the help of a man named 'Uncle.'"

"So does that mean that Maria told her mother about Peter's research? Is that the connection?"

"I believe so," replied Brucelli, on a roll, "because it seems that when Peter had dinner with Maria and her mother, Anna, his research on Nazis on the run came up. He did not go into detail. It's my understanding that Anna was very uncomfortable with Peter's research. And based on some of the information we got through Anna's first hypnosis session, it is quite possible that the man Maria and Anna are calling 'Uncle' seems to be a former Nazi. You must be upset by the attack on your office and I am so sorry you lost your research papers, but I think this means we are close to solving the case."

"That's excellent," said the professor, "I am very happy to hear about your updates. I am still so devastated by the murders of Peter and Brother Paolo. But by the way, I think I forgot to tell you that Peter recognized Maria's uncle as a former Nazi on the run, named Heinrich Schmidt. He was a guard at Auschwitz. He recognized the scar from an old photo that Simon Wiesenthal has, and Brother Paolo sent us the same photo."

"Oh, really? That's a lucky break. Let me jot down that name. Heinrich Schmidt, you said?" said Brucelli.

"Yes, sir. I wish Peter and Brother Paolo were still here and we could have prevented these murders."

"I agree, Professor. Well, at least we have some progress," said Brucelli, disappointed, as he continued to pace back and forth. "It looks like we have more pieces of the puzzle. Thanks for the name of Maria's uncle.

"Again, I am sorry, Professor. I should have reached out to you sooner," Brucelli said.

"That's okay, I know you've had your hands full. And I was so distracted, I forgot to tell you that Peter met Uncle, 'Heinrich Schmidt,' at Maria's house in Rome, a few days before the murder–I think it was a Sunday. He came to see me the next day, terrified out of his mind, as if he'd seen a ghost. He recognized Heinrich from his facial scar. But by the time Peter went to see Brother Paolo in Bolzano, I was out of town for the next two weeks.

"I didn't hear about the murders until I came back. I'm so sorry. I could have helped you so much more when I first met you. But I was a broken man. I sobbed day and night in a fetal position. And my guilt was insurmountable. I played that rose garden scene in my head over and over again. It should have been me who died, not Peter. I never should have asked a graduate student to take such a big risk. I put Peter in touch with Brother Paolo. It's my fault. My devastation left me despondent. I stayed at home with the shades drawn and just stared at the wall. But I went to my office today and the break-in and warning in blood sure woke me up!

"So, if you could send someone out to my university office in Perugia to collect fingerprints or photos, it would be much appreciated. I won't touch anything that might make it difficult for your forensic team to gather evidence or any clues that might make a difference. All the books on the shelves were opened and thrown on the floor. My locked file cabinet was smashed and pulled apart so they could steal all my files and research papers, most of which are irreplaceable. Anyway, the entire office is a complete mess. They went through everything. Thank God I wasn't here."

"Wow, these folks are vicious, out for revenge, and dangerous," said Brucelli. He started to panic and continued his new habit–pacing back and forth on the wooden floor of his office. "I promise I will send a police team out to your office right away. I am so sorry, I should have been more careful and given you some protection. But I, too, have been out of commission after my attack a few weeks ago–a few broken ribs, a ruptured spleen, and also a strong warning. Mine was 'stay away from monasteries.' One of my attackers had a facial scar."

"Oh, no," said the professor as he froze up and clenched his jaw. "Again, I'm so sorry to hear about your attack. I guess we have stumbled into a hornet's nest. Peter and Brother Paolo were the first casualties; let's hope there aren't any more. We'd better watch our own shadows," the professor said as he stroked his long, dark grey beard. "I'll wait here for your police detail to arrive. Thanks in advance."

"No problem, it's the least I can do," responded Brucelli. "I promise I will keep you posted if anything new comes up."

"Okay thanks, Sergeant. Ciao."

"Giacomo," Brucelli yelled as he walked out his door and down the hall, "send someone out to the University of Perugia right now. We need to collect fingerprints and take photos of Professor Giovanni's office. There's been a burglary and a warning written in blood."

The professor drowned his sorrows in hot chocolate while he waited for the police to arrive.

As soon as Abie and Sasha got back to their hotel suite, they froze. It had been ransacked. Clothes were thrown all over the place, suitcase panels were cut up, and books were scattered, even the French version of *Atala* .... The entire safe which held their passports was picked up and stolen from their room.

"We have to change hotels right away," Sasha said to Abie. He complained to the management and then phoned Brucelli.

"You're the second call I've gotten today about a break-in related to this case. I just got a call from Peter's professor that his office was burglarized and all of his research was stolen." Brucelli sighed, frustrated, as he pounded his fist on his desk.

"Oh, no. How awful," said Abie, covering his mouth.

"You must change hotels now and don't leave a forwarding address, Abie."

"Okay, can you recommend a safer hotel nearby?" asked Abie, his heartbeat throbbing in his throat.

"How about La Savoia?" Brucelli suggested. "I will send a protection team out to La Savoia. Better safe than sorry."

"Don't you think you should send a unit to our current hotel to see if you can get any fingerprints? And also, we'll need to replace our passports," sighed Abie as he rubbed his sweaty hands on his pants.

"Yes, they're already on their way. Don't touch anything. Leave all items as they are. We will gather everything up and bring them to you later. We'll help you get new passports," replied Brucelli, determined to juggle all these break-ins and issues.

Maria returned home after she completed her errands at the library and grocery store. She discovered her house had been turned inside out. Maria tried not to freak out, but she glanced around to survey the damage. All of her clothes and even her mother's clothes were thrown on the floor. Her books and papers were rummaged through and left upside down. It seemed like the intruders were on a search for something specific. Everything was knocked off the walls and cupboards were bare. Someone did a thorough job. Maria took deep breaths. A rush of fear mingled with her blood. She had to call Brucelli.

"I figured you'd be surprised, Sergeant Brucelli,' said Maria.

"Nothing surprises me about this case anymore. Your professor and Peter's family called to report the same experience. And I was attacked. Someone or a group of people are on a mission. They are looking for something or they desire to scare those of us related to this case in some way. Did Peter keep any of his notes at your house?"

"No. Everything is in his filing cabinet in his dorm room at the university."

"I think we'd better go check," Brucelli said as he spoke through his teeth with forced restraint.

"I'm willing to go with you, Sarge," she said.

"Great, I'll pick you up in about half an hour."

It was a bit of a drive but they needed to be sure that none of Peter's work or research had been stolen. Also, Brucelli was concerned. He didn't want Maria to go by herself in case there was a blood warning on the wall there. They arrived and discovered that Peter's room was turned upside down, too.

"Do you think they got what they needed?" asked Brucelli with a heavy sigh.

"I'm not sure," Maria said as she shrugged her shoulders and glanced around.

Brucelli needed to play catch-up. He was overwhelmed. He needed to search *all* these places for fingerprints and photos. What a train wreck.

"We must be getting very close because the intruders seem desperate. We must be vigilant and determined in order to solve this case. We have to get those fingerprint experts to work overtime. If it is just one intruder and the prints all match up to one person, that will point us in the right direction, Maria. But I hope this isn't all a distraction," he cursed under his breath.

Brucelli sent out some experts to examine each location. He was impatient to get the results. Several days later the analysis came back. Brucelli pulled his team together.

"The fingerprints for the break-ins not only belong to the same person, but they are also the third set of fingerprints on the knife that killed Peter and Brother Paolo. We hit the jackpot." Brucelli smiled, pleased with himself. "Perhaps it's true that the knife was taken from the Romano kitchen.

"Wow. Breakthrough time. The key is to find those sneaky little fingers who left all those fingerprints," Brucelli said to Bacci and Amaro. "We are on a roll now. Why wasn't the intruder more careful? He must've been in a big hurry. Or maybe he desires to taunt us or feel in control. We're almost there...We can't give up," Brucelli smiled with excitement, his heart pounding.

The question then arose what the holdup was with the fingerprint collection from the monks in the Roman monastery. The answer came crashing down on him. Brucelli never got the warrant to collect those fingerprints because he was in the hospital. The officer got the name of the Roman monastery from Maria but Brucelli had never taken care of it. He waited to hear from Maria, but he could have asked the professor. Why didn't he? *Wow*. That was a big mistake. How could he let that order slip through the cracks? Brucelli started to doubt his ability to handle such a hugely important case.

Too late to worry about it now... Time to get the warrant and send several strong policemen out to the monastery that Maria mentioned and collect those fingerprints. That would take several days, even with four officers, because it was a very large monastery. Brucelli was not sure how cooperative the Abbate would be.

Brucelli had a feeling, based on his own attack, that there must be more than one Nazi war criminal hiding there. This monastery had very close ties to the Vatican while other monasteries had broken ties and hid Jews, Gypsies, etc. during the war. This Roman monastery had close connections with Father Hudal, who was well-known for hiding Nazis. Hudal also supplied them with false ID papers from the International Red Cross.

After the warrant came through, Brucelli announced, "Be ready, everyone. We'll be heading out to the monastery together tomorrow."

By the time they got there, the note on the main entrance of the monastery said they were having a silent retreat and would not be open to the public for the next three days. Brucelli was furious and he pounded his fist on the hood of his car.

"We've lost so much valuable time." Brucelli was frustrated and pulled his hair out. He had to do something. He couldn't sit still. What could he do that would make a big difference in the case?

Simon... Vienna!

Since he had few days to kill, Brucelli came up with a new plan. He called Simon Wiesenthal at his newly renamed Jewish Documentation Center in Vienna. This organization was set up to hunt down Nazi war criminals. Simon offered to meet with him the next day. Brucelli bought a roundtrip ticket to Vienna to do some research himself. He did not mention this to anyone. Brucelli just said he needed a few days off.

The plane ride was uneventful, but he had a very productive meeting with Wiesenthal.

"First, I have some terrible news," Brucelli confessed with a heavy heart.

"What's that?" Wiesenthal answered as he braced himself and leaned back in his chair.

"That young man Peter Wolf who came to see you a few weeks ago was murdered, along with Brother Paolo, in the rose garden at the Bolzano monastery."

"Oh, my goodness. I didn't know. I came to love that passionate young man even though I only met him for a day.

What a waste of talent and dedication. But Brother Paolo I have known for years. They were both such committed Nazi hunters. What a shame," he said. He suppressed his great sadness. He could always cry or break down and sob later.

"I'd like to see the photos of all high-profile Nazis on the run who might be hiding in a monastery in Bolzano or Rome. I am determined to solve the murders but I need your help," Brucelli's words rushed together with a heavy sigh. "Especially Heinrich Schmidt," he added, frustrated, clenching his teeth. Wiesenthal brought down his picture collection of Nazis on the run.

"Just remember as we look through these photos and you see the names listed, most of these Nazis will have changed their names after the war. The Red Cross gave them false ID papers to hide their identity. Those IDs weren't hard to obtain if a church or monastery vouched for the Nazi claiming to have lost his papers due to the war," said Wiesenthal. "Sorry if I am very emotional. I am still in shock about Peter and Brother Paolo."

"That's understandable," said Brucelli. "I didn't even know them and I feel very emotional about this case. When I catch this Nazi and there's a trial, I am going to need to connect with witnesses who were former inmates from a specific concentration camp. I think it might be Auschwitz if the killer is Heinrich Schmidt, the one with the scar."

As they studied the album, Brucelli gasped. "That's him. That's the man who attacked me. That's the man with the scar."

"That's Heinrich Schmidt, alright," confirmed Wiesenthal. "You're correct. He was a guard at Auschwitz."

"As soon as I arrest Heinrich Schmidt, we will get ready for a War Crimes Tribunal. I am convinced Heinrich Schmidt committed crimes against humanity. I will get back in touch because I will need some Auschwitz survivors to testify at the trial."

"No problem. I am sure they'd be happy to put him away for good."

"Would I be able to borrow some of these photos of Heinrich to help with an upcoming trial? I promise to return them myself after the trial."

"I am hesitant because I usually don't loan out my photos, but I will in this case," Wiesenthal said. "Thanks, Sergeant, for your help. I feel hopeful you will catch this Nazi. We owe it to Peter and Brother Paolo. I look forward to testifying with my witnesses at the trial. It will do my heart good."

The two men shook hands. "Till we meet again."

"Ciao."

The question was could Brucelli catch Heinrich Schmidt and were his fingerprints on the knife? Hopefully he hadn't left the country. Brucelli experienced a heavy time crunch.

***

Brucelli was elated by the experience in Vienna.

"I have a good photo of Heinrich Schmidt–scar and all–so now we just have to find him and match up his fingerprints. I can't wait to dig into that monastery. It should be open to the public by now," Brucelli said as he ran his fingers through his hair.

"But Sarge, we've already gotten all the fingerprints. The forensic expert analyzed all of them and none of them matched the third set on the knife."

"Wow. That's terrible news. I have been afraid he already left the country. I feel so frustrated. How is this possible?" said Brucelli as he pounded his fist on the desk then shook it up toward God. "The only logical explanation is that Uncle is hiding somewhere else."

Frustrated, the Sergeant went to pay a visit to the Roman monastery himself with a few detectives just to check if they missed anything. Most monasteries raise honeybees for the virgin wax to make candles. There was a monk in the bee yard tending to the bees so Brucelli asked his detectives, "Has that man been fingerprinted?"

"No," replied the detectives.

"Why not?"

"That monk travels back and forth to Bolzano bringing wax and honey to the monks. It just happened that he was not around at either location when they collected the original fingerprints." Brucelli was shocked by the answer.

"*Wow*. This is the very monk who should have been fingerprinted," he yelled as he waved his fist.

Brucelli said in a loud voice, "Fingerprint that monk now," as he pointed to the monk in the bee yard.

As the officers approached the beekeeper monk, he bolted and headed for the stables. The police followed him but the monk was way ahead and flew out of the stables on the back of an Arabian horse, galloping towards the forest. Brucelli and his men followed suit by jumping on the other horses in the stable. Within an hour they had cornered the monk near a cave. He slid off his horse and slipped inside the cave.

The rebellious monk was finally captured after forty-five minutes in the cave. He was read his rights, brought to jail, and kept in isolation.

"Please be Heinrich Schmidt," Brucelli said under his breath as he stared at the sky.

They fingerprinted the monk in spite of his attempts to attack them. After two days the results of the fingerprints came back.

"They are identical to all the fingerprints in every burglary associated with this case and they also happen to be the third set of fingerprints on the knife from the Romano kitchen. This part of the long journey appears to be over," Brucelli announced.

That afternoon Brucelli showed the mugshot of the monk, taken during his arrest, to both Anna and Maria. They both identified Uncle as the man in the photo. So Brucelli had his man. Brucelli was in a celebratory, boastful mood. He was so proud of himself. *But wait*. Just finding the same prints on the knife did not mean that Uncle killed Brother Paolo and Peter. It just confirmed that Uncle had used the knife to cut a piece of bread at the Romano house. Other than that, Uncle's fingerprints just tied him to the rash of burglaries. Brucelli almost punched the wall. While he tried to calm down he bit his fingernails.

So, they had to go back to Anna's hypnosis sessions again to delve deeper. Did Uncle kill Peter and Brother Paolo? Was he a Nazi on the run? If he was guilty could they get a conviction? Brucelli had nothing proving that Uncle was in Bolzano on the day of the double homicide.

Chapter 22
Another Layer of Secrets

Anna had been placed on some new psychological medication for a few weeks and seemed to be in a more stable and less volatile condition. Dr. Rabino arranged a second hypnosis session.

"I love this lounge chair, soft pillows, and comforter," said Anna, with a happy smile. The doctor guided Anna into a trance-like relaxation state before starting his questions.

"Would you please state your name for the record?"

"Anna Romano."

"Do you know where you are?"

"I am not sure, but everyone is nice and I feel better."

"That's great news, Anna. You mentioned during our last session that a man named Uncle owned a Nazi uniform with medals on it and a swastika tie tack. Where was this uniform kept?"

"In a secret hiding place in the attic," said Anna.

"Where is that secret place?"

"I am not positive, but I think it is behind a wooden bookcase on the right-hand side of the attic."

"Excellent," said the doctor. "So if we go there, we should be able to find the uniform?"

"As far as I know, but I have not been home in a while."

"That's okay, Anna. And do you recall who the uniform belonged to?"

"I think it belongs to Uncle."

"Does anyone else know about this secret hiding place?"

"I don't think so. Sorry I cannot be of more help. I have trouble with my memory."

"That's okay, Anna. Let me put it this way: do you think Maria knows about his hiding place?"

"Maybe."

"Is there anything else in the hiding place, besides the uniform, medals, and tie tack?"

"There is a flag with a swastika on it."

"Okay. Is it okay to talk about Bolzano now?"

"I am scared to talk about it."

"Why are you scared?"

"Because if I tell, Uncle will kill me."

"Why do you think Uncle will kill you?"

"Maybe...because he has a certain spell over me. If I don't do what he asks, he forces me to go into the bedroom. And I do not like what happens in the bedroom. Mean things happen in the bedroom. I have to do whatever he needs me to do. And I am still so frozen with him after all these years, so I just have to do those things."

"Can you describe what he does to you in the bedroom that is scary?"

"Well, it is hard to explain. Sometimes I have to lie on my back; other times I have to lie face down. And sometimes he makes me bend over."

Dr. Rabino and Brucelli glanced at each other, stunned that Anna had been sexually abused by Uncle, perhaps for a long time. And despite all of this, she still needed to protect him. Anna then explained that sometimes she locked herself in the bathroom; other times she caved in and did whatever Uncle desired.

"So, it sounds like," said Dr. Rabino, "that going into the bedroom was a kind of punishment. Is that right, Anna?

"I guess so."

"Did you ever have children, Anna?"

"I think so."

"How many children did you have?"

"I think I just had one child."

"Was it a boy or a girl?"

"Wait, it was definitely a girl."

"What was her name?"

"Her name is Maria."

"You sound like you are starting to get your memory back."

"Yes."

"Is Maria still alive?"

"Yes, definitely."

"Is Uncle Maria's father?"

Anna paused. "Yes," she said, finally.

"Does Maria know that Uncle is her father?"

"No, of course not!"

"Why doesn't Maria know Uncle is her father?"

"Because that's a family secret."

"I see. Well, why is it a family secret, Anna?"

"Because for a long time Uncle did not know that Maria was his daughter."

"When did Uncle find out that Maria was his daughter?"

"When he came to see me in the hospital, a few months ago."

"And how did he react when you told him Maria was his daughter?"

"He got very angry, called me a bad word, walked out of the room, and slammed the door!"

Brucelli quietly slipped Dr. Rabino a handwritten note. The doctor read the note and nodded.

"What language did you speak when Uncle called you a bad word?"

"Polish."

"What was the bad word Uncle called you?"

"I don't like the word, but he called me a *whore* in Polish."

"Okay, that's helpful, Anna. Why was he so angry that he called you a whore?"

"Because he did not know Maria was his daughter and he *never* planned to have children."

"Did he think Maria was someone else's child?"

"Yes. After we moved to Italy I married Guglielmo Romano. I was in the early stages of pregnancy, so Uncle just assumed that Mr. Romano was the father when Maria was born. Oh, please promise me you won't tell Maria. This is one of the family secrets."

"Yes, I promise you. Is Mr. Romano still alive?"

"Oh, no, he died right after Maria was born."

"What did he die of?

"He died under mysterious circumstances–a car accident where it appeared that the brakes might have been tampered with."

"Did they ever find out who might have tampered with the brakes?"

"No, but I have a strong feeling that someone paid off the police."

"Do you know who paid off the police, Anna?

"Uncle."

"Why do you think Uncle killed your husband?"

"He was jealous of him and Uncle desired to have me all to himself. He could not stand to share me."

"So, you think that Uncle got away with murder, Anna."

"Oh, yes, many times."

"So, since we are talking about murder, is it okay to talk about Bolzano?"

"I'd rather not."

"Okay, Anna." Dr. Rabino brought her out of the hypnotic state.

After Anna left the room, Rabino and Brucelli compared notes.

"I'm encouraged and hope that next time we can get some information about who killed Peter and Brother Paolo," Brucelli expressed.

"Yes, that would be great," said Rabino. "I just can't push her too hard. She is on her way back towards her normal self and I can't frighten her. We cannot afford to have Anna slip back into a more unstable place."

"I understand. I'm just so anxious to solve this case. Sorry, I guess I am just frustrated," Brucelli apologized.

Rabino nodded. Was Uncle the murderer? If so, why didn't he flee the country? That did not make sense. Brucelli had to solve the puzzle.

***

After Anna's second hypnosis session, Brucelli went to visit Uncle in jail. Brucelli had Uncle brought into an interrogation room. Uncle was handcuffed and was seated opposite Brucelli. He was no longer cloaked in a monk's robe but dressed like every other prisoner in the jail.

Brucelli turned on the tape recorder and stated his name, the date, and time. He then said to Uncle, "Please state your name for the record."

Uncle refused to state his name and asked to speak to his attorney. He also demanded that a telephone be brought into the room. Brucelli was frustrated but he brought in the phone. Uncle asked the Sergeant to leave the room but was aware that there was a good chance Brucelli could hear what he planned to say.

Uncle's lawyer, Antonio Russo, arrived ninety minutes later, dressed in an expensive Italian silk suit. The two men started to speak in another language. Based on Anna's comments, Brucelli assumed they spoke Polish.

Brucelli kicked himself for not anticipating this tactic. He should have brought a Polish interpreter to the police station. But since he had neglected to do that, he ran around the station in a panic asking if anyone spoke Polish. No one did. A legal assistant offered to make some calls for him.

In the interrogation room, Uncle and his lawyer were relaxed and playful. They laughed at how stupid the policeman was.

"I didn't have anything to do with these murders," Uncle said with a deep laugh as he leaned back in his chair. "I'm glad someone killed them," he continued with a sly smile, "but it wasn't me." He laughed.

"Do you think it was one of the other Nazis in Bolzano or Rome?" asked Russo.

"I don't have a clue," said Uncle, "but I must admit many of the monks hated Brother Paolo and were convinced he was a spy. It really could have been any one of them. I'm not worried; I know it wasn't me. Let the police waste their time. They are on a wild goose chase. They're searching for a ghost."

"I just fooled around with a little burglary to seek information. Some of my friends helped me out," said Uncle. "I left my fingerprints because I don't care if I get caught for that. If I spend a year or two in jail, it would be a nice change of pace from the monastery. To tell you the truth, I'm a little bored. At least in prison I could hang out and brag about all the murders I've done, like in Auschwitz as a senior guard. I am sure that would scare all the inmates in any jail they'd send me to for the burglaries."

"Don't brag too much. It may backfire on you if there's a snitch in jail."

"Yeah... you're probably right. I think I can brag and still cloak the location where my crimes took place. I'm not an Eichmann. I'll be careful. I won't get caught."

Uncle and Russo continued to hang out and enjoy each other's company for a while longer. It was fun to spend time together. They hadn't seen each other in a while.

Brucelli ran back to the two-way mirror with a female interpreter to see if she could glean anything. At this point all she could figure out was that the two men were laughing. Brucelli guessed Uncle had some scheme up his sleeve. Perhaps he had already convinced his lawyer that he was not involved in the double homicide. Brucelli was about to jump out of his skin–he was so frustrated. He was filled with self-doubt and self-criticism for all his mistakes.

Was this case over his head? Would he ever solve it? Or would Uncle win the day? Brucelli had no way of proving that Uncle murdered Peter or Brother Paolo. All he had was fingerprints for the burglaries. His prints on the knife could have easily happened when he cut himself a slice of bread. Brucelli needed more information.

***

Several days later Brucelli got a letter that disturbed him. It said, "Stay away from monasteries or you'll be *next.*" The envelope was postmarked Bolzano. It was not typed or handwritten. The person who composed the warning had cut out each letter from a magazine and pasted it on the paper one alphabetical letter at a time. There were no fingerprints anywhere on the letter or envelope so the sender must have worn gloves. Brucelli experienced an eerie chill go up his spine.

Who in the world could have sent this letter? Uncle was in custody in Rome. But it was postmarked in Bolzano. Was it possible Uncle sneaked the letter out through his lawyer? Brucelli was impatient. There must be a Nazi conspiracy at work. He needed strength to carry on.

Brucelli called the professor. "I'm ashamed to admit that I feel like this case is way over my head. I've never dealt with a case that has such a wide-ranging dynamic. I've also never met a Nazi war criminal before. Most of my cases were more straightforward–burglaries, assaults, petty theft, and an occasional murder, but ones that had clear parameters and were easily solved. To tell you the truth, professor, a great many of my cases could be solved by a fifth-grader. But even a Ph.D. student would have trouble with this one."

"I hear you, Sergeant. My advice is to hang in there and just put one foot in front of the other. Eventually you will find a crack in the darkness where the light comes through."

"Thanks, Professor, for your encouragement."

"No problem. Call anytime."

As Brucelli hung up he recalled what his grandfather would've said: "Vut you kin do?" He threw up his arms. Was it possible that Uncle was set up or agreed to be a patsy and chose to leave his fingerprints at the scene of these burglaries while others wore gloves?

Exasperated, Brucelli showed Maria and Anna the photos borrowed from Wiesenthal's Association in Vienna. He met Maria in the conference room at the hospital.

"Hi, Maria. How have you been?"

"Okay, I guess, under the circumstances. I still miss Peter a lot...and the house feels pretty empty without Mother."

"I'm sorry to hear that. Are you sure it's a good day to go through some old photos?"

"Yes, it's okay, I'm just a little lonely," Maria shrugged.

Brucelli took out a series of old photographs and asked Maria if she recognized any of the men. "Did any of these men kill Peter?"

She hesitated. "It's possible. Maybe or maybe not."

"Okay, I'll do my best, but it feels scary."

Maria took out her glasses and studied each photo with care. "Wait a minute. These are old photos of Uncle. Why would Uncle kill Peter and Brother Paolo?"

"That's a good question. I haven't figured that out yet." Brucelli asked Maria to wait in the conference room while he showed the same pictures to Anna.

"Hello, Mrs. Romano. How are you feeling?"

"Much better, Sergeant," said Anna as she twirled her hair.

"Would you like to look at some old photos?"

"Sure." Brucelli gave Anna the photos he'd gotten in Vienna.

"Oh Jesus, Mary, and Joseph. These look like a younger version of Uncle to me. Now that's a shock. Was this a trick?" she asked.

"No. It looks like Uncle to me, too."

Brucelli asked Anna if he could bring in her daughter Maria. "She can't wait to see you. She misses you. I just showed her the same photos and she picked out Uncle too. What do you think? Is it okay if I bring in Maria?"

"Okay," said Anna.

Brucelli went back to the conference room. "How would you like to see your mother, Maria?"

"Are you sure she is comfortable with me entering the room? The last two times she guessed I was her nurse."

"Let's give it a try. She agreed to see you."

"I hope it works out okay."

Brucelli and Maria entered Anna's hospital room. "Hello, Mother."

"Hi, sweetie," said Anna with outstretched arms. "Where have you been? I've missed you!"

They had their first embrace since they were first separated by the police. Maria didn't mention any of the times she visited when her mother was nasty or didn't recognize her. She was just glad to have her mother back.

Brucelli left the women alone to reconnect and he took some time to reflect. The photos showed Uncle, Heinrich Schmidt, at Auschwitz near the infirmary. According to Simon Wiesenthal, Heinrich was a very high-profile Nazi war criminal. He was a sadistic and cruel senior guard at Auschwitz. Wiesenthal was confident that he had several credible witnesses who were still alive and could put Heinrich Schmidt at Auschwitz as a guard during the war. They were all Holocaust survivors from Auschwitz, plus one Nazi doctor acquitted at Nuremberg.

The pieces of the puzzle were falling into place. Perhaps one more hypnosis session with Anna might reveal answers that would confirm who was responsible for the double homicide in Bolzano. Brucelli needed to nail this down.

Brucelli reconnected with the district attorney in the province, “Anna’s not fit to stand trial. She had a mental breakdown. She might be a witness, a perpetrator, or an accomplice in these murders. In order to continue to gather information and find the perpetrator of this double homicide, I promised Anna that she could stay in a locked ward in the hospital, and she would have immunity. That was our plea deal. Are we still in agreement, sir?”

“Yes, I’m on board. The original plea deal stands. I look forward to a successful end to this murder investigation, Sergeant.”

“Me too, you have no idea. I’m exhausted.”

But would Brucelli actually be able to pull it off? Would he be able to connect all the dots? Or was this case over his head? Brucelli continued to pace back and forth in his office as he tried to piece together the puzzle.

Chapter 23
Hard Questions

A week before Anna's third hypnosis session, Dr. Rabino increased Anna's medications to a higher dosage. He needed her to have more mental clarity but also the ability to be able to handle the hard questions and answers they needed. When he sensed Anna was stable, he set up the same lounge chair with the same soft pillows and comforter. He guided her into a trance-like relaxation state before beginning his questions.

"Please state your name for the record."

"Anna Romano."

"Do you know Uncle's full name?"

"I believe his name is Heinrich Schmidt."

"You're doing great, Anna. Why do you call him Uncle?"

"To hide a family secret."

"Would you be willing to share that family secret?"

"As long as you don't tell Maria."

"Okay. I promise I won't tell Maria."

"We call him Uncle because he is Maria's uncle."

"And that makes you...?

"I am Uncle's sister."

"And am I right that you said that Maria is your daughter?"

"Yes, she is my daughter and a good girl."

"Is it possible that Maria is both Uncle's niece and his daughter?"

"Yes."

"Okay, Anna, that is very helpful. I won't tell Maria."

"Great."

"I am really proud of you for being able to tell family secrets."

"Thanks. It's still hard but I think I will feel better if I do it."

"So, Anna. We need to talk about Bolzano. Do you feel like it is a good time to do that now?"

"Well, I do not think it will ever be a good time to talk about it because I am afraid to talk about it. Do you still promise I won't get in trouble and I can stay in the hospital so that I am safe? Uncle might hurt me or send any of his friends to hurt me. I need to be safe."

"I promise," said Dr. Rabino.

"Okay. Could you ask the questions and I will answer?"

"Yes. Okay, so let's start with the morning you told Uncle about Peter's research. What is the first thing you can recall?"

"Uncle and I were having coffee and I remember telling him that I was worried because Peter was doing research on Nazi war criminals hiding in monasteries. And that Peter was meeting with Brother Paolo, and Uncle did not like Brother Paolo."

"And what happened next?

"Uncle was very angry with me. I don't understand why. But then Uncle forced me to do Bolzano... No... wait... that's not right... I did Bolzano to protect Uncle. I have to protect Uncle or he'll kill me."

"Okay, let's go a little slower. What happened after you told Uncle about Peter's research and Brother Paolo and then he got angry?"

"I am really a little mixed up about what happened next."

"Okay, just give it a try, one idea at a time."

"I got very upset. I forgot who I was."

"Okay, that's great, Anna. What's the next thing you can picture?"

"The next thing I recall was a monk was driving the car and Uncle got in. And somehow the car got all the way to Bolzano. "

"*Wow,* that's a long drive. Did the monk drive the whole way?"

"Yes, I can see in my mind's eye a monk driving the whole way."

"What happened next?"

"A monk arrived at the Bolzano monastery. Then a monk got out of the car and waited for Peter and Brother Paolo to arrive in the rose garden."

"Did Uncle wait in the car?"

"Maybe...but I don't really recall that part."

"Okay, what happened next?"

"A monk focused on Peter in the rose garden first. A monk hit Peter over the head with a rock and Peter fell down. Then a monk stabbed him with a knife so he was really dead and could not hurt Uncle."

"Okay, and then what happened?"

"A monk went after Brother Paolo and then a monk stabbed Brother Paolo. Then a monk ran back to the car."

"Was Uncle still in the car?"

"I am not sure...but I don't think so... Oh, I am not sure, I am sorry, I forgot."

"What happened next?"

"A monk drove far away and into the forest. A monk took off the robe and threw it into the water. Then a monk had to hide the knife. It was hard to find a good place to hide it but then there was a wooden cabin. And it was lucky because there was a place to hide the knife under the floorboards."

"That's really good, Anna. Take your time. What did the monk do next?"

"I don't remember anything next, except being in my kitchen and Uncle was there. "

"What did he say?"

"He said he was proud of me and that I did a really good job."

"Was Uncle in the car with the monk on the way back from Bolzano?

"I am not sure. I think a monk dropped Uncle off at a monastery but no, wait...not sure."

"Which monastery, do you recall?"

"I think the one in Rome. Wait, no...it could have been Bolzano. But I am also a little mixed up. I'm not sure."

"I am a little mixed up too, Anna. Let me see if I can get some clarity. This is a hard question and just do the best you can to answer it. Just say the first thing that comes into your mind."

"What did the monk look like?"

"A monk with brown robes and a hood."

"Okay... Then what did the monk look like after he threw the robe into the water?"

"That's a hard one. Let me think... A monk became invisible."

"Okay. That's good, Anna. Did the monk look like Uncle?"

"Not sure."

"Did the monk look like anyone you know?"

"Maybe. Sort of...not sure."

"Okay... Anna, do you think the monk was a man or a woman?"

"Oh, that's easy. Women can't be monks."

"But is it possible that a woman could put on a monk's robe?"

"I guess so."

"Is it possible a woman could dress up like a monk to hide her identity?"

"It's possible. But I'm not sure."

"If you had put on a monk's robe to protect Uncle, do you think that might have worked and helped Uncle?"

"Yes, I think I did that to protect Uncle."

"Did you as the monk kill Peter and Brother Paolo to protect Uncle?"

"I think so–no, I don't think so...but I don't remember... Oh, sorry...not sure."

"Are you sure Uncle was in the car or the rose garden with you–I mean, the monk?"

"I am not sure. I think I might have been alone in the car and the rose garden, after I dropped Uncle off at the monastery. But I am really mixed up. Not sure about this."

"Did you or the monk try to protect Uncle when you said he was not with you in the car and the rose garden?"

"Yes, a monk and I killed Peter and Brother Paolo in order to protect Uncle. But Uncle told me what to do and he did it, too. Maybe we did it together...or maybe I stayed in the car? Oh... I'm not sure. Sorry."

"And one last thing, was Uncle a Nazi guard at Auschwitz?"

"Yes, he killed a lot of people there. It was called a camp, some kind of camp. He used to brag about it when he drank after the war was over. Oh, my God, he will kill me if he finds out that I told you all of this."

"Thank you so much, Anna. You have been a big help as we try to solve this puzzle."

Dr. Rabino brought Anna out of the trance-like state.

Then Anna went back to her room, totally unaware of what she had disclosed in the session.

Would Brucelli have enough answers to charge Uncle with the double homicide? That was the question that haunted him.

Chapter 24

Switching Gears

Brucelli and Dr. Rabino had a heart-to-heart talk. "It seems that Anna may have killed Peter and Brother Paolo while she was in a fugue state of mental confusion in order to protect Uncle. Is that right, Doctor?"

"I'm not sure. I actually think Uncle could have committed the murders. But to protect himself he found a way to confuse Anna. He might've had her wait in the car, also in a monk's robe. If we hadn't done the hypnosis sessions and if Anna hadn't been brought down to the police station, she would've been unaware that she was involved in a double homicide. And she and Uncle would have gotten away with it."

"It has been a bit of a wild goose chase, Doctor. Uncle's fingerprints were on the knife used in the double homicide. But it could've been just his everyday prints when he cut a slice of bread in the Romano kitchen. The fingerprints on the knife are not enough to convict him of the double homicide. And we have no concrete evidence, besides Anna's comments, to prove Uncle was in Bolzano or committed the murders."

"Are the only charges you can bring against Uncle that string of burglaries where his actual fingerprints were found?" asked Dr. Rabino.

"Well, I was worried about that. But it just occurred to me that Anna and Maria handed me an even bigger criminal case: crimes against humanity. Uncle, Heinrich Schmidt, is a Nazi war criminal who needs to be tried and convicted in an Italian Court. That is way more important than burglary charges tried in a lower court. Oh, my God."

"You're right, Sarge. Wow. What was I thinking?"

"Yes, I was so focused on the double homicide that I was blind to the big picture. I need to call Simon Wiesenthal and find a good prosecuting attorney in Italy. We cannot lose this case because then Uncle will get away with thousands of murders. I better call Simon Wiesenthal now. Ciao," said Brucelli.

"Hello, Simon. It's Sergeant Brucelli. We've found a Nazi in hiding," he yelled into the phone, as he puffed his chest out and threw a fist in the air.

"Which one?"

"Heinrich Schmidt," yelled Brucelli, almost jumping out of his skin.

"Mazel Tov. Fantastic."

"Hey, Simon, that means we're going to need witnesses from Auschwitz and a brilliant prosecuting attorney in Italy who's familiar with Eichmann's trial. Can you help me?"

"Okay, give me a few days and I'll get back to you."

Wiesenthal sobbed with joy into a pillow, "One more Nazi will be behind bars, thank God. All this work I've done for all these years was worth it, but so sad Peter and Brother Paolo had to die," whispered Simon into his pillow.

Brucelli was ecstatic and danced with joy. He was over the moon. If someone had seen Brucelli as he beamed, swayed, and swooned, they'd have guessed Brucelli was in love. And as Brucelli drove in his car he screamed aloud, pounding on his steering wheel.

"Your time's up, Uncle. You've been well hidden for eighteen years. Your time as a free man is over. We gotcha."

Two days later, Wiesenthal called. "I've lined up several Auschwitz survivors who would love to come to Rome to testify against Uncle. Nazi physician, Dr. Hans Munch, who was acquitted at the Nuremberg Trials, is ready to help. He met 'Uncle' in Auschwitz."

"Fantastic," exclaimed Brucelli.

"I also found an excellent Italian prosecutor who attended the Eichmann trial. His name is Alberto Marco."

"Great, I'll talk to the current district attorney to see if Marco can assist him. If so, I'll set up an appointment with Marco right away. Once we have a trial date I will let you know. Thanks so much, Simon. You're a gem. I don't know how to thank you."

"The best thank you would be a guilty verdict," said Wiesenthal as he cried silent tears.

"You bet, I look forward to a celebration with you!"

Brucelli called the district attorney and asked if Alberto Marco could assist him at trial. "As far as I'm concerned, he can run the whole show. I have no experience with a prosecution of a high-profile Nazi. If you can get Marco, grab him."

"Thanks for your encouragement, sir," Brucelli replied, relieved.

Oh, God! Brucelli now had so many more phone calls to make: Marco, Sasha Wolf, Giovanni, and Maria. He would have to explain that the person who killed Peter and Brother Paolo was either an unstable woman–Maria's mother, who was in a fugue state of confusion and tried to protect her Nazi brother hiding in a Roman monastery–or Anna might have just been an accomplice and Uncle might have committed the double homicide. And they might never know. But the good news was that they now had a Nazi war criminal in custody and a trial was about the begin. Italy was about to accuse a Nazi of crimes against humanity, something Peter and Brother Paolo would have loved.

Abie and Sasha were heartbroken. Sasha shook and sobbed out of control on her knees.

"Peter's murderess will go unpunished, but at least she'll stay in a locked ward at the hospital and will never be able to hurt anyone else. And at least the Nazi they caught was someone Peter was looking for."

"How soon do you think the trial will begin, Sergeant?"

"I don't really know for sure, Abie. We have an excellent prosecuting attorney who observed the Eichmann trial. And I will be meeting with him to discuss the case in a few days. I will keep you posted."

"Thanks, Sergeant."

Sasha threw herself on the bed. She cried and thrashed around. She beat up the king-sized pillow as if she was punching that Nazi himself.

"God damn you. You took my Peter away from me. I hope you rot in hell and hang so all your relatives feel the pain that I feel. And God, if you're up there, how dare you take my father and Peter away. I don't believe in you anymore. How could you let the Holocaust happen? And Nazis are still around unpunished. The war is over and no one can stop the old and new Nazis. It's beyond unfair and too much for me to bear. I cannot take it anymore. Why do these Nazis get to rule the world?" Sasha then wailed without words and punched that pillow until it fell apart.

Abie tried to console her to no avail. She pushed him away.

"Why my Peter? Why did they have to kill my Peter?" Sasha argued with God.

"I think it was because Peter was a smart and clever investigator who found a Nazi war criminal hiding in a monastery," Abie replied. "Peter would be overjoyed that this Nazi will stand trial for crimes against humanity. He created a brilliant discovery and even though he's not here to reap the rewards, we can still be so proud of him, my dear."

"But I was already proud of him. I didn't need him to die to be proud of him," Sasha sobbed.

"I'm sorry. You're right. It's beyond unfair," Abie responded.

Again, she pushed Abie away. Where was her Michael? Sasha needed her Michael. Only Peter's real father would understand.

Abie began to pray in silence that his spiritual daughter would find a way to cope with this unspeakable pain and double trauma. How awful to lose a father and a son... How would Sasha be able to cope with so much sorrow?

"I will never see Peter get his Ph.D., or get married and have a wedding, or even have children. I will never be a grandmother. Ever. I only had one son. And we never found Michael. Michael never got to know him. We must find Michael. I will not spread Peter's ashes until we find him."

"Okay, Sasha, we'll find Michael."

"A man can't really understand what it's like for a woman to not be able to have grandchildren. It's both a biological and psychological need."

"I'm sure you're right. Sorry, my dear."

"It's unbelievably important for me. It feels like a dagger in my heart. I'm never ever going to be a grandmother and cuddle Peter's new baby and watch him or her grow up." Sasha attacked another pillow and ripped it to pieces.

***

Professor Giovanni burst into tears. He confided in Brucelli because he had no one else to talk to.

"I feel so guilty. It should have been me. I never should have let Peter go to Bolzano; it was too risky once we figured out he'd met Uncle, Heinrich Schmidt. What was I thinking? I must have been insane. Peter was such an excellent student. I loved taking him under my wing, like the son I never had. He was a younger version of me. He was excited to go, and he tried to protect me by going himself, Sergeant."

"Don't be too hard on yourself, Professor," Brucelli said. He didn't know what else to say.

"It's all my fault," Giovanni continued. "I was the one who taught Peter about the monastery routes... And that information got him killed. I'm just so heartbroken. I feel helpless."

To cope with the guilt and loss, Giovanni had to do something. He couldn't just sit around, hug his pillow, and cry. His first solution: hot chocolate. Then he stared in his mirror. Would he just cave in and give up his mission to be a Nazi hunter? No! He had found the courage and continued on, no matter the sacrifice. Then Giovanni got busy and put his office back together. He scrubbed hard and wiped all the blood off the walls. He was sure there were more Nazis hiding in those monasteries. This was just the tip of the iceberg. He would have a chance to help capture other Nazis in the future. His secret wish was for Peter to be proud of him. But, for now, all he could do was prepare for the trial. He would cry himself to sleep many nights to come.

***

Brucelli had to call Maria.

"Oh, hi, Sergeant," said Maria.

"Hi, Maria, how have you been?"

"Pretty good, and you?"

"I am doing well. I have some updates, but they might be hard to hear."

"Okay," said Maria, bracing herself. "Well, as you know, your mother has been doing much better, but she had been in a rather unstable place up until recently. We've been using some hypnosis techniques to help her recover some memories. Dr. Rabino increased her medication to help her regain her mental clarity. This has really helped. But...it came out during a hypnosis session that she had been traumatized by Uncle for years, and as you know she has been very afraid of him. When you mentioned to your mother that Peter was doing research on Nazi war criminals hiding in monasteries in Rome and Bolzano, she became very upset."

"Oh, no. I am sorry I upset her; I didn't mean to."

"It's not your fault, Maria. You see, your family has many secrets. Your mother tried to protect Uncle because he had a secret so big, it couldn't risk exposure."

"Okay, this sounds a little scary but please continue."

"Well, it seems that Uncle was a senior guard at Auschwitz."

"Oh, no. How terrible."

"There are quite a few eyewitnesses who will come forward and state that they observed Uncle kill, torture, and maim Jews, Gypsies, and other 'undesirables' at Auschwitz."

"So, what does this mean?"

"Mr. Alberto Marco, a prosecuting attorney in Rome, is preparing a case against Uncle as a Nazi war criminal who committed crimes against humanity."

"Oh, wow. On the one hand, I'm shocked, but on the other hand, I think deep down I figured he was capable of something like this. I just couldn't face it. I was in denial."

"I'm so sorry to bring you this news but you said to keep you in the loop. I needed to tell you this before you were told by someone else. We hope to keep this out of the media spotlight, so please do not share this information with anyone else. Your mother brought it up in her last hypnosis session, but she will not recall it. There is some more bad news and I think it would be better to share it with you in person. Do you have any time today or tomorrow to come down to the station, Maria?" asked Brucelli.

"I am free right now, Sergeant. I could be there in about thirty minutes."

"Okay, great. See you then."

Maria entered the precinct and found Brucelli's office.

"Hi, Maria. Thanks for coming in. This is not an easy topic to talk about. But before I begin, let me say in advance that you didn't do anything wrong."

"Okay, I'll try to remember that."

"As I said on the phone, your mother has been stabilized with medication prescribed by Dr. Rabino. Before she regained some of her mental clarity and stability she was in a 'fugue state of consciousness.'"

"What does that mean...'a fugue state'?"

"It's almost like sleepwalking or doing things that you don't remember, like a 'blackout.' For example, you could be unaware that you got up in the middle of the night, cooked a meal, left dirty dishes in the sink, and then went back to bed. When you woke up in the morning you had no memory of doing any of those things at night. Then you're mixed up as to why the dishes are in the sink...because you know you didn't leave them there yourself."

"I get it," Maria said.

"We all know that your mother was very scared of Uncle and that he was really mean and abusive to her. Your mother became very traumatized from an early age. But in spite of all this, your mother had a very strong psychological need to protect him because she was afraid of him. Once your mother found out that Peter was meeting Brother Paolo in Bolzano to discuss Nazis hiding in monasteries, she had a very deep-rooted psychic need to protect Uncle. Your mother became frightened and told Uncle about Peter's research."

"Did Uncle kill Peter and Brother Paolo?" asked Maria, her chin beginning to tremble.

"Well, it's a little more complicated than that, Maria. Uncle got very upset and somehow in the midst of his rage, your mother went into a fugue state of confusion, and we think either she was the one who drove to Bolzano and killed Peter and Brother Paolo... Or she drove Uncle there and he killed them. We are not sure who really killed them."

Maria was silent after hearing this story. Brucelli was not sure what to say or do next. Maria was breathing heavily and beginning to sweat, so Brucelli started to reach out and touch her hand but he hesitated. He had put a box of tissues on the table, but she didn't reach for one. Maria fainted and fell on the floor. She hit her head on the edge of the table on the way down. He tried to revive her, but he panicked and called for an ambulance. Before the medics arrived, he put a pillow under her head. Brucelli had no idea Maria would react this way. He expected she might cry and sob, but not remain silent or faint.

The ambulance arrived and the medics used smelling salts to revive Maria. They gave her some water, too. They brought in a stretcher, but Maria refused.

"I'd rather not go to the hospital," she said.

"I'm sorry, Maria," said a kind nurse, "but because you hit your head, we have to take you in. You need to be seen by a doctor to make sure you don't have a concussion."

Maria lay down on the gurney and was wheeled into the ambulance.

Brucelli paced back and forth in his office as he worried about Maria. He had to remind himself that he didn't do anything wrong and Maria was going to be okay. He called the hospital to check on Maria, but the doctor hadn't seen her yet.

About three hours after Maria was wheeled out of the police station, Brucelli got a call from the doctor.

"She has a mild concussion but nothing to worry about. We are going to keep her for a night or two just to observe her. But Maria asked me to tell you a secret," said Dr. Sacchi, excited to share the news.

"Oh, okay," said Brucelli as he leaned forward. Now Brucelli was curious what kind of secret it could be. His mind wandered. *Could Maria know that Uncle killed her father?*

Could she know that Uncle was her biological father or...on and on... This family has so many secrets... They never end...

Then Brucelli was startled because he himself was in a fugue state. He needed to listen to Dr. Sacchi.

"Could you repeat that, please?" Brucelli asked, embarrassed.

"Sure, Maria is about four to five months pregnant with Peter's child."

"Oh, *wow.*" Brucelli exclaimed, his eyes bulging wide. "That's amazing news."

"Yes. Mother and baby are just fine but to be on the safe side we'll have to keep Maria here for a few more days. Please remember to keep this revelation a secret for now."

"I will. Thanks so much for the call. I've been worried."

"You are very welcome."

Maria, pregnant–how would Sasha react? Would this be a gift for Sasha or more of a heartache?

***

Brucelli obsessed about Maria's plan to tell Sasha and Abie that she was pregnant with Peter's child. Sasha was very upset that Maria's mother might have killed Peter or at least might have been an accomplice to the killing and she was not going to jail. Sasha was upset that Maria told her mother about Peter's research. Sasha blamed Maria for Peter's death. Sasha even blamed Peter's professor for his research about the monastery routes. But the real truth underneath the surface was that Peter was obsessed with Nazi war criminals because his grandfather and other relatives were killed by Nazis.

Brucelli was aware that it was no one's fault and there was no reason to blame anyone for Peter's death, except the murderer. This was Peter's life's work and he died as he sought the truth. Peter was an innocent young hero archetype. He did not plan to die at a young age. He was on a quest. And now a Nazi war criminal would get what he deserved. All the people he killed along the way would scream out, "Hurrah!" from their graves, from the dust in the crematoriums, and from the ashes in the sky. They would not have died in vain. They would not be forgotten. Even as ashes, they will rise again like a phoenix from the flames.

Brucelli dreamed that Peter and Maria's child would live on to tell the tale when most of them were gone, many years from now. That child would learn about whether they won or lost the case.

Brucelli was a poet at heart. One would never guess it if you stared at him from the outside. Dressed in his neatly pressed uniform, he appeared like any other sergeant or policeman on the force. But inside that uniform there was a deep soul yearning to be free. He was the son of a partisan who fought for his country, one who died along the way but "fought the good fight" and would never be forgotten.

As he straightened up his office for his meeting with Mr. Marco the next day, Brucelli hummed the famous Italian Partisan song, "Bella Ciao":

Sta mattina mi son svegliato,
O partigiano portami via,
o bella ciao, bella ciao, bella ciao ciao ciao!
Sta mattina mi son svegliato
e ho trovato l'invasor.
o bella ciao, bella ciao, bella ciao ciao ciao
o partigiano portami via
che mi sento di morir.

E se io muoio da partigiano,
o bella ciao, bella ciao, bella ciao ciao ciao,
e se io muoio da partigiano
tu mi devi seppellir.

Seppellire lassù in montagna,
o bella ciao, bella ciao, bella ciao ciao ciao,
seppellire lassù in montagna
sotto l'ombra di un bel fior.

E le genti che passeranno,
o bella ciao, bella ciao, bella ciao ciao ciao,
e le genti che passeranno
mi diranno «che bel fior.»

Questo è il fiore del partigiano,
o bella ciao, bella ciao, bella ciao ciao ciao,
questo è il fiore del partigiano
morto per la libertà

***

One morning I awakened
Oh goodbye beautiful, goodbye beautiful, goodbye beautiful, bye, bye!
One morning I awakened
And I found the invader
Oh partisan, carry me away,
Oh goodbye beautiful, goodbye beautiful, goodbye beautiful, bye, bye!
Oh partisan, carry me away
Because I feel death approaching

And if I die as a partisan,
Oh goodbye beautiful, goodbye beautiful, goodbye beautiful, bye, bye!
And if I die as a partisan
Then you must bury me

Bury me up in the mountain,
Oh goodbye beautiful, goodbye beautiful, goodbye beautiful, bye, bye!
Bury me up in the mountain
Under the shade of a beautiful flower

And all those who shall pass,
Oh goodbye beautiful, goodbye beautiful, goodbye beautiful, bye, bye!
And all those who shall pass
Will tell me: "what a beautiful flower."

This is the flower of the partisan,
Oh goodbye beautiful, goodbye beautiful, goodbye beautiful, bye, bye!
This is the flower of the partisan
Who died for freedom.

Would Brucelli die for freedom? Or would he succeed in a new career as a Nazi hunter?

Chapter 25
Preparing for the Trial

The next morning Brucelli was ready to meet with Mr. Marco. Brucelli had gathered all his notes, rewritten those that were stolen, had them all typed and ready to hand to Marco. Brucelli recalled that this trial would be different from the trial that would have taken place about the double murders. Instead this was a trial about a Nazi war criminal who'd been hiding since 1945 and was caught. The cast of characters who were involved or affected by the Bolzano murders would be the same. But there would be additional individuals who'd be involved in a trial against a Senior Guard at Auschwitz for crimes against humanity.

Brucelli briefed Mr. Marco on all the relevant events that led up to this new trial. He went through all of the background information, even if it did not seem on the surface that it pertained to the new trial. Marco appreciated Brucelli's thoroughness.

"You never know when a detail here or there might make a difference in the way I would approach a witness or the case in general. Just to give you an example," Marco said, "the fact that Peter's grandfather and other relatives were killed by Nazis might not enter the transcript of the court stenographer, but it might make me more sensitive in my line of questioning, because I know that Peter's mother and Abie will be in the audience. At the same time, I also have to be conscious of the fact that there will be actual eyewitnesses in the courtroom who will give sworn testimony that Heinrich Schmidt committed crimes against humanity in Auschwitz. I need to be sensitive to them, too."

"Yes, I understand."

"So, here are the problems I see with the case," Marco continued. "Except for the eyewitnesses, almost the whole case appears to rest on the answers given under hypnosis by what the court might see as 'an unstable woman who was in a fugue-like state,' who was also sexually abused by her incestuous brother, and now accuses him of many murders during the war, based on his 'bragging.' The court might see this same witness as someone who could have faked an illness to get back at her brother for this 'sexual abuse,' based on her own description under hypnosis. And even her claim that her brother fathered the child named Maria is based on our belief that Schmidt and not Romano was the child's biological father."

"To be truthful, unless we get a very sympathetic judge and have some amazing and believable eyewitnesses, this case may fall apart. I pray you have some superstar eyewitnesses–otherwise there is a good chance we will not be happy with the outcome of this trial. We may all be disappointed except for Mr. Schmidt–Uncle–who will get the last laugh."

"Oh, I can guarantee you," said Brucelli with confidence, "that the eyewitnesses will be some of the most outstanding ones you can find on the planet. We know that most of the eyewitnesses died many years ago, but Simon Wiesenthal has promised me these are very convincing witnesses. I am sure you will need to prep them in advance for the kinds of questions you will ask, but also the questions they need to be prepared to answer during cross-examination."

"Oh, yes, of course," Marco agreed.

"Okay, so I would like to meet with Professor Giovanni, Anna and Maria Romano, and Sasha Wolf and Abie Gabriel this week if possible."

"I am sure I can arrange that."

"Then the following week I would like to meet with all the eyewitnesses. Once I complete those interviews, I will have a better idea how long it will take me to get ready for the trial. We'll also need a list of documents and photos that we will introduce at trial, for example the transcripts of the hypnosis sessions and the photos Simon Wiesenthal shared with you that Maria and Anna identified as Uncle."

"No problem. I am at your disposal. I will get you whatever you need."

"Excellent."

"Oh, and one last thing. I will need a list of any witnesses the defense plans to call upon and also any documents they plan to introduce to the court."

"Of course." And with that the two men concluded their meeting with a handshake.

The fundamental question was would the judge be sympathetic, and would the eyewitnesses be powerful enough to overcome any weaknesses in the case? Brucelli became concerned.

***

Brucelli arranged for Sasha and Abie to meet with Marco. Sasha's heart raced and she had labored breathing in the car on the way to the police station. "Will you protect me, Abie?"

"Sure, sweetie."

Brucelli was only there as an intermediary to introduce them to Mr. Marco, but Sasha was glad he stayed for the interview. Marco himself was confident but not overconfident.

"First, I am so sorry for the loss of your beloved Peter, and also for the loss of your father, Sasha–and your best friend,

Abie, your beloved Philip Wolf." Sasha and Abie nodded in appreciation.

Mr. Marco said, "I don't want to get your hopes up. We will have to go with the flow. The eyewitnesses need to be front and center of the trial. We need a sympathetic judge because much of the case rests on information gleaned from hypnosis sessions of an unstable woman who may or may not have committed two murders without knowing it."

"Oh, *wow*," said Sasha, terrified. "I never guessed this would be a risky case. I must be very naïve...although I should be cynical by now. I'm not even sure I can be in the same room with a Nazi war criminal. My father's Nazi murderer was never caught and now Peter's murderess will probably never go to jail. It's all so cruel and unfair. On the other hand, I assumed that Peter's research would have been so thorough and foolproof that it could stand alone even without him present. I feel embarrassed for being so foolish."

"But wait, Sasha. This case is not doomed, only a challenge. As long as we handle it well and our eyewitnesses are stellar, I feel like I can make a very compelling case. I will have a better idea after I meet with each individual eyewitness. If I play my cards right, I can touch the judge's soul enough to give us a fair hearing," replied Marco as he tried to convey hope to them.

"How soon can you meet with the eyewitnesses?" asked Abie, his foot tapping under the table.

"I hope to meet them all next week."

"Great, but now I'm concerned that Peter's research was stolen and that it may be very hard to prove the arc of his research," Sasha worried.

Brucelli piped in and reminded everyone that Uncle's or Mr. Schmidt's fingerprints were found in Peter's dorm room at the university.

"This might work to our advantage," said Marco, and Brucelli nodded his head in agreement. "Since we know that

Uncle stole both Peter's research and his professor's papers, the fingerprints are screaming out that Uncle has something to hide," Marco continued. "The burglaries may come in handy after all, although it's a shame to lose all that research."

"Do you need anything else from us at this time, Mr. Marco?"

"I think I'm all set for now, but I know how to reach you." Both Sasha and Abie shook Marco's hand and then drove back to their hotel.

"So, what did you think of Mr. Marco?" Sasha asked. "He seems very confident but also honest. Do you think he will do a good job?"

"I hope so. I need a miracle right now. I would love to be able to sing 'Hava Nagila' and dance the hora in the street when the trial is over and Uncle hangs like Eichmann," Sasha said.

After lunch, Brucelli introduced Professor Giovanni to Marco, who explained the weaknesses of the case against Uncle and his hopes for the eyewitnesses to shine and save the day. The main thing that Marco needed to hear from the professor was that the research that Peter was doing was credible.

"Did Peter ever mention Heinrich Schmidt to you?" Marco probed.

"Yes," said the professor. "He met Uncle, Mr. Schmidt, by chance at a dinner in Rome at the Romano family home on Sunday, June 7th. He recognized him from secret photos, which he'd studied for months. He told me that he recognized the scar on Uncle's face from the photos. He was upset about meeting him and came to me on June 8th to discuss his concern, or maybe I should say his terror.

"We were in contact with Brother Paolo in Bolzano, who had been in a Hitler Youth Camp," the professor continued. "He'd never harmed anyone but was very uncomfortable with other monks–Nazis in hiding–in Bolzano and Rome who had worked as guards in concentration camps or were part of the SS. If Brother Paolo were still alive he could have handed over more Nazis in both monasteries but his critical insight died with him in the rose garden that day.

"Peter already discovered where Heinrich Schmidt was. If Brother Paolo had lived, we would've had access to many more high-ranking Nazis in hiding. Brother Paolo was even more of a threat to Uncle and the others than Peter, who was going to meet Brother Paolo to get the names of those Nazis on the run or 'hiding in plain sight.' And then Peter planned to bring those names to me when he returned to Perugia on Thursday. We had planned to fly to Vienna to meet with Simon Wiesenthal after Peter returned with names from Brother Paolo. But the house of cards collapsed."

"I see," said Marco. "So, you didn't lose any names of Nazis in hiding during the burglaries, just the research establishing the monastery routes?"

"Yes, that's correct. Do you think that you will need me to testify?"

"I think so, to establish the importance of Brother Paolo and to explain the monastery routes."

"Okay. Just keep in mind that if you ask me how Peter and I met Brother Paolo, I won't be able to answer because it will compromise another confidential informant and I cannot take that risk again."

"I understand. I will anticipate that and respect your boundaries. I will not push that agenda. I just cannot promise what the defense attorney will do."

"I understand," the professor nodded as he stroked his grey beard. "I wish you the best of luck, Mr. Marco."

"Thanks so much, Professor. I think I'm going to need it!"

"I think you'll be great."

Would Marco need that luck? Would Anna's credibility be questioned? Would the eyewitnesses be stellar? Would justice be served?

***

The next day Brucelli brought Marco to the hospital. Brucelli carried a bouquet of flowers into Maria's room. She was going home that day, but he wanted to do something nice for her.

"Hello, Maria. Congratulations."

"Thanks. But remember, mum's the word."

"No worries...just don't scare me again with your dramatic fainting." They both laughed.

"So, Maria, this is Mr. Marco, the prosecuting attorney for Uncle's trial."

"Hello, Mr. Marco. Welcome to the family."

"Thank you."

"Marco is curious, if it turns out to be necessary, if you'd be able to testify on the witness stand."

"The answer to that question may depend on the date of the trial since I am now four to five months pregnant. But I am happy to help if I can. Do you have any idea how soon the trial will take place?"

"Not really, it all depends on how long it takes to gather all the information I need and prepare the eyewitnesses from Auschwitz."

"Oh, I see. I am not sure how much I can help you, Mr. Marco. I was just aware that Peter had a research project with our professor. I was unaware of any specific names of Nazis and I didn't even know that I had upset my mother by bringing up Peter's research. The only things I know about those topics were things Sergeant Brucelli brought to my attention.

"It seems like I was really in the dark about everything. My house was burglarized, I think by Uncle, because they found his fingerprints... But then again, his prints would have been all over the house anyway because he spent a lot of time there. I am not 100% sure that Uncle was involved in the break-in.

He had the key, so he didn't really have to break in, but maybe he chose for it to look that way..."

"Oh, wait, Maria," Brucelli interrupted before he forgot, "could you look in the attic for the secret hiding place to see if Uncle's Nazi uniform is still there with medals and a tie tack, and also maybe a flag with a swastika?"

"Sure, I'll take a look and see if I can find it. I will let you know either way."

"Thanks, sorry to interrupt."

"Okay," Marco said, "I will be in touch, Maria, if I think of anything else or if I need to put you on the witness stand. I wish you all the best with your pregnancy and delivery."

With that, the two men moved on to Anna's room on the locked ward. As soon as they entered Unit B, they ran into Dr. Rabino. Brucelli introduced Marco to Anna's psychiatrist right away.

"Can I help you, Mr. Marco?"

"As a matter of fact, I might need to pick your brain so I can understand Anna's condition a bit better. But the first thing that would help me would be to know if any of your hypnosis sessions were filmed."

"Oh, yes, indeed. All three sessions were filmed."

"Oh, that's great news."

"The only thing is that some segments of the sessions were only able to take place because I promised Anna that I would not tell Maria about a particular family secret... So those sections might have to be edited out."

"Okay, that seems reasonable."

"Is it still your medical opinion that Anna is not competent to stand trial or handle being on the witness stand?"

"Yes, definitely. Anna is not competent to stand trial. Everything she said to me in the hypnosis sessions is already gone from her mind. She has no conscious memories of her own about what happened in Bolzano, or what she said about Uncle. They are memories we tapped into, but she does not remember any of that now. She would not be able to confirm anything she said during the sessions."

"I think it might be okay if you talked with her one-on-one, but if she starts to get frightened or startled I would stop. We can't afford her to slide backwards too soon after she has become stabilized."

"Do you think it would be okay to just pop into her room and say hello?"

"I think that would be fine." They shook hands and Brucelli brought Marco into Anna's room.

"Hello, Anna," said Brucelli. "How are you feeling today?"

"Okay, I guess." Anna glanced up and became aware of Mr. Marco. "Who are you?"

Before he had a chance to answer, Anna asked Brucelli, "Would you hand me my crayons and coloring books?"

"Yes, Anna."

Brucelli took Marco out into the hall. "The comment about the crayons and coloring books always comes up when Anna does not care to talk about something or if she doesn't know you."

"No problem. I won't take it personally."

Brucelli's mind already raced to whether Maria could find the secret hiding place and the Nazi uniform. Would the uniform, flag, etc. still be there? Or did Uncle seize it during his break-in? Another challenge...

***

Maria arrived home and put the flowers Brucelli had given her in a cobalt blue vase. That was thoughtful of him. That's the kind of thing Peter would have done. Her baby would be born four to five months from now, sometime around mid-February.

Maria missed Peter. How would she deal with all of this alone? A hot torrent of tears poured down her cheek.

A pot of ginger tea in her favorite clear glass teapot was her solution. She adored this teapot. Peter had given it to her, but she also loved to gaze at the beads of condensation that bubbled up on the glass walls and lid when she poured the boiling water in. This can't be seen in an opaque teapot. She loved to stare at the steam as it rose up and as the water turned golden brown from the teabag. She needed to set up a baby's bedroom, but did she plan to stay in Rome? Should she go back to Perugia? That might make her feel closer to Peter. So many decisions.

Maria remembered Brucelli asked her to inspect the secret hiding place in the attic to check if the Nazi uniform was still there. She went up the stairs to the attic. Was the flashlight near the door? Yes. Was the hiding place on the right or the left? It wasn't on the left wall. Oh wait, she spotted the old familiar bookshelf. It's behind that. Oh, man. There was no way she could move that bookcase, even if she weren't pregnant.

Maria went downstairs and called Brucelli, but he was gone for the day. She left him a message.

"Hi, Sergeant. This is Maria Romano. I need someone to come over and help me move the bookcase in order to check out the secret hiding place."

Frustrated and out of breath, she sat down and poured herself a cup of tea. But it wasn't hot. She warmed it up. When she finished her tea, Maria took a nap. It sure was good to be home in her own bed.

Her nap turned into a starlit sleep and by the time she woke up it was morning. Maria must have needed it. She lounged in bed for a while. The phone rang.

"Hello."

"Hi, Maria. How are you feeling?"

"Oh, hi, Sergeant. I'm feeling so much better. I had such a wonderful night's sleep."

"I am so glad to hear that. I got your message. When would be a good time for me to stop by and help you move that bookcase?"

Maria glanced at the clock. It was already 9 a.m. She needed to take a shower and get dressed. "How about 10:30?"

"10:30 is perfect. Have you eaten breakfast yet, Maria?"

"I haven't, sir."

"Okay, if you make some coffee, I'll bring some cornetti."

Brucelli arrived as promised. They sat at the dining room table and had coffee and cornetti.

"Hmmm, this is delicious."

"Yes, I get them at the pasticceria near the police station and all the officers seem to love them."

"I can see why."

"Do you plan to share the news about the baby with Sasha and Abie?"

"That's a good question. I'm not sure. You know them better than I do. I've never met them."

"I'm sure that Sasha is upset that your mother may have killed Peter."

"Exactly, and I was the one who told her about Peter's research."

"I understand. It's true that Sasha's devastated. She mourns for Peter and his whole future, and everything a mother looks forward to when she has a child. But his life was cut short. Sasha believes she'll never have a grandchild, so she craves one even more. If you share the good news about the baby at this moment in time, Sasha would receive the greatest gift you could ever give her. I think Abie will be supportive."

"I would like them to find out, but I'm scared to be the one to break the news myself, Sarge. I'm aware they might be upset at first. Or maybe they won't ever be happy about the baby because we weren't married yet. Would you approach them about this topic without me there?"

"Yes, of course. I'd be happy to do that. I can see why a plan like that would work best. If I talk with them alone, they will feel safer. I have a gut feeling that after a few days, Sasha will come around. Your child will give her a sense of Peter's immortality."

"That works for me."

"Okay, I will set up a time to meet with Sasha and Abie in the next few days. I will let you know the outcome."

"Thanks, Sergeant."

After coffee, Brucelli remembered they needed to go up to the attic.

"Let's check out the secret hiding place. But you just have to promise me that you won't lift anything heavy, Maria."

"Okay. I am curious if the uniform is still there, but I am worried that it's not. If that happens, then Uncle or his 'friends' got what they came for. And it might appear that my mother dreamed it up, Sarge."

"Well, let's wait and see what happens."

Before they went up to the attic, Maria found the key to the secret hiding place. It was in her mother's drawer by the side of her bed in the jewelry box. Then the two of them went up to the attic.

"Let me turn on the flashlight. Okay. Here's the bookcase."

"Great. Thanks, Maria. I'm going to put on some latex gloves. Here goes nothing. Boy, this bookcase is heavy. I'm glad you didn't even try to move it."

"Yeah, me too."

"Could you shine the flashlight over this way, Maria? Thanks. Okay, I see the door to the secret hiding place now. Hand me the key and keep the flashlight focused on the lock."

"Here's the key, Sergeant."

"Okay, the lock and door are now open. Try to shine the flashlight all the way back. Great. Thanks."

"Oh, my God. Eureka! It's here."

Brucelli pulled out the uniform with care and was sure that all the medals and the swastika tie tack were attached. There was also an SS hat.

"Maria, can you shine the flashlight further back into the hiding place? I need to look for the Nazi flag with the swastika," Brucelli asked. "Thanks, I've got it. This is a lucky day."

"Wow. Mother was right."

"She sure was, Maria. You can be proud of her. She led us to a big discovery. Oh, can you get me a plastic bag from the kitchen? I can't contaminate anything. Thanks."

Maria came back upstairs with the bag.

"I believe, Sarge, that whoever broke in did not know where the key to the secret hiding place was hidden. Either Uncle forgot or he forgot to inform one or more of his 'friends.'"

"I agree. Either way we found something he tried to keep hidden."

"What's the next step?"

"I call the fingerprint expert and get him to swab every surface on the uniform, hat, medals, and flag."

Brucelli locked the hiding place and moved the bookcase back. He tied the large plastic bag with a knot so nothing would fall out. Then he removed his latex gloves. Brucelli and Maria, triumphant, walked down the stairs to the kitchen.

"Will the contents of the secret hiding place be the final nail in Uncle's coffin or will he weasel out of this discovery, too?" said Brucelli.

"The suspense is killing me," Maria replied.

Chapter 26
Good News

Sergeant Brucelli was flying high on his newfound evidence; adrenaline was pumping through his veins. He needed to make some calls. His first call would be to the fingerprint expert to come and pick up the contents of the secret hiding place. He would pick them up tomorrow. Next, Brucelli phoned Sasha and Abie and set up a meeting for the next day. He was glad they could make it. Brucelli reached Marco.

"Was the SS uniform and Nazi paraphernalia there?" asked Marco, bracing himself for disappointment.

"Yes, indeed. We struck gold."

"Fantastic."

The next morning Brucelli met with Sasha and Abie. Sasha began, leaning forward in her chair, "What's new?"

"Quite a bit has come to light. In one of Anna's hypnosis sessions she mentioned that there was a secret hiding place in her attic. It turns out it was hidden behind a bookcase. I went over to the house and Maria was nice enough to let me in. She helped me find the key to the secret hiding place. We were thrilled to find an SS uniform, medals, a swastika tie tack, an SS hat, and a German flag with a swastika on it. Everything was exactly where Anna said it would be."

"Wow, that's exciting," said Abie.

"What's the next step?" asked Sasha.

"The fingerprint expert picks everything up today and we will have some answers soon."

"That's great news."

"How is Maria?" asked Abie.

"Why did you bring up Maria? Don't mention her," said Sasha, annoyed.

"Well, Maria received some news," Brucelli interrupted, raising his hand.

"I'm not interested in anything to do with Maria, Sergeant. It's all her fault. She told her mother about Peter's research. Peter's dead because of Maria. Please take me back to the hotel, Abie."

"Okay," said Abie as they left Brucelli's office and got into the car.

"Why in the world would you bring up Maria, Abie? She betrayed Peter. It's because of her Peter will never come home. And I'll never be a grandmother," mourned Sasha.

"I brought it up because Brucelli described how Maria had helped him find the key, the hiding place, and the SS uniform. I'm sorry I upset you."

"Please don't ask about her again. We won't even have a trial about Peter's murder. Another Nazi gets away scot-free."

"But there will be a trial of a Nazi war criminal that Peter discovered. Peter's memory will stay alive that way. Peter loved Maria, so she must be devastated."

"I tried to like her, but I just can't right now, Abie. I need a nap. I need to escape."

Abie went to the hotel lobby. He called Brucelli to find out how Maria was doing.

"I am so glad you called, Abie. When Maria was in my office a few days ago, I had to give her some bad news. She fainted and hit her head on the table. The doctor called me a few hours later to say Maria had a slight concussion but he also added that Maria was four to five months pregnant."

"Oh, *wow*. I see. That's quite a new development, Sergeant," exclaimed Abie. He really hoped this would lift Sasha's mood.

"Maria was excited to share the good news with the two of you, but she was concerned she might upset you. I offered to be the peacemaker. I feared Sasha's first reaction would have been similar to what she said this morning. Perhaps in a day or two, Sasha might find a way to be happy about the baby. Abie, didn't Sasha say a while back that she was sad because she'd never be a grandmother?"

"Why, yes. That's one of the things she is most upset about right now."

"I'm not sure how to bring this up to Sasha, Sarge. Maybe I'll pray about it and see if I can find an opening."

"I wish you luck, Abie. You are in a tough position. You have to be supportive of Sasha but at the same time you have some new information that might make her happier," said Brucelli. "Keep me posted."

"I will."

***

As soon as Brucelli hung up with Abie, there was a knock on the Sergeant's door.

"I'm here to pick up the bag from the secret hiding place. I hope I can bring you some good news."

"Me too, thanks." Brucelli replied.

The Sergeant then paced back and forth in his office–his new way of dealing with anxiety–as he wiped his sweaty hands on his pants. Brucelli would be very happy if Uncle's fingerprints were on the buttons, medals, and tie tack. As for the cloth of the uniform and flag, they could have been washed, which might degrade the prints. But this expert was superb.

Brucelli needed some more evidence to help convict Uncle. Would he get lucky or would all the fingerprints have been wiped clean? Would someone else's fingerprints be on there? Or would all the prints be Uncle's?

***

Sasha woke up from her nap and stretched her body. The aroma from Abie's coffee cup sweetened her nose.

"I feel so very melancholy, Abie."

She just couldn't shake this overwhelming sadness. "I wish I could wave a magic wand and bring Peter back to life. I feel like I'm not a mother anymore. I will never be a mother again. I am nobody's mother. I am nobody." She cried silent tears.

"I am so sorry that we lost Peter. If somehow we could wave a magic wand and you could still be a grandmother, would that help?"

"That's impossible."

"What if I said that a miracle happened?"

"I would not believe it. And I just can't let myself have that kind of hope because it's not possible and it's painful."

"Sweetie, let me say it in a different way. What if I said you are about to become a grandmother? Would you believe me? And if so, would it help, Sasha?"

"I think it would help." Sasha paused. "Wait. Is this your way of letting me know that Maria is pregnant with Peter's child?"

"Yes, Sasha. This is my way–"

"Really? For real?"

"Yes..."

"Wow, oh, my God, that changes everything. How far along is she?"

"About four to five months. If all goes well the baby will be due in mid-February."

"Oh, wow. I feel so different now. I will be a grandmother. When can we meet with her?"

"I think Brucelli has her number. Shall I telephone him now...?"

"Yes! Oh, my God, I'll be a grandmother. Oh, my God, I can't believe it. Maria's pregnant with Peter's child. Peter will live on. What a miracle."

"Hi, Sergeant, would it be possible to get Maria's phone number? We would love to talk to her."

"So, Sasha came around?"

"You bet. Big time."

"That's great news. How about this plan–I would feel more comfortable if I called Maria and gave her your number. Is that okay?"

"Sure. That's fine."

"Hi, Maria, this is Sergeant Brucelli."

"Oh, hello. I hope you have something good to share."

"I do. They'd love to see you, Maria."

"Really? That's such great news. When can we get together?"

"Call them right away. Here's their number."

"That's so great. Thanks so much, Sergeant."

"You're very welcome."

Maria washed her face and took some deep breaths before she called. She was aware that Sasha desired a grandchild. This was a miracle. Maria prayed to God to help her say the right thing to Sasha.

"Hi, Abie, it's Maria Romano."

"Oh, hi, Maria, we are so glad to hear from you. We are ecstatic about the baby... Sasha needed this miracle."

"I think I needed it too, Abie. I miss Peter so much."

"We do too... We would like to invite you for dinner tonight at our hotel. Are you available?"

"Yes, I'm free. What hotel are you in and what would be a good time to meet?"

"How about 7 p.m. at La Savoia."

"Okay. Such good news, Abie."

"How will we recognize each other, Maria?"

"I have long, dark hair and I'll wear a navy-blue dress and a matching scarf."

"Okay, thanks for the tip. I'll wear a blue tie."

Maria glanced through her closet, choked up and on the verge of tears. She chose her clothes with care since she needed to make a good first impression. She'd gained some weight due to her pregnancy, so she needed this blue dress to still fit her. Oh, good, it did. She glanced through several scarves to see which one would complement her dress. She picked a pretty floral scarf with red roses.

They all met in the lobby of the restaurant. Everyone was all smiles and happy tears, the women's black mascara smudging.

After their meals were ordered, Sasha began her declaration, "Thank you so much, Maria, for this wonderful gift. I just cannot believe it. It's a miracle. A chance to be a grandmother means the world to me. And you have given me that opportunity, when all hope was gone. I cannot thank you enough, Maria.

"Please don't worry about money, medication, furniture, or hospital bills. We will pay for everything, even the crib and a dresser."

"Wow. Thank you so much, how generous of you."

"Well, it's the least we can do, Maria. Oh, and also maternity clothes–we will buy you all that you need. Just say the word and we can shop together, Maria."

"Oh, my God. Thanks so much."

"It's too bad that Peter didn't know he would be a father. What a shame."

"But Sasha, after the first month when I missed my period, I mentioned to Peter that I was worried I might be pregnant. He was excited and told me not to worry because–and these were his exact words–'my mother would love to be a grandmother.' We talked it over and we figured if it turned out that I was pregnant, then we would celebrate the news with everyone and get married right away. We both planned a big wedding in our minds."

"I would have loved a big wedding, Maria. I am so glad Peter understood you might be pregnant."

"I am sorry we did not manage to give you a big wedding," Maria apologized. "I think on some level Peter was afraid that he and the professor had started a project that was very dangerous," Maria continued. "But they both were compelled to complete their research."

"I was afraid that Peter's project would put him in harm's way. I have been worried about this for many years," Sasha said.

"Yes, I was scared for Peter too. People hide for a reason and they'd rather not be found," Maria added.

"When Peter and I understood that I might be pregnant and he commented that you'd love to be a grandmother, I believe–and I could be wrong–that Peter was aware that if anything happened to him, you would at least have a grandchild."

"Wow," said Sasha. "I wish I could have had it all."

"That would have been wonderful for all of us," said Abie.

Sasha changed the subject. "Do you have an OBGYN yet?"

"No, not yet but I think I can get a referral from the hospital," Maria said.

Sasha said, "We will get you all the vitamins you need. Please drink plenty of water. Listen to your body. If it says rest, you need to rest. Eat good, healthy food.

"When I was pregnant with Peter, my mother wasn't supportive. She wasn't there for me. She became very angry and withdrawn because I wasn't married. I understand your mother is in the hospital and she won't be able to help you, Maria. You will not go through this pregnancy alone. I may not be able to legally adopt you, but please feel safe. You can lean on us. We will adopt in spirit. You can always come and live with us in America, but no pressure. The gift is not only a grandchild, but a daughter as well. I hope you will be able to relax in our care," said Sasha.

"I will. I was so worried you would shun me. I am so glad you are happy and you'll include me as family."

They spent so much time on conversation that their dinners got cold. But they didn't care. Within a span of one day they went from total strangers to a family. They ate their cold meals together. The restaurant was fairly empty, so they weren't worried about talking too much or too loudly. They laughed and cried together. For the first time in a while they all had a sense of family.

"I feel so lucky," said Maria.

"We are lucky, too," said Sasha. Abie agreed.

"Would you like some dessert?" asked the waiter.

"How about gelato?" Maria suggested.

"Oh, yes," said Sasha.

Maria and Sasha chose chocolate hazelnut, while Abie chose espresso gelato. They all had hot chocolate. When they were done, Abie paid the bill while Maria and Sasha went to the ladies' room.

"I'm sorry that I haven't reached out to you before," Sasha apologized. "I have just been so devastated that I couldn't reach out to anyone, even Abie."

"I totally understand," said Maria. "Peter was my very first boyfriend. You raised a wonderful son. He was so kind and thoughtful. He created an aura that allowed me to feel very safe. He must have learned a lot from you and Abie about how to be a real gentleman."

"Thank you, Maria. We believe that Peter's father died in the war. He was in the resistance and we lost track of him. We didn't want Peter to get his hopes up, so we explained his father died in the war."

"Yes, Peter told me that his daddy died in the war. My 'Daddy' died in the war too, so we had that in common."

Sasha then explained the significance of the hot chocolate and told her a little bit about Michael. Sasha confided in Maria that deep down she hoped Michael was still alive and she planned to try to find him after the trial.

"But every time I drink hot chocolate, it's one more prayer that Michael is still alive and that I'll find him before I die."

"Thanks for sharing your secret desire with me about finding Michael, Sasha. Now I understand why Peter always ordered hot chocolate." They both smiled.

Maria and Sasha met Abie in the lobby. They threw some coins for good luck in the fountain. They said their goodbyes and hugged one another. They walked Maria to her car in the parking lot.

After she drove away Sasha said to Abie, "This was the miracle I needed–my heart's aglow. Let's call Grandma and Grandpa Wolf."

"Great idea."

"Mazel Tov, Sweetie. It's a real miracle," said Grandma Wolf when she heard the news.

It was a miracle, but would Sasha be able to forgive and accept Maria on a deep level despite the fact that Peter died because she told her mother about his Nazi research? Would the birth of Peter and Maria's baby help Sasha break through her anger and sadness? She almost didn't recognize herself in the mirror. Sasha was facing a doorway of no return. She could either move forward or give up. And there was no way she was going to give up after coming this far.

It would also help Sasha feel close to Michael. She was curious where Michael was and what he was doing now. She did not focus on the fact that he might be dead. When she lost Peter, Sasha lost a piece of Michael, too. That's why this new grandchild gave her back a sense of closeness to Michael.

Sasha promised herself that after the trial she would find Michael. How would she do this? She had no idea. It had to be done. She would not return to America until she found Michael. No matter what. After she found Michael, she could go back to America where she could continue to hunt for her father's killer.

Chapter 27
Moving Forward

Brucelli received the news he'd waited for. The fingerprint expert, Pasquale, dropped by the station to go over his findings. Just by chance Marco was in the office.

"I hope you have good news for us," said the Sergeant.

"Indeed, I do," Marco replied.

"Okay, tell us everything," said the Sergeant. They turned on the tape recorder to capture all the details.

"The uniform buttons, medals, and tie tack with the swastika, all have one set of fingerprints–Uncle's," said Paquale.

"Excellent," said Brucelli. Marco was silent.

"The cloth uniform itself had some partial fingerprints that could be Uncle's, but remember the uniform was washed, so some of the fingerprints may have degraded. The hat and the hatband only have Uncle's prints. And the flag has several of his finger and palm prints.," said Pasquale.

"That great news, right?" asked Brucelli.

"Maybe," said Marco.

"What do you mean 'maybe'?"

"Well, Uncle could say that a Nazi at the monastery or somewhere else gave him all those items to hide in his attic. Or perhaps Uncle bought them as memorabilia of a bygone era. If that is the case, the original owner could have wiped everything down and then handed it all to Uncle. Then maybe Uncle tried everything on and that's where his fingerprints came from. But let's assume for a minute that all of these items belonged to Uncle during the war. There is still a possibility that Uncle's defense lawyer could claim that everything belonged to someone else and that the fingerprints are only there because Uncle touched the items when placing them in the secret hiding place."

"Do I think that these items were Uncle's?" asked Marco. "Yes. But we need to prepare ourselves for anything and everything under the sun. Nazis are clever, sadistic, cunning and baffling. And they will try any trick in the book, and not just 'Mein Kampf.' So, hold onto your hats, fellas. I believe we are in for a wild ride. I predict it will be a roller coaster."

"I hope you're wrong," said Brucelli.

Before Marco left the police station, he asked Brucelli to set up the eyewitness interviews as soon as possible. Brucelli called Wiesenthal to see how soon this could be done. It seemed like most of the survivors from Auschwitz lived in Israel except one, who would be coming from America. Almost all of them survived because they were twins and part of Dr. Josef Mengele's experiments. Brucelli needed to work with Simon to set up some flights. The highlight of the trial might be Dr. Hans Munch. He was the only high-ranking SS medical officer who was acquitted at the Nuremberg trials. Munch would be coming from Bavaria. He was a Nazi doctor who did not participate in Mengele's experiments.

Brucelli pressed Wiesenthal to set up the interviews during the next week if possible. Wiesenthal said he would do his best but there were some Jewish holidays coming up. Brucelli planned to set up the interviews right away because the sooner they were done the sooner the trial would start.

Would those witnesses be as stellar as Wiesenthal promised? Would the judge be moved by their testimonies?

How good would Uncle's lawyer be? Would the witnesses be intimidated by Uncle or his lawyer?

***

The following interviews were recorded to gather as many details as possible from eyewitnesses. Most of the names of the witnesses have been changed to protect the innocent.

1. Marco began with Evelyn. She and her twin sister were from Hungary and were sent to Auschwitz in 1944. She lost all of her family except for her sister, Judith. Since they were twins, they became part of Mengele's experiments. They called him the Angel of Death because in spite of the horrific experiments, many of the twins survived due to the fact that Mengele needed to keep them alive. Based on all the details Evelyn gave him, Marco was convinced she would be a very effective witness. She was courageous, strong, and found a way to survive. She lived the impossible dream–freedom. Evelyn selected Uncle from the photographs Marco had shown her.

2. Next, Dr. Hans Munch arrived. Although a doctor, he never worked with Dr. Mengele. He was acquitted at the Nuremberg trials because he saved so many Jews and they testified at his trial. He did not drop the Zyklon B pellets in the gas chambers, but he did have to sign the death certificates. Munch still had nightmares about Auschwitz and was depressed because of it. Munch picked out Uncle and the infirmary in the photos. Munch was compassionate and brave and would make an excellent witness.

3. Marco then interviewed Jonathan. He was a Mengele twin who was unable to experience any real joy in his life after Auschwitz. Jonathan picked out Uncle from a series of photographs Marco received from Wiesenthal. Jonathan was a kind person who seemed very traumatized by his experiences

at the camp. He seemed like someone who would touch the heart and soul of the judge.

4. Samuel Rosenstrauch was almost as powerful a witness as Dr. Munch. He had lived in Zyrardow just outside of Warsaw, Poland before he went into hiding. He recognized Uncle because of the large scar on his face. Uncle had killed his cousin in a pogrom before the war. Samuel had spent years in search of the man with the scar and then they both ended up in Auschwitz. Samuel was an inmate. Uncle was a senior guard. Samuel now wore a patch on one eye, and his face was scarred because he was attacked by Uncle's German Shepherd at the camp. Samuel seemed to know more about Uncle than the other eyewitnesses because he had seen Uncle and searched for him before the war even began. Samuel was very believable and would make a very credible and powerful witness. He was a man with a mission.

Marco told Brucelli that he was almost ready to begin the trial. They just needed to make some extra copies of the hypnosis sessions for the defense lawyer and the judge, as well as a list of witnesses, and extra copies of the photos he got from Simon Wiesenthal. He might need to use Wiesenthal as a witness to validate where the photographs came from.

Brucelli seemed pleased that Marco was almost ready for the trial to begin. He could not wait for it to start and, better yet, for it to be over. It had been a long few painful and frightening months. They had not informed the media yet. They waited until the day before the trial to hold a press conference. Brucelli almost forgot that he needed to ask the judge if some media coverage would be allowed inside the courtroom. He was looking forward to looking back on all of this. He just needed there to be a good outcome and not too many surprises.

He notified all witnesses that he guessed the trial would start in a week or two. The local witnesses were prepared and ready to go. All of the out-of-town witnesses remained in

Rome. Brucelli just needed to invite Simon. He also asked the judge to pick a date or a series of dates to begin the trial that would work for the court's schedule. Brucelli discovered from Marco that he would be called as a witness himself. This might be the biggest case of his career. Just the idea of it sent a shiver down his spine.

What if the witnesses fell apart under cross-examination? What if the evidence wasn't strong enough? What if the judge wasn't sympathetic? Everything hung on a slender thread.

***

Uncle met with his lawyer, Russo, to prepare for the trial. They spoke in Polish. Uncle said he was only going to answer to the Italian name that he got with the false ID papers from the Red Cross.

Russo then asked, "How are you going to deal with the issue of Auschwitz?"

"What's Auschwitz?"

"Are you planning to deny everything?" said Russo.

"Yeah, why not play cat and mouse with them? They can't prove it," said Uncle.

"Okay. Well, just be prepared for all possible questions and how you will answer them. You are prepared to commit perjury and lie under oath?" Russo asked.

"What have I got to lose? I will make my lie believable. I am already in jail... So if I lie, what can they do, put me in jail again?" Uncle laughed and then Russo started to laugh.

"Let's get serious now. If they can prove you were a senior guard at Auschwitz, you could hang," said Russo.

"My life is rather meaningless right now. If they find out, I could choose to deny it or admit the truth. I have done my part to help the Germans get rid of the undesirables, so I've accomplished enough with my life."

"Don't talk that way. If you win this case, they can't try you again and maybe you could leave the monastery for good and have a normal life," said Russo.

Uncle replied that he had no desire to get married or have children.

"What would a normal life look like for someone like me? I don't really have anything to look forward to, except maybe drinking beer with some young Neo-Nazis in Bolzano. I am bored and don't care to hang out with that crowd. They are too young for me. Maybe I'm just better off dead."

"Uncle," said Russo, "you are too focused on the negative. There is more to life."

"If you say so."

"You sound depressed."

"No, just more realistic. The height of my career was in Auschwitz. All of that power went to my head. I was important. I created a difference in the world. I am nothing now, except a pretend monk who keeps bees for the monastery."

"Don't you enjoy your work with the bees?"

"I guess so. It's just something to do. Sometimes when I get bored, I just smash the bees against the hive. I love to kill them."

"But then you'll lose some of the honey."

"Who cares? Sometimes I just need to let out my rage, that's all. I am not a good beekeeper. I just pretend to be."

Russo understood there was no real point in a discussion with Uncle anymore. He spoke in circles and riddles. Russo needed Uncle not to give himself away. But he was who he was...and he had every right to answer the questions the way he desired. Russo didn't know what he would do if he were on trial. Who was he to judge Uncle? Russo got up, threw his silk jacket over his shoulder, and walked out of the room.

Russo's goal was to prevent Uncle's conviction. They had gone through too much together. Russo planned to win the case and become famous. How could he set Uncle free? Would Russo be able to rise to the occasion?

Chapter 28

The Press Conference

They had a very intense day ahead of them. Sasha and Abie went to pick up Maria at 3 p.m. to head over to the press conference in front of the courthouse. Sasha was happy that Maria wore one of her new maternity outfits and a raincoat. They had a couple of umbrellas in the car. The weather had started to turn a bit colder and a storm was on the horizon. None of them had any idea what would happen at the press conference. It would be the first time the media would hear the news of the trial of a Nazi war criminal who had been hiding in a Roman monastery.

Abie dropped Sasha and Maria off at the front of the courthouse and he went to look for a parking spot around the corner. He brought the umbrellas. Brucelli and Marco stood at the doors of the courthouse. They had a podium and a microphone, and they were covered by the portico. Everyone else stood on the stairs. There seemed to be about fifteen newspaper and TV reporters who had their own microphones. There were about twenty concerned citizens and witnesses as well.

"Welcome, everyone," said Brucelli. "We are excited to let you know that tomorrow we begin the trial of a Nazi war criminal for crimes against humanity. He was hiding in a

Roman monastery as a monk. He was a senior guard at Auschwitz. We will have some local witnesses and we've flown in some eyewitnesses from other countries.

"As long as we have order in the courtroom, the Honorable Judge Bianchi has agreed to allow the media in the gallery. It is possible that the courtroom will be very crowded, so we recommend you get here early. The trial begins at 9 a.m. Please bring your media press passes with you."

"At this time, we will take a few questions from reporters," said Marco.

A journalist from the *Corriere della Sera* asked, "How did you find this Nazi?"

Mr. Marco replied, "We've searched for him for four months, but many others have searched for him much longer."

An *RAI* reporter asked, "How did you know he was hiding in a monastery?"

Brucelli answered, "There has been some research that Nazis escaping Germany, Poland, and Austria took refuge in monasteries in this country on their way to Genoa to board ships for South America.

"The most famous Nazi we know of who hid in a monastery in Bolzano as a safe house was Eichmann. Some Nazis stayed in Italy and just went into hiding in specific monasteries. This was called the 'monastery route.' Okay. We will take one more question now," said Brucelli.

A famous journalist from *Le Monde,* Jean-Francois Martin, asked, "Who is representing the accused?"

"Antonio Russo," said Marco. "Okay, everyone. This concludes our press conference for today. Thank you for coming. We hope you will be able to attend some or all of the trial."

Sasha, Abie, and Maria walked back to the car and headed out of the parking lot. Brucelli caught them just as they were about to leave the driveway.

"How do you think it went?" he asked.

They all chimed in, "Very well. You did not give out too many answers and you left them craving more."

"Great," said Brucelli. "See you in the morning."

Abie replied, "Right you are!"

Abie drove back to the hotel. They entered the lobby and went into the restaurant called La Fanciulla del Mare–the Sea Maid–for an early dinner. They figured they were going to talk during dinner, but they were determined not to let their dinner get cold like last time. They glanced at their menus and for some reason they all ordered salmon with ginger sauce and asparagus. It came with spaghetti. And it was delicious. Sasha and Abie had a special white wine, Meursault, that Albert Camus named one of his characters after. Maria just had water. The restaurant was filled with flavorful aromas. They all had the same gelato again, plus hot chocolate.

They did not let their dinners get cold. Maria could see why Sasha loved Abie so much. He was kind, compassionate, and a good listener. He had a nice smile, dimples, sweet eyes, and curly grey hair. Sasha was lucky to have him as a father substitute. Sasha had told Maria that at one point she desired to marry Abie. Maria now understood why.

Everyone remarked about how wonderful the restaurant was–the lush wallpaper of landscaped gardens and the marble floors were elegant. They continued their ritual to throw coins in the lobby fountain for good luck.

They had a joyful evening and they tried to distract themselves from the upcoming trial. Abie drove Maria home.

"Thank you so much for everything," Maria said to Abie as she sat next to him in the front seat.

"No problem. You are part of the family. It is almost as if we have Peter here."

"What a nice thing to say," she said as she yawned. "Sorry, I guess I am sleepy."

"Sleep well. We'll see you tomorrow."

"I think I will take my own car, so I will just meet you at the courthouse. Please save a seat for me so we can sit together."

"Okay, that sounds fine," replied Abie.

When they got to Maria's brick house, Abie waited for her to unlock the front door and go inside before he drove back to the hotel.

They were all worried about the trial. They'd distracted themselves tonight but once tomorrow arrived, they would not have that luxury. How would each of them handle the different aspects of the trial? Would their wounds bind them together or pull them apart?

Chapter 29
The Trial Begins

Everyone rushed to get to the courthouse early so that they were assured to get a seat. Maria, Abie, and Sasha all sat together in the third row.

When the time came, one of the bailiffs announced, "Please rise."

A door swung open in the front of the courtroom.

"The Honorable Judge Bianchi has entered the courtroom," the bailiff continued. "You may be seated."

There was a court stenographer at the front of the room. The air was filled with the smell of well-oiled wood.

Since this was not a jury trial, the prosecuting attorney Mr. Marco gave his opening remarks to the judge.

"Your Honor Judge Bianchi, I will prove to you without a reasonable doubt that Heinrich Schmidt was a senior Nazi guard at Auschwitz from 1942 to January of 1945. He has committed crimes against humanity. I have many eyewitnesses and researchers who will prove on the witness stand that they know in their bones that Mr. Schmidt murdered and tortured many inmates in Auschwitz with great pleasure and then spent almost eighteen years hiding in a monastery in Rome. He is a vicious criminal who needs to be punished to the fullest extent of the law."

Mr. Russo then began his own opening remarks. "Your Honor Judge Bianchi, by the end of this trial I will prove to you without a shadow of a doubt that my client spent the entire war in Warsaw, Poland working in a machine shop. He has never murdered or tortured anyone. After the war he joined a monastery in Rome. He wasn't hiding from anyone. He is not a criminal and does not need to be punished. This whole trial is a fabrication of the police and Simon Wiesenthal's center in Vienna, and has no basis in reality.

"By the end of this mockery of a trial, we will sue the court for slander and libel with intent to smear an innocent person with false allegations. It is our intent by the end of this trial that we will have proved our case successfully, and you, in your great wisdom, will agree. Thank you very much, Your Honor." Mr. Russo sat down next to his client.

The judge stated to the entire courtroom, "It seems to me that this case and trial may be very volatile and intense. I would like to ask everyone in the audience to refrain from jeers, clapping, shouting, or other demonstrations in support of or against any comments made by witnesses or attorneys. If I do not get your full cooperation with these instructions, you will be asked to leave the building or even held in contempt of court. I implore you to follow my commands; otherwise we may not be able to continue this trial in a timely manner. I will give you one warning and after that you will be accused of contempt or escorted out of the building. Thank you in advance for your willingness to have order in this courtroom." Then he deferred to the prosecuting attorney, "You may now proceed."

"Thank you, Your Honor," Marco began. "I call to the witness stand Mr. Heinrich Schmidt." Uncle at first refused to go up to the witness stand.

"That isn't my name," the defendant whispered to his lawyer.

"Just explain to the prosecuting attorney that isn't your name."

"Okay," Uncle sighed. "But this is under duress."

Uncle went up to the bailiff and put his hand on the Bible. The Bailiff asked, "Do you swear to tell the truth, the whole truth, and nothing but the truth, so help you God?"

"I do."

"You may be seated."

Marco asked the defendant, "Please state your full name for the record."

The defendant then stated, "Tommasino Ricci."

"I am confused," said Marco, "then who is Heinrich Schmidt?"

"How should I know?" said Ricci as he shrugged his shoulders and leaned to the side. "You put the wrong man on trial, sir."

"I do not believe so," said Marco, and continued, "When did you acquire the name Tommasino Ricci?"

The defendant replied, "I have always gone by that name. When I left Warsaw in 1945, I lost my papers on the way to Rome and the Red Cross issued my new ID papers in approximately June of 1945."

"So, if we were to contact your last employer, he would know you as Tommasino Ricci, is that correct?"

Ricci replied, "That machine shop closed in early 1945, so I doubt anyone would answer the phone."

"Have you ever been a senior Nazi guard at Auschwitz?" asked Marco.

"What's Auschwitz?" the defendant laughed.

"Have you been drinking this morning? I smell alcohol on your breath," asked Marco.

"Objection, Your Honor," yelled out Russo.

"Sustained," said the judge. "The defendant is not on trial for alcohol abuse." Marco was exasperated but tried not to let it show.

"I am about to show you some photos from Exhibit A. Please inform me if they look familiar," asked Marco.

"No, I have never seen them before," Ricci replied.

"Do you know what Oswiecim was?"

"I think it is a little town in Poland not too far from Krakow," Ricci answered.

"Have you ever been there?"

"No," Ricci replied.

"Are you aware 1.5 million people died near Oswiecim?"

Ricci acted startled and said, "Oh really, that's a shame." The entire audience was stunned.

Then Marco stated, "Your Honor, I am done with this witness for the moment, but I would like the opportunity to recall him later in the trial."

"Granted," said the judge. "You may return to your seat," the judge said to Ricci.

At this moment, the reporter from *Le Monde* left through the back door of the courtroom, almost unnoticed.

"I now call to the witness stand Dr. Hans Munch."

Munch slowly walked up to the witness stand and the Bailiff swore him in. Dr. Munch then sat down.

Marco asked the witness, "Please state your full name and where you currently reside for the record."

"Dr. Hans Munch–Bavaria, Germany."

"Thank you," said Marco. "Will you please tell the court what you were doing during the war?"

"Yes, of course. I was a Nazi doctor and a high-ranking SS officer at a concentration camp called Auschwitz. I was there from 1942 to January of 1945."

"What was your job at Auschwitz?" asked Marco.

"I signed the death certificates."

"Did you drop any Zyklon B gas pellets into the gas chambers or murder any inmates in any other manner?"

Munch replied, "No," as he glanced down at his shoes.

"Did you participate in Dr. Josef Mengele's experiments on twins?"

"No, I did not," said Munch.

"Were you ever called to the Nuremberg trials?" asked Marco.

"Yes, I was, but I was acquitted."

"Why do you think that you were acquitted?"

"Because many Jewish people came to my defense, explaining that I helped them."

"What have you done with your life since you left Auschwitz?"

"That is my problem," answered Munch. "I've had nightmares about Auschwitz and I have had no great joy in my life. I have been very depressed."

"I am sorry to hear that, Dr. Munch. That's very sad." said Marco. Then he continued, "I would like to ask you to take a look at these photos from Exhibit A and tell me if you recognize anyone or anything in these pictures."

Dr. Munch put on his glasses that were in his pocket. He gazed at the photos with care.

"I recognize a man and also a building in these two photos," said Munch.

"Where were these photos taken?"

"They were taken in Auschwitz because I recognize this building, called the infirmary."

"And who is the man in these photos?"

"He was a senior Nazi guard at Auschwitz. At the time he went by the name of Heinrich Schmidt. I recognize him, as well as the scar on his face."

"Do you see that man in the courtroom today?"

"Yes, he is the defendant," and then Munch pointed to Uncle, who now went by the name Tommasino Ricci.

Marco was glad that he put Dr. Munch on the stand immediately after Ricci. He was stuck with Mr. Ricci and he needed someone with credibility to counter the defendant with strength.

"Thank you, Dr. Munch, for your very important knowledge and insight."

At this moment in the proceedings, the judge called a recess for lunch.

"We will reconvene in one hour and the cross-examination of Dr. Munch will continue at that time."

The audience started to move out of the courtroom. But Martin, the journalist from *Le Monde*, rushed back into the courtroom as he glanced around for Marco, Brucelli, and Wiesenthal.

"I must speak to all of you right now, and in private."

"What is this about?" asked Marco.

"I have confidential information about the defense attorney, Russo, via three different reliable sources."

Marco said, "Let's go over here in the corner of the courtroom."

Martin explained that Mr. Russo was the brother of the defendant. "His name at birth was Friedrich Schmidt. They grew up together and were employed at the Iron Works Machine Shop in Warsaw before the war. Friedrich Schmidt entered the monastery in Rome and received false ID papers from the Red Cross in the fall of 1944. In 1945 he was able to get safe passage for his brother, Heinrich, to follow him to the monastery."

"Are you absolutely sure your information is reliable and unimpeachable?" asked Brucelli.

"Yes, without a shadow of a doubt. I have been up all night. If I promise not to publish it, would it be possible to look at those photos with all of you from Exhibit A?"

They all stared at Wiesenthal, who responded, "And what reason would you need to look at them?"

Martin replied, "I just need to see if, by any slim chance, Friedrich Schmidt is in those photos."

"Why would he be in any of these photos?" asked Brucelli.

"He was an SS officer at Theresienstadt."

"You've got to be kidding me!" said the Sergeant.

"No, I am not, if only," said Martin.

They scoured the pictures and all of them recognized an SS guard who seemed similar to Mr. Russo, or Friedrich Schmidt. Wiesenthal turned the photo over and there, scrawled in pencil, was *Friedrich Schmidt, Theresienstadt, 1943*.

Wiesenthal said, "I can't believe I missed this."

Martin added, "And one more thing–Russo is not even a lawyer. We must speak to the judge in chambers and have Mr. Russo removed as the defense attorney."

Brucelli was incredulous as to why this wasn't discovered earlier. "Didn't anybody do a background check on Mr. Russo? I guess not. It's hard to believe."

They tried to go to the judge during the lunch recess but he had given strict orders not to be disturbed. They would have to wait until right before the judge came back into the courtroom. They waited in the hall near the judge's chambers. Forty minutes later, the judge's door opened.

"What is the meaning of this, an ambush?" asked the judge.

"We must speak to you in private."

"Well then, approach me at the bench in the courtroom after we reconvene."

"We can't, sir," said Marco. "We need to talk with you in private, out of earshot of Mr. Russo."

"This is highly unorthodox," said the judge. "It better be worth it."

"It is Your Honor, I promise you," said Marco. They had a heart-to-heart talk with the judge and explained everything.

The courtroom started to fill back up again after the lunch recess.

"Brucelli, Marco, and Wiesenthal aren't in the courtroom," said Sasha.

"They might be a little late on the way back from lunch," said Abie. Fifteen minutes later they were still not back, and the crowd started to get restless.

"Is something wrong?" asked Russo to a bailiff. The bailiff just shrugged his shoulders.

Another fifteen minutes went by and Russo said, "I demand to speak to the judge," but it fell on deaf ears.

Five minutes later the bailiff said, "All rise. The Honorable Judge Bianchi presiding. You may sit down."

Then Brucelli, Marco, Wiesenthal, and Martin entered the courtroom from the back door.

"What was that all about?" whispered Sasha.

Abie just shrugged his shoulders and said, "Whatever it was, it must be very important in order for the judge to delay the trial. I guess we shall soon find out."

The judge stated, "It has come to my attention that we cannot continue this afternoon's session, so we must adjourn for the day. We will reconvene as soon as possible. Everyone must leave the courtroom except for the defendant and Mr. Russo. Bailiffs, will you please escort everyone else out of the courtroom? Thank you."

Once everyone was gone, the judge was left alone with Russo, Ricci, and two bailiffs who carried guns.

"We have a big problem, Mr. Russo. I am now aware that you are not an attorney and you are also the brother of the defendant. Therefore, I must dismiss you from this case. Because you were also an SS officer at Theresienstadt, we need to arrest you as a Nazi war criminal for crimes against humanity. You will go to jail until such time as we can build a case against you and bring you back before the court." Russo was shocked.

"Where did you get all these crazy ideas?"

“It’s none of your business now. Bailiffs, would you please call in Sergeant Brucelli to take Mr. Russo to jail?”

Brucelli entered the courtroom and asked Russo to stand up and put his hands behind his back. Brucelli read him his rights. The bailiffs stood nearby. After the handcuffs were securely fastened, Brucelli walked Russo out of the building to a police car that awaited them.

The judge then addressed the defendant, “It is your right to have an attorney. If you cannot afford one, the court will appoint someone to represent you.”

Uncle said, “Under the circumstances, I would like to represent myself.”

“Do you understand how risky that is, since you are not a lawyer?”

“Yes, Your Honor, I am aware that I have not gone to school to train as an attorney, but I know my case better than anyone else. I would like special permission to represent myself.”

“Well, against my better judgment, I will make an exception in your case. You can return to jail overnight and begin to represent yourself tomorrow. You will not be able to leave the courtroom for any reason except to use the men’s room, accompanied by an armed bailiff. Please make arrangements to bring a packed lunch with you each day. You will eat in the courtroom in the company of one or more bailiffs.”

“Okay, sir. I understand. Thank you very much.”

The judge asked a bailiff to get the detective that Brucelli had arranged to enter the courtroom and handcuff the defendant. They left the room and headed outside for another police car that awaited.

The judge was relieved that the day was over, and he did not desire any more complications tomorrow. What a strange turn of events. Bizarre. That journalist from *Le Monde* did his homework in less than twenty-four hours. The judge created a mental note that if he ever needed a journalist, this was the man he would handpick.

Sasha, Abie, and Maria went to get hot chocolate at a nearby café before they left.

"What in the world is the problem?" asked Sasha.

"I guess we might find out tomorrow," said Maria. "Unless they do not reconvene."

"Wow. It must be something big," said Abie. Everyone agreed. "Does anyone have a clue what it might be?"

"Well," said Sasha, "Wiesenthal, Brucelli, and Marco were all out of the room after the lunch break and they came back right after the judge returned."

"But aren't they mandated to update the defense attorney if they are about to introduce new evidence?" asked Abie.

"Maybe it was something that they could not allow the defense lawyer to overhear at that time," said Maria.

"Oh, I think the judge ordered the defendant and his lawyer to remain in the room," said Abie.

"You're right," said Sasha, "so I bet it has something to do with Uncle or his lawyer. Wow."

"Some police cars just took two people away," said Abie.

"What a surprise," said Sasha. "I guess we'll find out tomorrow or very soon. How will we know whether to come back to the courtroom tomorrow?"

"Good question, Maria." said Sasha.

"Maybe we should call Brucelli and find out."

They asked the owner of the café if they could borrow the phone and they called Brucelli. He wasn't available but the desk officer said the trial would begin again tomorrow.

"If anything changes, Brucelli or I will call you," he said.

"Thanks so much," said Sasha. "We are back on track for tomorrow morning."

"That's great."

"I don't care for any more delays. I just can't wait to get the trial over with," Sasha complained. They finished their hot beverages and left the café.

Maria went home, took a bath, and went to bed. She pulled the covers over her and fell asleep as soon as her head hit the pillow. She had been very tired all day and not very hungry. Abie and Sasha went back to the hotel, took naps and showers, and then they went out to dinner at the hotel restaurant. It was super convenient.

"I'm really glad Brucelli recommended this hotel. We don't even have to dress up for dinner." Abie smiled and nodded. They threw coins in the fountain for good luck.

They didn't say anything, but they were both concerned that the recess that afternoon might foretell a dramatic end to this story. Whatever it was it must have been explosive. Neither of them slept well. Maybe the issues or problems would work out in their favor...but maybe not.

Chapter 30

Return to Auschwitz

Le Monde released a morning edition with a front-page article on Uncle's trial. It turned out that Mr. Russo was not only not an attorney but also the brother of the defendant. The judge dismissed him from this case. Russo was also an SS officer at Theresienstadt. Russo was arrested as a Nazi war criminal for crimes against humanity. They needed to build a case against him in the future. Everyone was shocked.

The bailiff in the front of the courtroom announced the judge's arrival. "Please rise. The Honorable Judge Bianchi presiding. You may be seated."

The judge announced that the defense attorney had been dismissed and that the defendant had petitioned the court to represent himself.

"Oh, my goodness. God help us," exclaimed Sasha, "what a nightmare." Sasha put her head in her hands.

"I hope he makes a total fool of himself and we win the case," laughed Abie.

"I like that idea," said Maria.

"Give him enough rope and he'll hang himself," chuckled Abie. "From your mouth to God's ears."

"Amen," added Sasha.

"I would like to cross-examine the last witness," said Uncle.

"Dr. Hans Munch, would you please return to the witness stand? You are still under oath," said the judge.

Dr. Munch returned to the witness stand. "You said you recognized me by the scar on my face? Did you not?"

"I recognized you without hesitation. We spent a lot of time together over two and a half years. I only mentioned the scar at the end of my recollection of you because it jumped off the photo's page at me."

"But many people have scars on their face and not all of them are me," Uncle responded.

"That may be true, but you were the only guard at Auschwitz who had a facial scar," Munch retorted.

"What makes you so sure that picture was taken at Auschwitz?" Uncle asked.

"I spent two and a half years there. The building in the background is the Auschwitz infirmary. I am a doctor. I spent a great deal of time in and around that infirmary. My time at Auschwitz was probably quite different from yours," replied Munch. "I did not enjoy my time there.

"You, on the other hand, seemed to enjoy your ability to kill and torture inmates. We are two very different types of people," said Munch.

"How did you know what I was like in Auschwitz?" asked Uncle.

Munch replied, "That bewitched smile on your face and your body language when you shot inmates at point-blank range, as well as when you tortured people. Your cackling laugh is unforgettable. You also seemed very happy while you drank beer with your fellow officers."

Uncle replied, "That means nothing. It could have all been an act."

"I don't think normal people cackle and laugh while they murder innocents. That is not an act; that is very real. It is a sign of the mind of a criminal. I think you were caught up in the Nazi myth and the whole Jewish and 'undesirable' propaganda. You could not stop yourself from the way you carried out your allegiance to Hitler," said Munch.

"Okay, I've had enough of you, Dr. Munch. You may return to your seat."

"Thank you," said Munch as he walked back to his seat with a measured pace.

Brucelli and Marco both winked at him. Dr. Munch must have done a good job. He did not yet grasp the coup he pulled off as he cornered Uncle into his admission that he'd spent time in Auschwitz. Uncle didn't even deny or cover up that he'd been there around the same time as Munch. Everyone was overjoyed.

"I don't think that Uncle even understood what just happened. He got caught up in the moment. I am sure Marco will be able to use this later," Sasha rejoiced.

It was Marco's turn to call the next witness. He called Evelyn up to the witness stand. She was a short woman with honey golden hair. She wore her signature royal blue suit and scarf. She appeared very professional.

"Please state your name and where you reside for the record."

"My name is Evelyn Moses and I live in America."

"Were you an inmate in Auschwitz?" asked Marco.

"Yes, I was one of the Mengele Twins."

"Would you explain what a Mengele Twin was for those in our audience who are new to that expression?"

"Sure. Dr. Josef Mengele was often called the 'Angel of Death.' He loved to do research and he was in charge of the medical experiments at Auschwitz. He used twins because we were a perfect control group. He would inject one of us with a serious illness to see how we would respond. For example, if I died, he would have injected my twin sister Judith with a lethal injection of phenol into her heart and she would have died instantly. Then he would do the comparative autopsies to see what he could learn.

"Quite early on he injected me with something very powerful. I ended up in the infirmary. I was very sick with a high fever. I found out there was a water faucet at the opposite end of the room. I crawled because I was so weak, but after many hours I got to the water and boy, did it taste good. Then I had to crawl all the way back to my bed. By the end of that journey, I whispered, 'I must survive, otherwise Mengele will kill Judith.' The next day he came by with some other doctors and said in German, 'Too bad... she only has two weeks to live.' I became frantic and terrified. If I died, Mengele would kill Judith. I *had* to survive.

"I was more like Judith's mother than her sister. I was so responsible for her. So, I spoiled Mengele's experiment. I survived. I triumphed over him. But I hovered between life and death. The injections Dr. Mengele gave to Judith stunted her kidneys and they never grew to a normal size. They remained the size of kidneys of a ten-year-old girl. Years later I gave Judith one of my kidneys," concluded Evelyn.

"I am so sorry. What are you doing now?" Marco asked Evelyn.

"I got married a few years ago and now I have two beautiful children, a boy and a girl. But just because I am free of the Nazis does not remove the pain they have inflicted upon me. When we got out of the cattle car and we were on the selection platform, the Germans were yelling 'Twellinge, twellinge'–'twins, twins.'

"Judith and I appeared alike, and we were dressed alike. They asked if we were twins and we did not offer any information. But they guessed in that moment that we were twins. They pulled me and Judith to the left and my mother and the rest of the family were pulled to the right. I can still see my mother's arms outstretched towards us in total despair and then in a minute she was gone. As I said before, we called

Mengele the 'angel of death' because although he did terrible experiments on us, the reason we are alive today is due to him. Rather ironic."

"Do you have any memory of Heinrich Schmidt from your time in Auschwitz?"

"Yes, for sure. He seemed callous and cold as he slaughtered inmates. His facial scar was very distinctive. As a ten-year-old girl, his scar gave me the shivers. He wasn't nice like Dr. Munch, who really cared about us."

"Would you be able to glance at some photos and see if any of them look familiar?"

"Sure," said Evelyn.

She found her glasses in her purse and studied the photos. Evelyn picked out the man people called Uncle.

She said, "It wasn't just the scar, but his face was like the face of the defendant. I also agree with Dr. Munch. That the building in this picture is the infirmary, where I spent way too much time."

"Oh, one last question, do you know what 'Canada' was?" asked Marco.

"In Auschwitz there was a building called 'Canada.' This was the place where everyone's belongings ended up. It was a cushy position to work there. No Mengele Twin got a chance to work there. They were too busy doing experiments on us. The inmates who were lucky enough to work in 'Canada' were out of the cold. They went through everyone's possessions and sorted them into piles based on categories, like clocks, gold, dresses, hats, money, coats, suitcases, etc. It was a source of wealth and prosperity. People called it 'Canada' because that building had the riches of the real Canada. And everyone dreamed they would survive the concentration camp and be able to move to the country called Canada."

"Thank you very much, Evelyn. You will now be cross-examined."

Uncle approached her. “So, you were aware of me in Auschwitz? What if I was a prisoner there?” Uncle laughed.

Evelyn said, “If you were an inmate you would have a tattoo like mine, and she raised her sleeve. Let me look at your arm,” she said to Uncle. Then she continued, “You see, you don’t have a tattoo.”

“I could have erased mine.”

“Well to me, my tattoo is now my badge of courage. Why do you play this cat and mouse game with me?” she asked.

“Just to throw you off your game,” he quipped.

“Well, this is not a game to me. You strike me as someone who used to have a lot of power and now you are a little nothing. That’s what I think. Do you know what ‘Canada’ was?” asked Evelyn.

“Yeah, the country.”

“Well, I do not think you are a very serious man. It was a mistake to represent yourself. You will lose.”

“But at least I can have fun with people like you,” cackled Uncle.

“I survived Auschwitz; I can survive you! I believe you will get what you deserve,” Evelyn said with sternness.

“You could be right, but I have some tricks up my sleeve. You can return to your seat,” Uncle said with a laugh.

The judge called for a lunch recess to last one hour. Sasha, Maria, and Abie went across the street to the café again.

“What a fool he is,” said Maria.

“Yeah, he admitted to Dr. Munch that he was in Auschwitz... so now he’s screwed himself,” said Sasha.

Abie agreed and stated a quote sometimes attributed to Abraham Lincoln: “‘Anyone who represents himself has a fool for a client.’ If you give him enough rope, he will hang himself.”

“I hope so,” said Maria.

After lunch they rushed back to the courtroom to get good seats.

The bailiff in the front of the courtroom announced the judge's arrival. "Please rise. The Honorable Judge Bianchi presiding. You may be seated."

Marco called Maria to the stand. She was sworn in. She had no idea she was the next witness.

"Please state your name and where you live, for the record."

"Maria Romano, and I now live in Rome." Marco asked her how she was related to the defendant.

"He is my uncle and he used to visit us quite often."

"Has he had that facial scar for a long time?"

"As long as I can recall, since I was a child."

"Okay. Let's switch topics for a minute. How old are you, Maria?"

"Nineteen years old."

"Did you ever know your father?"

"No, he died before I was born."

"How do you feel about your uncle?"

"I feel scared of him and he and my mother used to fight a lot. He is mean and crabby and brags about killing thousands of people during the war."

"Thousands?"

"Yes, thousands."

"Wow," said Marco.

"Okay, thanks for your experience of the truth. Is it okay if I ask how many months pregnant are you?"

"About four or five months."

"Do you know who the father is?"

"Oh, yes, my boyfriend, Peter Wolf."

"Is Peter happy about the baby?"

Sasha squeezed Abie's hand and Maria wiped the tears away with a handkerchief. "Peter was murdered in Bolzano in June," said Maria.

"Oh, I'm so sorry."

"But Peter's mother, and friend, Abie, have stepped in to comfort me and I am so grateful for that. They are my new family."

"Okay, Maria. It is time for your cross-examination. You're doing great."

Uncle swaggered up to the witness stand with his hands on his hips. "It's nice to see you, my dear. It's been a while. So, you said your father died before you were born."

"Yes, sir. It was what I was told."

"Who would have told you that?"

"My mother."

"What if I told you that your mother lied?"

"I would not be able to comment on that."

"Objection," said Marco.

"Is this relevant to the case?" asked the judge.

"Yes, indeed," said Uncle, "it will provide the motive as to why Maria and her mother have lied about me."

"Okay... Overruled, but get to the point."

"The truth is your father is still alive."

Maria was stunned.

"The reason I'm aware of this, although I am not happy about it, is because I am your father."

Everyone in the courtroom gasped, Maria included. "I don't believe it. That would mean that you committed incest with my mother because she is your sister."

"She never desired it to happen. I just pushed forward against her will."

"Oh, no," shouted Maria.

Then the judge repeated his question, "How is this relevant to the case?"

"It shows that Maria and her mother Anna will go to any lengths to lie about me and discredit me."

"But I haven't lied about you," Maria whimpered.

"I think you've done enough damage for today, Mr. Schmidt," said the judge, and he told Maria she could return to her seat.

Maria ran out of the courtroom and Sasha followed after her. Brucelli turned around as he stared at Maria and Sasha. He was concerned.

Maria sat on a wooden bench in the lobby and Sasha ran over. "He was so mean. Do you think it is true, Sasha?"

"I don't know if it is the truth, but it shows his true colors and his ruthlessness to hurt people."

"I feel like I can't go back in there."

"I don't blame you, Maria. What an awful experience. He is very cruel. If it is true, he could have told you a long time ago or at any time. Instead, he chose to grandstand and blast it out to the whole wide world."

"I am so embarrassed."

"You didn't do anything wrong and you said some wonderful things about Peter. I think the judge will see through him...but it doesn't help at the moment."

"I need to leave and go home and just get under the covers."

"Would you like me to come with you?"

"For now I'll say no. I will be okay. I have a lot to reflect on. And I need a good cry."

"That's for sure," said Sasha. "Okay... How about this plan–you go home and rest and if you are in the mood, you can meet us for dinner."

"That sounds like a good idea. But if I don't show up, will you promise not to be offended?"

"Absolutely."

"If for some reason you need to stay home tomorrow and you'd like some company, just let me know and I will come over. I don't like the idea of you home alone right now," said Sasha.

"Thanks. I appreciate all your support. I need you guys. I don't know what I would do without you."

"Okay, sweetie, you go home and rest and then just see how you feel."

"Yes, I will, Sasha. Thanks again." Maria left the courthouse lobby, ran to her car, fumbled with her keys, dropped them, and then at last opened the door, jumped in, and cried all the way home.

"What did I miss?" asked Sasha in a soft tone.

"Not much, they just swore in Jonathan, another twin who was tortured by Mengele in Auschwitz. How do these people sleep at night?" Abie whispered. Sasha shrugged her shoulders.

"What did I miss between you and Maria?"

"Oh, she is very upset with Uncle's cruel tactics. She went home to rest. She may join us for dinner, but I think she will just cry herself to sleep. If she cannot handle it, she may stay home tomorrow. But if she needs me, I will skip the trial tomorrow and just keep her company," Sasha murmured, and Abie nodded.

"Okay, Jonathan. What was the hardest part of Dr. Mengele's experiments?" asked Marco.

"We often had to stand there all day totally naked. I got very cold and also was very embarrassed. He would perform experiments all day long. Sometimes we were in groups and other times I was alone. He did experiments to try to change our eye color. He injected us with all kinds of diseases and poisons. If my brother died from one of those toxins, within minutes I would have been given a shot of phenol straight into my heart and I would have died within seconds. But I guess the hardest part was being scared of the unknown, whether we would live or die. I shiver when I think of it."

"If we ended up in the infirmary Dr. Munch came to see us and another man named Samuel also came and told us stories and poems he had memorized. We had the other twins, but they were often too scared themselves to comfort anyone else," said Jonathan.

"Okay. By any chance did you know the defendant over there, perhaps under the name Heinrich Schmidt?" Marco asked, pointing to Uncle.

"Oh, yes, sir. I was more terrified of him than of Mengele. He would shoot an inmate for no reason. You had to walk on eggshells around him. And that scar was super scary for a kid with no parents to comfort him. I tried to stay out of his way. I guess I succeeded until today. I will have to be confronted by him soon. I am already scared."

"I am so sorry it has come to this," said Marco. "I hope it is not too painful. Hold your head up and take the high road."

"I'll try," said Jonathan.

"Okay, it's time for your cross-examination. Good luck. We are all rooting for you," said Marco.

Uncle rushed up to the witness stand and said, "So you are scared of me, eh?"

"Yes, sir," said Jonathan as he squirmed in his seat.

"What have I ever done to you?"

"It's not what you have done to me...but what you have done to thousands of others that scared me the most. I tried to avoid you."

"Well, I don't have any recollection of you at all," he cackled. "You're just a little nothing, a nobody. You have nothing to be scared of. I need to make sure you were really in Auschwitz. Can you tell us what Canada was?"

"Yes, sir. Canada was a building where they sorted out clothing, gold, jewelry, candlesticks, watches, clocks, shoes, and other things that were in the suitcases of the people who arrived in the cattle cars. I was never there myself, but I was told it was special."

"Why didn't you ever go there?"

"Mengele Twins had one purpose and one purpose only, to serve Dr. Mengele and be involved in his experiments. We were not able to move around like the other inmates. We had a special building where all the Mengele Twins slept. We had very little food, or even water. That's why we were all so skinny, even our ribs showed."

"What have you done since you left Auschwitz?"

"I have been very depressed and like Dr. Munch, I have had no great joy. Even my children say I don't know how to be happy. I feel stuck in the past."

"Well, it's time to live it up, boy, and get on with your life."

"I have done the best I can, and I refuse to lie," said Jonathan.

"Okay, little nothing, I'm done with you now. You can go back to your seat. You are a little cry baby and a wimp. I have bigger fish to fry."

The judge said to Uncle there was no need to shame or intimidate witnesses. He explained to Uncle that he needed to be polite and more professional if he desired to represent himself.

Then the judge turned to the audience and said, "It's been a long day and I think this is a good time to adjourn. We will start again promptly at 9 a.m. tomorrow."

Sasha ran up to Jonathan and gave him a big hug. "You were great. Don't listen to that cruel man. His words and cruelness speak volumes about him and nothing about you. You were very brave, and we all rooted for you, and you won."

"Thanks," said Jonathan. "Were you in Auschwitz?"

"No," said Sasha. "But my father and other relatives were killed by Nazis. And now it appears that my son was murdered because he did important research on Nazis hiding in monasteries."

"I am so sorry. Your son was Peter Wolf?"

"Yes," Sasha answered.

"I am sorry to bring up a painful memory for you."

"It's okay, this is such a painful period in the history of mankind. It's hard not to cry when you think of it."

"Bless your heart, and thanks for the hug."

"My pleasure, and just let me know if you need more hugs," Sasha said.

"I sure will."

"Maybe one more hug for the road?" asked Sasha.

"Okay," said Jonathan, and they shared another sweet hug.

Was Uncle really Maria's father? Would she ever be able to come back to the courtroom? Would Uncle's tactics succeed and get him off the hook, or would he betray himself? What would Peter think if he were here?

Chapter 31
Twisted Cross

Sasha and Abie went back to the hotel, took short naps, and had their usual dinner. It became their evening ritual and they continued to throw coins in the fountain. Sasha secretly wished to find Michael after the trial. Abie hoped for Sasha to find happiness and peace.

"I wonder how Maria is, but I don't plan to call her and risk the chance it might wake her. I guess I'll just wait until morning and see if she calls. You can always fill me in on what happens, Abie."

"Sure. Yes, I think Maria should be our main concern right now."

Abie and Sasha slept well but Maria had nightmares. In the morning Maria called Sasha and asked her to come over and keep her company. Maria couldn't stand to be in the same room with Uncle.

"I totally understand," said Sasha. "I will have Abie drop me off in about thirty minutes."

"That's great," said Maria. "I just can't be alone today."

"That makes sense. I'll see you soon."

"Terrific. I will just stay in my nightgown and robe."

About a half an hour later Sasha arrived at Maria's door with two cups of hot chocolate, while Abie continued on to the courthouse. He got the last parking spot and the last seat in the back row of the courthouse.

The bailiff in the front of the courtroom announced the judge's arrival. "Please rise. The Honorable Judge Bianchi presiding. You may be seated."

Marco called his next witness to the stand, Professor Giovanni. He was sworn in and sat down. He was a distinguished and professional man with a long, dark grey beard which he stroked often. He carried himself with an air of confidence. He glanced around the courtroom to see if anyone reminded him of Sasha. No.

"Please state your name for the record," said Marco.

"Professor Giovanni."

"Where do you teach?"

"The University of Perugia."

"What kinds of classes do you teach?"

"I teach history and social justice. I also take on private students to help them with their research projects."

"What kind of research are you focused on at the moment?"

"Nazi war criminals hiding in monasteries."

"Have you had any luck with your research?"

"We have moved forward with great strides and forged ahead until Peter Wolf and Brother Paolo were murdered in the rose garden of the Bolzano monastery in June of this year," he said as his voice broke.

"So, was Peter one of your students?"

"Yes, we were collaborators on this particular research project. He was a brilliant student who had a great career ahead of him, which was cut short by a killer who must have stalked him. We were so close to the key names of Nazi war criminals on our list...so close. My heart just breaks for Peter's family. He was an exceptional student who was filled with drive and passion. He was committed to his research 150%. I wish he were here today to see this trial in action. This trial would not have happened without Peter's research and subsequent murder. It helps me to believe that Peter is here in spirit with us today and every day," said Giovanni.

Marco thanked the professor for his honesty and explained that he would now be cross-examined. The professor nodded his head.

"So *now* we meet," said Uncle. "I have anticipated with glee a chance to meet you. You're the one who twists the little minds of gullible children," said Uncle.

"I beg your pardon?" Giovanni asked.

"You convince your students, who respect you and who want to get good grades, that if they agree with you and follow your research that they will excel."

"That is absolutely untrue. I have some skeptical students and others who are fascinated to learn about the monastery routes, safe houses for Nazi war criminals. Some of these Nazis continued to Genoa to escape to South America. Eichmann was the most famous one we're aware of. Others stayed in Italy for a variety of reasons."

"I don't agree with you," said Uncle.

"You have a right to your opinion. But it seems to me that you are the one on trial, not me," the professor said.

"Yes, but it is a mistake," said Uncle, "I am innocent and aim to prove that. I am glad that Peter and Brother Paolo were murdered. They were too close to the proof of your incorrect research."

"If it was incorrect research, there was no reason to be afraid of Peter and Brother Paolo and therefore no need to murder them."

"Well, I see that I am at a stalemate with you, so you may as well go back to your seat. I am done with you. You are not even worthy of the title 'professor,'" Uncle concluded.

Giovanni was relieved to be done with this nonsense and headed out of the courtroom with grace. Abie tried to follow him to shake his hand and thank him, but he was too late. The professor had already left the courthouse. Abie was glad that Sasha was not there to observe this mockery.

The judge announced that there would be a sixty-minute recess for lunch. Abie had a sandwich at the café.

He whispered under his breath, "I am so happy that both Maria and Sasha were not here for this charade today. Uncle is so ruthless and cruel. I'm concerned it will just get worse as we get closer to the end of the trial."

Abie picked up a copy of *Le Monde* on the way out of the café. He found a good seat because he got to the courtroom a little early. There was a small article on the first page stating that Uncle, and his various names, had represented himself and it was more of a mockery than a trial.

"He continues to make a fool of himself," the reporter stated.

Abie was happy that some new reporters had arrived, one from the *New York Times* and a very famous writer from *The New Yorker*, Dr. Hannah Arendt, who had covered the Eichmann trial and was one of Sasha's mentors.

Sasha listened to Maria's pain with gentleness and love. She now considered Maria her own daughter. She had always desired a girl and now she had one. She encouraged Maria to cry whenever she needed to.

"I can't stand the idea of him as my father. I lost Peter and my mother, but I gained a father I despise. I am so embarrassed by him. I hope he gets convicted and they throw away the key or maybe even better he gets hung. I'd like to go to the trial, but I can't be around him. It's kind of a double-bind."

"Yes, so true. I guess we'll take it one day at a time."

"Yes. That sounds like a good plan." Maria went back to sleep for a bit while Sasha read a book.

Back in the courtroom, the bailiff in the front of the room announced the judge's arrival. "Please rise. The Honorable Judge Bianchi presiding. You may be seated."

The judge stated, “Mr. Marco, are you ready to call your next witness?”

“Yes, I am.”

“Please proceed.”

“I call my next witness, Samuel Rosenstrauch, to the stand.”

Mr. Rosenstrauch painfully walked up to the stand. “Please state your name and where you reside for the record.”

“Samuel Rosenstrauch, Tel Aviv, Israel.” Samuel wore an eye patch and part of his face was full of scars.

“Are you in pain right now?” asked Marco.

“Oh, yes, sir,” said Samuel. “When I was in Auschwitz they broke my legs twice, so when the weather gets damp, the pain increases.”

“I’m so sorry,” said Marco. “Were you a Mengele Twin?”

“Oh, no, sir but I recited poems and stories to them at night. I was found hiding in a cave for a few years with several other Jews outside of Warsaw. We were discovered and sent to Auschwitz. Before I went into the cave I lived in a little shtetl, a small village, not too far from Warsaw. During one of the pogroms in my village my cousin was killed by a man with a deep scar on his face. He tried to kill me but didn’t succeed. I spent about a year in search of this man without any luck, before I went into hiding in the cave.

“A unique irony, we both ended up in Auschwitz. I was an inmate and he was a senior guard. I was determined to kill him, whatever the cost. He robbed me of my whole life in so many ways. The first day I was aware of him in Auschwitz I was elated. It was my chance! I ran right towards him and head-butted him in the stomach. But he sic’d his German Shepherd on me and that’s how I got these awful scars on my face. The dog scratched out one of my eyes, that’s why I wear this patch.”

"I am so sorry," said Marco. "Would you be so kind as to glance at some of these photos and determine if you recognize anyone."

Samuel pointed to Uncle's photo right away. "This is the man who killed my cousin in a pogrom. It's the same face with the scar. He was the very man I hunted for so long. And then I found him in Auschwitz. He was the same man I punched in the stomach. I figured I was a dead man in Auschwitz anyway, so I had nothing to lose."

"Do you see this man in the courtroom today?" asked Marco.

"Yes, sir," said Samuel. "He is the defendant, and he is seated right over there." Samuel pointed straight at Uncle.

"Thank you, Samuel. No further questions."

Before the cross-examination began, the back doors of the courtroom swung open in a blaze of gunfire.

The judge said with haste, "Take cover, everyone."

"Sieg Heil," said the intruders as they saluted Uncle, but very few people were aware of the events. They'd ducked for cover.

The judge was able to see everything through the hole at the foot of his desk. The bailiffs were poised to take down these young Neo-Nazis. They shot at two of them and missed because the Neo-Nazis moved around with deliberate speed. The invaders shot back and hit one guard in the chest and another in the arm.

Brucelli said, "We need to call two ambulances for the bailiffs who were shot."

"Okay, but no one else leaves this courtroom," said the ringleader.

Brucelli used his walkie-talkie and called for two ambulances *stat*. While they waited for the ambulances, the intruders waved their flags, marched around, and sang, "The Horst Wessel Song."

Abie was so glad that Maria and Sasha were not there. What a nightmare. How would everyone get out of this crazy scenario alive? Neo-Nazis had taken over the courtroom. Abie hid. He was so glad that Hannah Arendt had arrived today. This should make front-page news back in New York. The ambulances and EMTs came with two gurneys to wheel out the wounded bailiffs.

"I command you not to call the police, so just take them to the hospital. That's it. And don't tell them they were shot in this courtroom. Am I clear?" the ringleader warned. The medics nodded their heads.

But the ambulance crews were already aware that the police waited in the lobby of the courtroom ready to barge in any minute. The EMTs told the officers that there were four Neo-Nazis in full regalia with flags by the front wooden rail of the courtroom. The six policemen were armed with riot shields and gear, bulletproof vests, and submachine guns. Their goal was not to kill anyone but to arrest the intruders. But the minute they burst into the courtroom they became aware they'd have to wound the Neo-Nazis in order to gain control of the situation. They each shot an intruder in the arm or leg. The Neo-Nazis started to shoot back, and the audience was helpless. They were afraid to move. Some of the bullets ricocheted but fortunately no one was hit except the Neo-Nazis.

At this point the intruders ran out of ammunition and were too weak to stand, so the riot police were able to go to the front of the room, take away the Neo-Nazis' guns, and handcuff them. They called some ambulances that arrived in twenty minutes. Some people started to sit up when they understood that the danger had passed. Everyone was so relieved and yet still very traumatized by the experience. Once the Neo-Nazis were taken out of the room by ambulance crews, everyone breathed a sigh of relief.

The judge said, “I think we’ve had enough excitement for today. Let’s adjourn until tomorrow, but be advised that we will have many new bailiffs and they will wear bulletproof vests. Also, all those who attend will have to show their press passes and regular citizens will have to show some form of ID, for example, a passport or driver’s license. Two armed bailiffs will be stationed in the lobby for the duration of the trial and at least two armed bailiffs will also be in the courtroom. Please prepare to be frisked and to empty your pockets for the rest of the trial. Thank you and God bless! You are all free to leave now.”

Abie ran out of that room as fast as possible.

It was much later than most afternoon sessions and Sasha had begun to worry. What could have delayed him so much? Was he in an accident? She and Maria had no idea what had taken place. Abie arrived at Maria’s house about thirty minutes later.

“I have been so worried. Did something happen?”

“Let’s just start with the fact that I am so glad the two of you weren’t there,” said Abie.

They went out to a local pizzeria near Maria’s house. Abie updated them on the professor, Samuel, and the shoot-out.

“Wow. That must have been hard to deal with.” Sasha’s heart raced.

“Sure happy I wasn’t there,” Maria added. “It would have been the last thing I needed today.”

They dropped Maria back at home after dinner and said that they’d pick her up in the morning.

“What was the professor like?” asked Sasha as they drove away from Maria’s brick house.

“He was very professional, with a dark grey beard,” said Abie. “He complimented Peter on his passion and dedication to his research project. He was confident and did not let Uncle get under his skin. But I know deep down he’s devastated.”

"That's sad. I wish I could have empathy for him; he must be hurting. But he did send Peter on a risky mission and I'm not sure I can forgive him," said Sasha.

"He was a very sweet man. You might like him if you met him in person. He left the courtroom with great speed after his cross-examination. I ran after him just to shake his hand. But he was already gone. I was so disappointed," Abie sighed.

What Abie did not know was that the professor sobbed alone in the men's bathroom.

"And what about Samuel?" asked Sasha.

"He is a very kind-hearted soul," Abie explained. "He lost his cousin in a pogrom near Warsaw. The man who killed his cousin had a big facial scar. Samuel spent about a year looking for him without any luck. After the Germans entered Poland, Samuel went into hiding with some other Jews in a cave. After a few years he was discovered and ended up as a prisoner in Auschwitz where he met Uncle, the man he'd searched for who killed his cousin. It's a long story but he punched Uncle who then sic'd his German Shepherd on him. He will be back for cross-examination tomorrow. So be prepared that he has an eye patch and a bunch of scars on his face created by the dog attack," Abie explained.

"Okay, thanks for the heads-up. It sounds like a rather dramatic day, but I am relieved I wasn't there. I would have been on the edge of tears with the professor and Samuel and then the Neo-Nazi event would have taken my breath away. It gives me the shivers when I picture it. I don't know how I would have survived that," said Sasha.

"It was a blessing that you and Maria were not there, too. It would have been traumatic and something you would never forget. But I was worried about Maria being pregnant and I would have been terrified if she had been shot. We just cannot lose her or the baby. She's like a granddaughter to me. I have lost so many people over the years, I cannot stand to lose anymore."

"I understand, me too."

They arrived back at their hotel drained and exhausted. They each went to their rooms, took hot showers, and went to bed early. Tomorrow would be another day.

Would Maria be able to come back to the courtroom? Would there be any surprises? Would Uncle be nasty and make the audience cringe? Would the judge be sucked in by Uncle and let him off the hook? They all had shivers up and down their spines.

Chapter 32

"This Man is Delusional"

The next day everyone was ready for the trial to continue. Sasha and Abie went to pick up Maria. None of them got much sleep. The events of the day before had shaken them all to the core.

"Based on the instructions and new rules the judge ordered I don't think there will be any outbursts," said Abie.

"That's great. I hope you're right," said Sasha.

They picked up Maria. "You look so pretty," said Sasha.

Maria smiled and said, "Thank you."

Although they got to the courthouse with plenty of time to spare, there were no parking spots left in the courthouse lot. Abie dropped the two women off in front of the courthouse, so they could try to get good seats. Then he went to look for a nearby place to park. They got into the lobby and the new rules were in effect. The bailiff asked for their IDs and frisked them to make sure they had no weapons. Then they were allowed into the courtroom. There were only three seats left. Thankfully they were all in a row, so Sasha grabbed them. Dramatic events sell newspapers, so that added to the increased audience size.

The new bailiff in the front of the courtroom announced the judge's arrival. "Please rise. The Honorable Judge Bianchi presiding. You may be seated."

"Before we begin, I need to give an update on the two bailiffs who were shot by the intruders yesterday," said the judge. "It is with great sadness to report that the bailiff who was shot in the chest passed away early this morning. Our hearts and prayers go out to his loved ones. And may their memories be a blessing." The audience sighed. "The bailiff who was shot in the arm is on the mend. Let's take a moment of silence for the bailiff who died." Quietude filled the courtroom.

"Okay, we will pick up where we left off at the cross-examination of Samuel Rosenstrauch."

"I call Mr. Rosenstrauch back to the witness stand," said Uncle.

"You are still under oath. Oh, I see you have worn a hat today."

"Yes, sir. I feel like it hides my scars and my eye patch. I am very self-conscious."

"That's too bad. So, you said you found me before the war."

"Yes, near Zyrardow, Poland."

"Impossible, never been there. Not a place I'm familiar with. How are you sure it was me?"

"I never forget a face. I searched for you in Warsaw for about a year, but I never found you until we both ended up in Auschwitz. You walked around with a German Shepherd. On one of my first days there, I was thrilled to encounter you and I went right up and punched you in the stomach and you sic'd your dog on me."

Uncle gazed out at the audience and said, "This man is delusional. I never had a German Shepherd in Auschwitz. This witness is a liar." He turned back to Samuel and said, "You're dismissed. Go back to your seat, Mr. Weasel Liar."

Samuel walked right out of the courtroom without a glance back. That poor man. Sasha kicked herself. She could have gotten up and given him a hug. The judge admonished the defendant again because he shamed a witness.

"You're on thin ice here, Mr. Schmidt," said the judge.

"I have ice skates. I'm not worried," cackled Uncle.

Then Marco called Simon Wiesenthal to the stand and he was sworn in. "Thank you for the photos you provided us for this trial. It was very helpful that the names of the locations were written on the back of each photo. May I ask where you got these?"

"Of course. The ones from Auschwitz were hidden in a drawer at the camp itself. The others came from an archive that people have compiled for many years, with hopes to catch some Nazis on the run. It was one of the ways Eichmann was discovered."

"Thank you, that was very helpful," said Marco.

"Do you feel ready to be cross-examined at this time?

"Yes, sir, I do."

Uncle wandered up to the witness stand. He began, "Those are not real pictures. Jews know how to fake things."

"You're the one who fakes things," said Simon. "That's a perfect answer to deflect from the real issue."

"I have only spoken the truth and nothing more."

"Well, even if you found some long-lost pictures of me, how does it prove that I was in Auschwitz?"

"Those photos were found in a desk at Auschwitz. It does say Auschwitz on the back of it and the year 1944. And many people here have commented that the building in the background was the infirmary in Auschwitz."

"Okay, then my question is how much did you pay these people to lie to get me in trouble?"

"Nothing, sir."

"Go ahead and lie. People like you lie and fake. You can go back to your seat." Wiesenthal held his head high.

Marco then called Sergeant Brucelli to the stand. He was sworn in and stated his name and occupation. "Is it true that you found some of the defendant's fingerprints on wooden and metal surfaces, as well as on some clothing, medals, and a tie tack?"

"Yes, sir, there were some break-ins where we found the defendant's fingerprints on doorknobs, desks, and filing cabinets. In addition, we found a Nazi uniform and hat in a secret hiding place in the attic of his sister's home," said Brucelli.

"Were you ever attacked by the defendant?"

"Yes," said Brucelli, "I was attacked by a group of men, including the defendant, in a dark alley behind the police station after a late night at the office. This defendant is a cruel and ruthless criminal, who will stop at nothing to get what he desires."

"Thank you, Sergeant," said Marco. "I am done with my questions. Are you ready to be cross-examined?"

"Yes, sir," said Brucelli.

Uncle meandered up to the witness stand. "What's the big deal of a few fingerprints?" he asked.

"Two people lost all their research and others were frightened," Brucelli answered.

"Maybe that research was not worth anything and should have been thrown in the garbage anyway."

"But it wasn't yours to throw away. People spent hours and hours and maybe years on that research," Brucelli explained.

"Well, it's not the end of the world," said Uncle.

"What's the end of the world to you?" Brucelli asked Uncle.

"Hmmm, I don't know..." grumbled Uncle.

Then Uncle deflected and switched topics, "And that story of you getting roughed up could have happened to anyone in Rome. And just that one man had a scar–it doesn't mean it was me. And as for the uniform, it was given to me to hide by a friend. I tried it on, too. So, if my fingerprints are on the uniform, that's why... Oh, by the way, are you Jewish?" asked Uncle.

"I choose not to answer that," Brucelli replied.

"You see, ladies and gentleman, *all* Jews lie." With that he sent Brucelli back to his seat.

At this point all the witnesses had been called, but Marco had planned to conclude with his questions for Uncle at the end so he could use everything that happened in the trial.

Marco said, "I now wish to recall the defendant to the witness stand."

Uncle walked up with reluctance and was sworn in. "You chose to represent yourself after your brother was dismissed. May I ask why?"

"Yes," said Uncle. "I am the only one who knows the full story and no lawyer would be able to defend me the right way."

"What is the full story?"

"As I told you before–I guess you don't have a good memory–I was in Ausch... I mean Warsaw during the war and worked at the Iron Works machine shop."

"I think you made a Freudian slip there," said Marco.

"What's that?" asked Uncle.

"Never mind. We have it from a reliable source that you and your brother only worked at the Iron Works machine shop before the war and then both of you left."

"Who is that reliable source?" asked Uncle.

"The owner of the company," answered Marco.

"Another liar. All these Jews lie."

"You also said you did not have a dog in Auschwitz, but it sounded like you did not deny you had been in Auschwitz without a dog."

"You're a liar, too. Are you Jewish?"

Marco just continued. "When you talked to Dr. Munch, you dismissed him from the witness stand since you didn't like his answers. They were too close to the truth. Also, you reached a stalemate with the professor and dismissed him with speed."

"That's because they are all Jews and I don't like Jews."

"And with Wiesenthal you accused him of lies and fake photos. And called him a Jew. Is there something wrong with being Jewish? If so, that connects you with Nazi propaganda. So, if those are the best answers you can give me, I am convinced I won't get any answers that will help me, and we will go in circles. You could cross-examine yourself. That would be bizarre," said Marco.

Uncle then got off the witness stand and stated for the record that he had no need to cross-examine himself. But he asked the court to provide him with the recordings of Anna's hypnosis sessions to peruse in his jail cell over the weekend. The judge agreed to make those recordings accessible and suggested they all adjourn for the day and reconvene on Monday morning.

Everyone vacated the courtroom. Sasha, Abie, and Maria went across the street to the café. Maria said, "I am so afraid if Uncle has time with those taped sessions of my mother, he'll be furious. I have not seen them myself, but I've been told they are explosive."

"Oh, no," said Sasha.

"Well, let's just enjoy the weekend off," said Abie. The women agreed. After lunch they picked up some newspapers and *The New Yorker* to read Hannah Arendt's article.

The weather was beautiful all weekend long and Maria gave them a guided tour of Rome. On Saturday they walked down the Spanish Steps and threw coins in the Trevi fountain in hopes of a good trial outcome. Sasha again wished to find Michael. As the warm wind blew the watery spray from the fountain in their faces, they were refreshed.

They visited the ruins of the Colosseum, an architect's dream. Dramatic ruins of history and a bygone era. Ironically, with what was at stake in the trial, they had a glimpse of the ancient equivalent of the concentration camps. Mussolini, like Hitler, needed to use the history and mythology of his country to create newer, tougher, less empathetic people. "I will restore the Roman Empire to you," the Duce had said. Eerie.

After a while they were tired of the tourist scene. From time to time they stopped at outdoor cafés for sandwiches and hot chocolate. Sasha kept an eye out for Michael. She tried to picture what he might look like some twenty-five years later. She guessed it would be too much of a coincidence to find him in Rome. But she glanced around anyway. She couldn't help herself.

They bought flowers, especially those huge sunflowers from the local stalls that Peter had loved, and enjoyed the open-air markets. The cobblestone streets nearby wound through the local neighborhood which allowed them to gaze in shop windows and at frescoes on buildings. The churches and stained-glass windows were spectacular. They bought strands of garlic, picked out tomatoes, and herbs because Maria had promised to make them homemade pasta, sauce, and garlic bread for dinner that night at her house. They discovered she was a very good cook for someone who was only nineteen.

The aromas from the kitchen were spectacular. Garlic permeated the air and thrilled everyone's nostrils. However, Sasha was uncomfortable in Maria's home. It was colored by a strange, eerie vibration that haunted her. Peter had been here before he died. This was also where Maria's mother and Uncle spent a lot of time. Hard memories to process. The house was just okay. It was kind of old-fashioned with built-in wooden shelves and figurines in the combined dining and living room. The kitchen seemed rather dark and run down with old appliances. If Maria stayed in Italy, would she sell this house with so many negative memories or would she bring the baby up here? Sasha's secret wish had originally been for Maria to move to America. But now Sasha herself planned to stay in Italy to work with Professor Giovanni to carry on Peter's research. Or maybe to work with Simon Wiesenthal, or both...

On Sunday, they went to the Pincio Park and gardens that overlooked the whole city. They had a picnic lunch together on a red and white checked blanket. It was a very relaxed weekend. They pretended they were tourists. But it was the hardest on Sasha since she had just lost her son. She put on an act, but deep down she was grief-stricken.

That night they went to dinner at an outdoor, sidewalk restaurant. The meal was delicious and they all enjoyed people watching. They tried to distract themselves from the agenda for Monday–to go back to the courtroom.

"The trial is almost done," said Abie. "What will you do when it's over? Will you go back to America, Sasha?"

"I have some mixed feelings about that. I know I have to clean out Peter's room at the university."

"I will help you with that, Sasha."

"Thanks, Maria. If only we could find Michael, we could spread Peter's ashes in the river Seine. But that seems like a pipe dream," said Sasha.

"I feel like I need to be here for the birth of your child, Maria–my grandchild. I plan to stay here and help Maria before and after the birth. It's important for me to be a real grandma. I will get Maria the best doctors around and make sure she has everything she needs."

"Oh, wow. Thank you. That's sweet of you."

"I also would love to continue Peter's research. I have no reason to go back to America. My life is really here."

After Sasha and Abie left for the hotel, Maria had a lot to consider. Deep down, Maria appreciated Sasha's help, but it was important not to be dependent on Sasha to survive. She needed to sell the house in Rome to support herself. If she found a little cottage in Perugia, she might feel closer to Peter and the professor. But nothing would ever bring Peter back.

Maria did not know how she would solve this dilemma. If Uncle were found not guilty there would be no way Maria could stay in Italy. Would Uncle be set free? Would he hang? Or would he get life in prison? If so, he might find a way to escape. Maria would not be safe if he escaped. Everything hinged on the verdict and sentence.

Chapter 33
Closing Arguments

Sasha and Abie left the hotel the next morning to pick up Maria. If there had been an anxiety meter in the car, the needle would have broken the glass lid. They were concerned what Uncle would say about Anna's hypnosis recordings. Maria was ready to go when they arrived. She had on a warmer jacket because the weather had turned bone-cold.

"How are you all doing?" asked Maria, trying to sound cheerful.

Sasha said, "We're fine." Sasha also masked her panic about Uncle.

"Today is a hot chocolate day," said Maria. Sasha nodded. They found a parking spot easily and got good seats in the courtroom.

The bailiff in the front of the courtroom announced the judge's arrival. "Please rise. The Honorable Judge Bianchi presiding. You may be seated."

Then Uncle said he needed to make a statement about his sister's recorded sessions. The judge agreed to allow it.

Uncle stated, "My sister is a complete and utter fool. She told the truth when she could have lied. She got herself in a lot of trouble. We are so different. I never would have confessed to a murder, a rape, and accused a relative of killing thousands. If she were here, I would have ripped her to shreds." Upon finishing his diatribe, he sat down.

"Okay, it's time for the closing arguments," said the judge. "Mr. Marco, please begin."

Marco stood up and said, "Your Honor, witnesses, journalists, and special guests. I believe I have shown you without a shadow of a doubt that Mr. Schmidt is a Nazi war criminal who has committed crimes against humanity. He is a ruthless and callous man who cares about no one but himself. At every turn he displayed both Nazi ideology and personal hatred. He didn't even try to disguise what he had done. If he tried to cover up his days at Auschwitz, he did not succeed. I believe the witnesses gave powerful testimonies and Mr. Schmidt fumbled his excuses. As far as I am concerned, Mr. Schmidt is guilty on all counts." Marco sat down.

Uncle stood up and began his closing statements. "I believe that the defendant is completely innocent and has been falsely accused of unimaginable cruelty. He was never in Auschwitz. The witnesses were paid off to lie. We all know that Jews *lie*. I beg the mercy of the court to see through the conspiracy of the Jew-lovers and render a not guilty verdict. In addition, I would like to affirm that the defendant's name is Mr. Ricci and not Mr. Schmidt. There has been an obvious mix-up. Maybe Mr. Schmidt did these things, but Mr. Ricci was never in Auschwitz. Thank you, Your Honor." Uncle sat down.

Then a bailiff approached the judge and whispered something to him. The judge announced that a bomb threat had been received and he needed to clear the courtroom so that the bomb squad and sniffing dogs could make sure it was only a threat. Many people ran to the doors, but there was a line.

"Let's get that hot chocolate," said Maria. They headed over to the café. There was no line there.

Thank goodness the courtroom was cleared and there was no bomb. Everyone went back into the building. The judge had come up with a plan.

"Ladies and gentlemen, we are done with all of our witnesses and closing statements. I will make a ruling on the guilt or innocence of the defendant after I have reviewed all exhibits and witness statements as typed by the court stenographer. We will recess until Thursday and then I will come back with a verdict. At that time, after I deliver my verdict, I will give you a date for the sentencing. Thank you all for your service and kind attention. I also appreciate the fact that you have not created any disturbances in the courtroom. Court is now adjourned."

The next few days flew by. They all couldn't wait to the end of the trial, as long as it had a decent verdict. They longed for a guilty decision. The prosecutor and the witnesses did excellent jobs. They were fairly confident in the outcome.

But, you never know, so they didn't keep their expectations too high, only to be disappointed. Would the judge be swayed by the witnesses or would he be fooled by Uncle's lies? Was the judge anti-Semitic? Would Uncle get away with murder...again?

Chapter 34
The Verdict

Thursday morning arrived. They picked up Maria and headed to the courtroom. The scene was chaotic as people milled about. Every journalist was there. Hannah Arendt arrived. Sasha had meant to talk with her since Hannah had been one of her instructors at the New School. Hannah was aware that Sasha's father had been murdered at Camp Siegfried and now her son was killed in June. Maybe after the hectic atmosphere of the trial, Sasha could connect with Hannah and talk some things out.

Then out of the blue, Hannah touched Sasha's arm. "Hey stranger," said Hannah.

"You were just on my mind," said Sasha. "I know you are busy now, but let's get together after this is over."

"I'd like to do a story on you," Hannah replied.

"Really?" asked Sasha. "I would be so honored."

"I think it's time that your story is written and told. I will make arrangements with my editor, just to get the clearance from the higher-ups. But a personal interest story like yours, linked to and following my report on this trial, will grab the readers and pull them in."

"That sounds phenomenal," exclaimed Sasha. "I can't wait." They hugged and then Hannah went to her seat in the front row.

Sasha was very touched. She told Maria and Abie that Hannah reached out to her.

"That gives you something to look forward to," said Abie.

"Yes, indeed!" Sasha said, excited.

Everyone braced for the verdict. The courtroom was crowded with journalists, all the witnesses, and spectators. The audience was bursting at the seams.

The bailiff in the front of the courtroom announced the judge's arrival. "Please rise. The Honorable Judge Bianchi presiding. You may be seated."

Everyone sat on the edge of their seats.

"I have reviewed all the exhibits and recordings," said the judge. "And I have gone over the statements exposed during the trial. And," he paused, "I have come to the conclusion that Heinrich Schmidt is guilty."

At which point most of the audience clapped and cheered.

Then the judge reminded everyone, "This is your first and only warning. There are to be no public displays by the audience. Thank you. The sentencing will be held tomorrow at 10 a.m. Everyone is free to leave at this time except the defendant," said the judge.

The elation was contagious. The courtroom was cleared by the bailiffs. By the time everyone was in the lobby and spilled out the stairs, they began to sing "Bella Ciao" at the top of their lungs. Then everyone sang "Hava Nagila" and danced a Hora. Italian, United States, and Israeli flags waved in the wind. Students and labor unions joined in. The demonstrations went on and on for hours. Everyone sang, danced, and hugged... The whole world was watching.

They never had dinner. They were higher than kites. But in the back of Sasha's mind she was concerned about the sentencing. Anything could happen. Would he hang like Eichmann or get life in prison?

Abie said, "I feel like the judge will do the right thing. In some ways this has really been a circus, with Uncle as the ringmaster."

"Sometimes he was so foolish and gave himself away and other times he was cruel and ruthless," said Sasha.

"I bet he organized those Neo-Nazis and the bomb threat. They were probably all his friends," said Maria.

"Definitely," said Abie.

At 10 p.m. they chose to have a late-night meal. They were all hungry. They went to the restaurant in the hotel. They all ordered their favorite meals.

"For some reason, this feels like 'the last supper.' I don't mean the last time we'll eat together, but the last meal before the sentencing," said Maria.

"You are so right," Sasha agreed. "Let's hope at this time tomorrow night we will all be very happy and can celebrate a victory." It sounded like a good goal.

Abie drove Maria home while Sasha took a long hot bath.

"Are you having mixed feelings about your uncle?" Abie asked Maria in the car.

"No, not at all. I have known him all my life and he is a cruel man. I didn't know all the details I know now. But I feel even worse about him than I did before the trial. I just need this drama to be over so I can enjoy the baby when he or she comes."

"Oh, yes, the baby," said Abie. "What a blessing."

Sasha became obsessed with the verdict and Uncle's reaction to it. Would she ever find out who killed Peter? Did Uncle have anything to do with it? Would she ever find the Nazi who killed her father? She had promised herself two things. She would get justice for her family and she would find Michael. Would the verdict help her solve the mysteries? Or would she have to start from scratch?

Chapter 35

The Sentencing

After they parked the car the next morning, Abie said he needed to run to the café and get some coffee. But he promised he would not be late. They saved him a seat so he could sit between them. Sasha sat on the aisle. She wore a white dress and Abie, who wore a bright red shirt, vibrant against his curly salt-and-pepper hair, sat to her left.

The bailiff in the front of the courtroom announced the judge's arrival. "Please rise. The Honorable Judge Bianchi presiding. You may be seated." The courtroom was filled to the brim.

The judge announced, "After careful consideration of the exhibits, the witnesses, the defendant's behavior in the courtroom, I have determined that the defendant will be hung thirty days from today." The audience stifled a huge cheer.

"It is customary for the defendant to be offered the chance to respond to the sentence." The judge asked the defendant if he would like to respond.

Uncle said, "Yes," and proceeded to stand up. The room fell silent.

Uncle began, "Sieg Heil!" and gave the Nazi salute.

He faced the audience as he puffed out his chest like a Napoleonic statue.

"I will tell the truth now, since I am to be hung and I do not plan to appeal the verdict. Brother Tommasino Ricci was a name given to me by the International Red Cross when I got my fake ID papers at the end of the war.

"I am proud to say that I am a Nazi war criminal. I was at Auschwitz as a senior guard. Hitler would have been proud of me. I personally killed over 33,000 Jews, Poles, degenerates, Gypsies, and political prisoners. I am honored to have served the mission of the Third Reich, with Hitler as its physician, healing the body and soul of the empire. I have no regrets and I would do it all over again if I could. It was the highlight of my life. I won. The Germans were victims of a Jewish conspiracy.

"Even the man who popularized the automobile, Henry Ford, also popularized the International Jewish Conspiracy, as described in the book *The Protocols of the Elders of Zion*. Also, keep in mind, Hitler built many of his ideas on American race laws and eugenics. The very center of Nazi ideology came from American racism and anti-Semitism. A large American corporation was at the heart of the Nazi machine. So those of you from the U.S. media and Peter Wolf's family should take a look at your own country before you point fingers at the Third Reich.

"And by the way, you think it's over. But it's not! Just because the Allies won the battle, does not mean they won the war. We'll be back. See you at the KKK rallies and cross burnings. See you at the next assassinations, riots, and bombings. We'll be there in the tear gas. You will see us march on your 'blood and soil.' Here's my warning: there are many Nazis on the run, Nazis in hiding, Neo-Nazis, white supremacists, anti-Semitic gangs, and some disguised as the KKK... Be on the lookout. They may be your neighbors, your grandparents, your uncles, or people bagging your groceries. You won't see us coming.

"Also, I predict that Camp Siegfried will be resurrected. And speaking of Camp Siegfried–now for the icing on the cake. My very first experience of killing a Jew happened at Camp Siegfried on German Day, in America in 1938." Sasha grabbed Abie's hand.

"I stabbed Philip Wolf and got away with murder."

Sasha stood up and screamed, "Murderer. You killed my father! I'm glad you will finally hang for your crimes."

After her comment, the judge asked Sasha to sit down. She did and held Abie's hand.

"I was the first Nazi to kill a Jew in America," he cackled. "Hitler was so proud of me."

A man went up to the front of the courtroom and tried to get the judge's attention. But the judge refused to listen, so the man sat down.

Uncle then continued, "But when I found out Peter Wolf was doing research on Nazi war criminals like me hiding in Italian monasteries, I did my own research on Peter Wolf. And I discovered that he was the grandson of the first Jew I killed in America. So, I had to kill Peter because I *had* to eliminate the seed of that family. Unfortunately, I did not know that my own daughter, Maria, was pregnant with Peter's child. If I had known, I would have killed her too."

Sasha screamed out, "No!"

Maria froze.

At this point, the same man from the audience who went up to the front wooden railing and pounded on it earlier, tried to get the judge's attention again.

"Order in the court," said the judge as he pounded his gavel.

"But Your Honor, I must speak out. I am beside myself. The defendant has expressed a cruel error and I must correct it."

The judge threatened the man with contempt of court.

"I don't care. I survived Auschwitz–nothing could be worse."

At this point Sasha figured out that the man who spoke was Samuel Rosenstrauch, due to his eye patch and scars.

"Okay, Mr. Rosenstrauch, you may proceed, but make it brief."

"I am furious that the defendant killed Peter Wolf. But the defendant did not get away with murder at Camp Siegfried. Philip Wolf survived the attack and came back to Poland to find him and kill him.

"The reason I know this is because I AM PHILIP WOLF!"

At this point, Sasha screamed out, "Daddy!" and fainted and fell to the right, into the aisle. Abie caught her by her knees and a monk across the aisle moved quickly and caught her under her arms.

"Let's take her out into the lobby and try to get her some fresh air," Abie said. "I think we should call an ambulance."

They did just that, and then came back to hold Sasha's knees, covered by her beautiful white gown. Then Abie glanced up and understood the monk was Professor Giovanni. He recognized the dark grey beard. And the monk recognized Sasha's locket.

Meanwhile, Sasha was going in and out of consciousness. The monk whispered in her ear, "I am your Michael."

Sasha smiled, yet continued to fade in and out. Then she whispered to Michael, "Peter was your son," as a soft, steady stream of tears rolled down her cheek. Michael wiped them away.

Sasha's soul ached and reverberated in her ears: *You have sealed your promises to find your father's 'murderer' and to reunite with your soulmate. Unfortunately, you paid the ultimate price and sacrificed your only son. But without Peter, none of this would have been possible. He was the crucible...the pearl of great price...bittersweet... Was it worth it?*

Then Sasha went semi-unconscious again and floated up to the ceiling. While partially awake, she glanced down and came to grips with the fact that the three of them had recreated the scene in the painting *Atala*. But instead of Abie, young Michael held her knees and Michael, as the monk, held her under her arms.

She'd always desired to be loved like that...someday.

Had Sasha come full circle to the intimacy she craved?

Or did forever just run out of time?

Chapter 36
One Last Chance

Sasha still drifted in and out of consciousness in her bed at St. Catherine's Hospital. She went into shock at the end of the trial and had to rest and regain her strength. The monk, Brother Angel, never left her side.

In and out of a dreamy sleep Sasha continued to repeat, "I have to find Michael... He was at the trial," she said with a sense of urgency.

"I will help you," said Brother Angel. Floating in and out, Sasha couldn't understand his words.

When she was more alert Sasha asked the monk, "Am I about to die? Are you here to give me last rites?"

"No."

"Then am I in Heaven?"

"Heaven on earth."

A few hours later Sasha asked, "Are you Father Aubrey?"

"Who's Father Aubrey?"

"He was the monk who held *Atala's* shoulders in my favorite painting."

"I see. I may represent Father Aubrey to you...but..."

"Then who are you?" interrupted Sasha.

"I am Brother Angel."

"Do I know you?"

"Yes. We met in the Louvre twenty-five years ago when you fell in love with *Atala*."

"That's interesting. I don't have any memory of meeting a monk. I fell in love with a painting and a man named Michael that summer... Can you help me find him? He was in the resistance."

"Yes, I can help you find that man."

"Really? That's wonderful. How soon can we find him? I've been longing all my life to find him again. You never forget your first love."

"I understand, Sasha. He has never forgotten you either. Every time he drank dark hot chocolate he longed for you."

"How do you know so much about Michael?"

"Because I am the man you are looking for. I am your Michael."

"You are? You are my Michael?" Sasha asked in disbelief. "Why are you wearing a monk's robe?"

"At the moment I am a monk. I joined the monastery when I lost you; I never desired to be with any other woman but you." Sasha started to cry. "But I needed a sense of community," Brother Angel continued. "We were able to save many Jews, Gypsies, political prisoners, and others at risk."

"Now I understand why they call you Brother Angel."

"Thank you. Yes, we created a real sanctuary."

"I was under the impression you had joined the resistance."

"I changed my mind and chose to save people rather than be involved in violence."

"But why were you at the trial?"

"I was Peter's professor. He was my research assistant at the University of Perugia. I loved him. I treasured his passion and creativity. I just didn't grasp he was my son," Michael sighed. "Some students called me Professor Giovanni. Others called me Brother Angel."

"You know, I never discovered your last name," said Sasha.

"Right, so you didn't connect me with Professor Giovanni. I was the one who taught Peter all about the monastery routes. He was my star pupil. And I feel that my research actually got him killed. I feel *so* guilty."

"Peter was my son," said Sasha. "Wait. If you are my Michael, Peter was your son, too."

"Yes, you whispered that to me at the end of the trial. If only... And now *I'm* crying," said Michael.

"It's time for a hug, is that okay?" asked Sasha.

"Sure." They shared a sweet hug and both cried. They had a son and never got to enjoy him together. They sobbed for what they had and what they lost.

"Can you ever forgive me, Sasha? It's my fault that Peter went to Bolzano. I will never forgive myself," he said with tears in his eyes.

"Give me your hands," begged Sasha. "It's strange but despite my fears and grief, I have already forgiven you because you are my Michael. You are and have always been my first great love, my one and only true love. I never forgot you."

Even Sasha was surprised by her own words. Her heart and soul went through an emotional and spiritual shift, an expression of new growth for her.

"Peter performed the ultimate sacrifice–to die while he pursued something courageous. That was his life's work. He was on a mission and he succeeded. Peter found a Nazi war criminal. That was his dream. His work on this earth was done. And perhaps part of his mission was to bring us back together."

"But I never should have sent him on that mission, Sasha. It was too dangerous once he met Uncle at Maria's house. I should have gone instead of Peter or at least we should have gone together. Maybe I could have protected him."

"Perhaps. But maybe you would have died, too. That would have been unbearable for me. My life would have been over. At least now I can move forward."

"Even in death Peter would be happy that he saved your life. He protected you from Uncle. He loved you, Michael. He would have done anything for you, even die for you."

"I'm so sorry I never discovered he was my son. With the last name Wolf and his love of dark hot chocolate, I had my suspicions. I even talked to the Abbate about it. If only I had asked Peter if his mother's name was Sasha."

"Yes, that's a shame. But he was sure you loved him and that's what counts. If he had understood you were his father, he would have protected you even more and would have given anything for you to find me."

"Wow. That helps me feel better. Thank you, Sasha."

"But Maria, Peter's girlfriend, is pregnant, so we'll be grandparents together," Sasha said, excited.

"Yes, I know. That's pretty incredible. Let's enjoy that little baby!"

"Absolutely. I plan to spoil that child."

"Oh, before I forget, would you come to Paris with all of us to spread Peter's ashes in the Seine, Michael?"

"Of course. I wouldn't miss it for the world."

"Thank you. I really need you there. That means everything to me," said Sasha. "You know Abie and I tried to find you when we were in Paris to spread Peter's ashes in June. We even put ads in the newspaper, *Le Monde*. And then when you didn't respond, I just had to come to grips with the fact that you were dead, that you had died in the resistance movement."

"Oh, my goodness. I have a funny feeling," said Michael, "that you came back to Italy from Paris exactly when I left Italy to go to Paris to spread my mother's ashes in the Seine, who died around the time that Peter did. So our planes literally crossed paths, mid-air."

"Oh, I didn't know that. I'm so sorry that your mother died. My deepest condolences. I guess there's a lot we have to catch up on."

"Guess what? I found out while she was on her deathbed that I am actually Jewish and we were in hiding."

"That is so strange. And you became a monk."

"Yeah, I told the Abbate I might have to do something about that after the trial."

"By the way, as long as we are catching up on things, I flew to New York in the summer of 1954 and went to the last address I had for you in Brooklyn, but I guess you had moved out long before that and I didn't have any way to find you. I called all the Wolfs in New York City but never reached anyone who was related to you. So I gave up and flew back to Italy."

"Oh, in the summer we were never home. We spent all our days with my grandparents at Brighton Beach Club. Peter loved it there. I wish you could have found me then. I needed you more than life itself. But just the knowledge that you tried to find me is an incredibly romantic story... My biggest regret was leaving Paris. I wish I had never left. I have cried so many tears."

"Me too, my beloved."

"Years ago I had a vision, Michael. I was a medicine woman. I saved my own tears in my tear-glass bottle and used those tears to help others."

"Your tears are healing me now, Sasha. A warm wave of forgiveness just came over me."

"That's wonderful."

"I've missed you so much and I still love you, Michael."

"I feel the same way."

"What are we going to do?"

"I have no idea. Don't you worry, we'll figure it out."

"I have no desire to return to America, Michael. I will stay here in Italy and help Maria get ready for the baby and help her after the birth. I would also love to follow in Peter's footsteps and help you, Simon, and Brucelli prepare for Uncle's brother's trial."

"The main thing right now is for you to start feeling better, Sasha. Everything else will follow," Michael reassured her. "Let me go tell the others you are awake, Sasha. And maybe I'll bring Abie in."

"Okay, Michael. But please come back, too."

"I will." Michael brought Abie in and they both sat down near Sasha's bed.

Abie reminded Sasha the reason she fainted. "Samuel Rosenstrauch is your father."

"I don't understand. I was convinced my father died in 1938 at Camp Siegfried."

"Well, your father was hurt then. He was stabbed and trampled. He ended up in the hospital on Long Island. I was with him. He survived. He forced me to bury an empty coffin and to tell your mother, you, and his parents that he died. I know you might be mad at me. I kept your Dad's secret."

"So, you're saying that my father is not dead?"

"That is correct, Sasha."

"We found out that the man who stabbed your father and tried to kill him flew to Warsaw, Poland. So when your father recovered from the hospital stay and he was able to fly, I paid for him to go to Warsaw to try to find this man. He went to live with your relatives about an hour from Warsaw. Then he lived in a cave. He was discovered and sent to Auschwitz. And had a new name, Samuel. Remember him from the trial?"

"Oh," said Sasha. "It's starting to come back to me a little bit at a time. So, the man with the eye patch and the scars is not really Samuel? He is my father?"

"Yes, that is correct, but Samuel Rosenstrauch and Philip Wolf are the same person."

"Wow," said Sasha. "That's quite a story. Is it really true?"

"Yes, your father is alive, Sasha."

"Well, you're right, I am mad, but I also love you. Send him in and I will give him a test to determine if he's really my dad. This must be a dream that I found Michael and my father due to the trial and Peter's sacrifice. But it was very real."

Abie brought Samuel into the room.

"Daddy, is that really you?"

"Yes, sweetheart. I'm so sorry," said her father. "I should've told all of you I was still alive. It's my fault. I asked Abie to promise not to tell anyone. Don't be mad at Abie."

"But Daddy, is it *really* you?"

"Yes. I just don't look the same. I went through hell and back. But I lived to tell the tale, though it's not a happy one. I'm sad that I never met my grandson, Peter. I'm sorry I left you alone with Mom. She was difficult. But I'm back and I'm here for you. If you're angry, I will understand. If you are not sure it's me, you can ask me questions that only I would know the answer to. I promise that Abie did not coach me."

"Okay," said Sasha, "where did we go on Saturday mornings when Mom was sleeping?"

"The diner on Ocean Avenue."

"What did I order?"

"Waffles and bacon, lots of maple syrup, and butter. Yes, extra butter."

"Okay. What did I do with my stuffed animals when I went to sleep?"

"You slept with a different animal every night and waited to see what your dreams revealed."

"What was the name of my favorite stuffed animal? And no cheating."

"Rhubarb."

"That's right," said Sasha. "Okay, I'll give you a hug, Daddy. I know it's you. By the way, we need to bury Peter's ashes by the river Seine in Paris. Would you come with us?"

"Sure," her father answered.

"Maria would like to come in and give you a hug," said Abie. "How about all the gentlemen leave the room so the two ladies may talk in private."

"Okay, send her in but don't leave the hospital without goodbye hugs."

"You look wonderful, Maria," Sasha said.

"Thanks. How are you, Sasha?"

"A little better."

"I would love to take a walk. I'm tired of this hospital bed. Can you ask permission for us to go for a little walk down the hall and back?"

"Okay," said Maria, "I'll be right back."

"Thanks."

Maria asked a nurse if Sasha could go for a walk down the corridor and back to her room. The nurse checked with the doctor. He said, "It's a good idea for her to stretch her legs."

"Can you get my robe from the closet and help me put it on?"

"Sure, no problem." There were railings on both sides of the hallway, so Sasha was able to hold on. They walked down the hall. At the end, there were some chairs.

"Let's sit down here, Maria."

"Are you okay?"

"I'm a little out of breath. I need to walk more each day to regain my strength."

"I think that's a good plan."

"How are you, my dear?" asked Sasha.

"I get tired," said Maria. "But I'm fine. I'm happy the trial is over. I'm glad you're better. I was worried about you, Sasha. I'm excited about the baby. But I miss Peter a lot."

"I understand. I miss him too."

"I guess we just have to focus on the future," replied Maria.

"You're right, dear. I couldn't have said it any better."

"We both have to be strong and keep his memory alive in our hearts."

"Do you think you'll be well enough to come with us to spread Peter's ashes in Paris in the Seine, Maria?"

"Oh, yes! Absolutely," she answered.

"That's great. Now I just need to regain my strength. I'll have to walk up and down these halls until I'm stronger. I think a physical therapist comes tomorrow to help me climb stairs. Once I'm released from the hospital I may have to rest up in the hotel for a few days before we all fly to Paris."

Sasha continued, "My goal is to come back to Italy after we spread Peter's ashes in the Seine, Maria. I will not go back to America. I would like to help you before and after the baby is born. I can't wait to be a grandmother. I am going to spoil that little baby. Do you think you will stay in your mother's house in Rome?"

"No. My mother's house now has bad memories. It's dark and empty there. I would like to sell the house in Rome. If I move to Perugia and the baby is born there, I will be closer to Peter."

"I understand. After we go to Paris, you, Michael, and I can return to Italy. Abie and Samuel will go back to America."

"Oh, I meant to congratulate you on finding Michael. I had no idea he was our professor."

"Yes, it's a miracle."

Sasha's physical therapy got her back on her feet. After a few more days at the hotel, Sasha had regained her strength and they bought tickets to fly to Paris.

Chapter 37

Bittersweet

Sasha prepared herself for a very poignant and bittersweet visit to Paris. The last time she was there she was in a lot of pain. She had just lost her son and missed Michael beyond words. She was desperate to find him. Her ads in the paper didn't work since he was in Italy. Without Michael she could not spread Peter's ashes. She was so glad she waited... Now she had Michael, her father, Abie, and Maria. It would still be hard to spread the ashes. She would keep some to take with her back to Italy.

The plane was ready to board. Michael, Sasha, and Maria sat together. Samuel and Abie sat side-by-side across the aisle. The next day was a time to celebrate Peter's life and to honor his passing. It was finally the right time to spread Peter's ashes. Sasha and Michael began the ceremony. They spread some ashes first in the Seine. Everyone followed the ashes as they floated down the river. Then Maria released some ashes. Next it was time for Abie and Samuel to continue the ritual. Everyone wept and hugged. Ashes flew through the air like snowflakes and landed in the water.

After the ashes were spread, the unlikely family group walked along the Seine. The sun's reflection sparkled on the water and refracted-rainbows and fireworks surrounded them. The sunset unveiled a sky that was filled with lavender and rose clouds. It was like a garden in the sky.

Sasha gave Michael a hug and whispered in his ear, "It means so much to me that you were here to help us spread Peter's ashes."

"I am glad I found you again so I could be part of this bittersweet ritual. But I am so sorry that I was not there to help you raise Peter. I feel like I failed you."

"There's a poem by Antonio Machado that might help you: 'Last night as I was sleeping, / I dreamt–marvelous error!– / that I had a beehive / here inside my heart. / And the golden bees / were making white combs / and sweet honey / from my old failures.'"

"So meaningful, Sasha–bittersweet."

"Together, Michael, we can repair the world. *Tikkun olam.*"

***

The next day they all went to the Louvre. Sasha showed everyone the painting that started her journey. They all loved it and they bought postcards of *Atala*. Sasha and Michael stayed in the gift shop after everyone else went out into the lobby. Michael asked Pierre, the salesclerk, if he still had that letter he had given him in late June that was addressed to Sasha Wolf.

Then Pierre said, "Yes, I have it right here in my drawer."

"Thank you," said Michael, and he handed the letter to Sasha. She opened the envelope and fell in love with Michael all over again. Her heart burst open.

"I'm so sorry you lost your mother. It's a terrible loss, isn't it?"

Michael had written the letter at a time when he was experiencing a very deep kind of loss. Michael had lost Sasha all over again, for the second time.

"The kind of love I feel for you," said Sasha, "is not something that has to be expressed physically. It's a much deeper love from the heart, from the soul. I will always be with you, Michael. You are my first great love. And nothing could ever separate us now. We had a beautiful child together and now we will have a grandchild soon. I look forward to hot chocolate together, just the two of us alone, for old time's sake and quality time. Someone told me that hot chocolate was a liquid form of love. Every time I've had hot chocolate in my entire life since I met you, I was healing my heart."

"Thank you, Sasha. I really treasure our love. You know, to the world, sometimes you can be just one person. But sometimes, to one person, you can be the world. You are my world, Sasha. And you will always be my world. I look forward to anytime we have together, even if other people are around. I know you love me on a deep level. I hold you in my heart, always. You are my first love and an old and dear friend," said Michael with tears in his eyes.

Sasha replied, "You can always make new friends, but you can never make old friends. Thank you for being my old and dear friend, my Michael and my first and only love, now and forever."

"Hey guys, we're getting ready to leave and go get some hot chocolate at the café. Do you care to join us?" asked Abie.

"Oh, sure," said Sasha. She had lost track of time and had enjoyed a few private moments with Michael.

It was ironic that there was a rainstorm and no one had an umbrella. They all got soaked as they ran to the nearest café, which happened to be the original café that Sasha and Michael went to. They had recreated the past in a new way.

Everyone ordered hot chocolate. Samuel, Maria, and Abie all got pastries. All Sasha needed was hot chocolate and Michael. The hot chocolate was her beverage of love and Michael was the food she needed to stay alive. Everyone else laughed and joked. Sasha and Michael were quiet and peaceful. They gazed into each other's eyes, no words needed. It was a miracle that they found each other. It was Peter who brought them back together. Peter paid the ultimate price. He sacrificed his life reuniting Sasha and Michael so their dreams could come true. What would've happened if Sasha's father had not been stabbed, and she hadn't left France in 1938? They probably would have eloped. But she couldn't turn the clock's hands backward.

Chapter 38

Forever

The next day Abie and Samuel took a taxi to the airport from the hotel. They were headed back to New York. Samuel could not wait to be with his parents again.

Sasha told her father, “I’m so glad you are still alive. What a miracle.”

She turned to Abie, “Thanks for everything.”

Michael told Abie, “Thanks for all your help. You were there for Sasha and Peter when I couldn’t be there.”

Abie whispered to Sasha, “I’m so glad you found your Michael again. I never imagined you would find him after all these years.”

There were hugs and tears all around. Even Maria wiped her tears away.

As their cab drove away, Sasha began to sob. “I may never hug them again.”

Maria and Michael tried to comfort her. “The only solution - hot chocolate,” said Sasha.

After they were done. Michael said he had an errand to run. Maria needed to rest.

“I’ll go up and keep you company, Maria.” Sasha read her *Atala* novel while Maria took a nap.

Michael went down to the lobby to use the phone. Then he jumped in a cab. When he returned, he said, "I'm going to take you on an adventure, Sasha."

"That sounds like fun."

Michael proceeded to go into the bathroom.

After ten minutes Sasha asked, "Have you turned into superman yet?"

"Very funny, Sasha. I'm almost ready."

Soon Michael called out from the bathroom, "Close your eyes, Sasha...and don't peek." "Okay. My eyes are closed."

Michael crept out of the bathroom. "I'm about to blindfold you, Sasha, with a soft, burgundy, velvet scarf."

"Okay. Seems like we're on a secret mission."

"Yes, we are."

Michael held Sasha's hand and arm and led her down to the hotel lobby.

"We are about to go into a cab, Sasha."

She was curious. After ten minutes the cab stopped.

"Time to get out, Sasha."

"I feel like I am on a wild goose chase, Michael."

"We are almost there."

They climbed the stairs and went room to room. Magic swirled in the air with the scent of old oil and dust.

"This place seems familiar," she said.

"Okay, you can take your blindfold off now."

That's when Sasha came face-to-face with the huge and startling painting she loved so much that started her on her journey. Its emotion still ignited the dream that had been with her forever–to be loved like that someday. The devotion depicted on the canvas jumped from its gilded frame, grabbed hold of her heart, and electrified her soul again–metaphysical lightning.

Then her eyes drifted down with grace from the painting to her beloved Michael. Sasha's heart melted like dark chocolate.

But wait–Michael wasn't wearing his robe! Oh, my God, Michael was on bended knee. A diamond ring sparkled in his hand.

The forever moment every woman dreams of.

You never forget your first love.

A sacred love.

A love to die for...

The End

P.S. To the Reader

Years ago, I had a vision I was a medicine woman. I saved my own tears in my tear-glass bottle and used them to heal others. My name became Amber. Amber was, to me, the tears of the pine tree. Under a million years of pressure, these tears hardened and turned into precious jewels. I've lived my life turning suffering into gold.

'Sacred Medicine' is another name for love. Alchemy presents the beautiful image of transforming lead into gold, suffering into beauty. Alchemists sought "The Pearl of Great Price." The pearl starts off as a grain of sand, an irritant inside the oyster's shell. The oyster deals with its pain by covering the grain of sand with a luster and continuing to do so, day in and day out, until the grain of sand becomes a pearl. The oyster transforms its suffering into a beautiful jewel. Our own suffering may be the seed of our greatest treasure. This seed may blossom into healing beyond our... wildest... dreams! How can you transform the very thing that's at the heart of your suffering and pain into a beautiful jewel? Only you know the answer to this question. If your life were a book, what would the title be? What chapter are you on right now? Remember, only you can write the next chapter. What did you come here to do? I promise you it is not too late to do what you came here to do. What is missing in your life? If you could wave a magic wand right now, what would you wish for?

My work is meant to inspire you to greater heights and challenge your greatest fears. We are all on a healing journey but sometimes we get lost. I believe that "all sickness is homesickness." And we are all 'Dorothys' and 'Totos,' just trying to find our way home again. This book offers you a personal invitation to remember who you are, to fall in love with life again, and to experience the alchemy of turning your suffering into gold. If I could wave a magic wand right now, I'd wish for you a MIRACLE!

Amber Rose

About the Author

Amber Rose has been a Holocaust scholar and healer all her life. Her advisor, Dr. Hannah Arendt, awarded her Special Honors in Philosophical Psychology at the University of Chicago for her thesis "A Soul's Answer to Suffering," including her work with Dr. Viktor Frankl and Dr. Bruno Bettelheim directly. After visiting Auschwitz, Amber wrote a play, *The Bride of Auschwitz*, which has been performed at Universities, Holocaust museums, synagogues, and libraries. Ms. Rose is a social worker, interfaith minister, singer-songwriter activist, classical and bee-acupuncturist. She has written four award-winning textbooks. *When I Am Ashes* is her debut novel about Nazi war criminals.

About Atmosphere Press

Atmosphere Press is an independent, full-service publisher for excellent books in all genres and for all audiences. Learn more about what we do at atmospherepress.com.

We encourage you to check out some of Atmosphere's latest releases, which are available at Amazon.com and via order from your local bookstore:

Insight and Suitability, a novel by James Wollak

Late Magnolias, a novel by Hannah Paige

The Saint of Lost Causes, a novel by Carly Schorman

Monking Around, a novel by Keith Howchi Kilburn

The Tattered Black Book, a novel by Lexy Duck

American Genes, a novel by Kirby Nielsen

The Red Castle, a novel by Noah Verhoeff

The Black-Marketer's Daughter, a novel by Suman Mallick

Within the Gray, a novel by Jenna Ashlyn

Where No Man Pursueth, a novel by Micheal E. Jimerson

The Hidden Life, a novel by Robert Castle

For a Better Life, a novel by Julia Reid Galosy

Nothing To Get Nostalgic About, a novel by Eddie Brophy

Alvarado, a novel by John W. Horton III

CPSIA information can be obtained
at www.ICGtesting.com
Printed in the USA
BVHW072159100621
609270BV00005B/787